PLACES

Jennifer Niven

a novel

ALFRED A. KNOPF ❧ NEW YORK

Dwarsligger® is a new book concept created by printer and publisher Royal Jongbloed BV (Heerenveen, the Netherlands).

This book is printed on Thinopaque paper provided by Tervakoski in Finland. Thinopaque is FSC certified, manufactured acid free from environmentally sustainable paper pulp. It is produced following the highest environmental standards.

MIX
Paper from
responsible sources
FSC
www.fsc.org
FSC® C013685

Visit us on the Web! GetUnderlined.com

Educators and librarians, for a variety of teaching tools, visit us at RHTeachersLibrarians.com

The Library of Congress has cataloged the original edition of this work as follows:

Niven, Jennifer.

All the bright places / Jennifer Niven.—1st ed.

p. cm.

Summary: "Told in alternating voices, when Theodore Finch and Violet Markey meet on the ledge of the bell tower at school—both teetering on the edge—it's the beginning of an unlikely relationship, a journey to discover the 'natural wonders' of the state of Indiana, and two teens' desperate desire to heal and save one another."—Provided by publisher
Includes bibliographical references.

ISBN 978-0-385-75588-7 (trade) — ISBN 978-0-385-75589-4 (lib. bdg.) — ISBN 978-0-385-75590-0 (ebook)

[1. Friendship—Fiction. 2. Suicide—Fiction. 3. Emotional problems—Fiction. 4. Indiana—Fiction.] I. Title.

PZ7.N6434Al 2015

[Fic]—dc23

2014002238

ISBN 978-0-593-12616-5 (mini)

Original cover design by Lucy Kim and Alison Impey. Cover design adapted by Jinna Shin.

Design adapted from the hardcover edition. Typesetting by 2K/DENMARK AS, Denmark

Printing and binding: Royal Jongbloed BV, Heerenveen, the Netherlands

10 9 8 7 6 5 4 3 2 1

First Random Mini Edition

For my mother,
Penelope Niven,
my brightest place of all

For my mother,

Penelope Niven

my brightest place of all

The world breaks everyone, and afterward, many are strong at the broken places.

—*Ernest Hemingway*

The world breaks everyone, and afterward,

many are strong at the broken places.

—Ernest Hemingway

FINCH

I am awake again. Day 6.

Is today a good day to die?

This is something I ask myself in the morning when I wake up. In third period when I'm trying to keep my eyes open while Mr. Schroeder drones on and on. At the supper table as I'm passing the green beans. At night when I'm lying awake because my brain won't shut off due to all there is to think about.

Is today the day?

And if not today—when?

I am asking myself this now as I stand on a narrow ledge six stories above the ground. I'm so high up, I'm practically part of the sky. I look down at the pavement below, and the world tilts. I close my eyes, enjoying the way everything spins. Maybe this time I'll do it—let the air carry me away. It will be like floating in a pool, drifting off until there's nothing.

I don't remember climbing up here. In fact, I don't remember much of anything before Sunday, at least not anything so far this winter. This happens every time—the blanking out, the waking up. I'm like that old man with the beard, Rip Van Winkle. Now you see me, now you don't. You'd think I'd have gotten used to it, but this last time was the worst yet because I wasn't asleep for a couple days or a week or two—I was asleep for *the holidays,* meaning Thanksgiving, Christmas, and New Year's. I can't tell you what was different this time around, only that when I woke up, I felt deader than usual. Awake, yeah, but completely empty, like someone had been feasting on my blood. This is day six of being awake again, and my first week back at school since November 14.

I open my eyes, and the ground is still there, hard and permanent. I am in the bell tower of the high school, standing on a ledge about four inches wide. The tower is pretty small, with only a few feet of concrete floor space on all sides of the bell itself, and then this low stone railing, which I've climbed over to get here. Every now and then I knock one of my legs against it to remind myself it's there.

My arms are outstretched as if I'm conducting a sermon and this entire not-very-big, dull, dull town is my congregation. "Ladies and gentlemen," I shout, "I would like to welcome you to my death!" You might expect me to say "life," having just woken up and all, but it's only when I'm awake that I think about dying.

I am shouting in an old-school-preacher way, all jerking head and words that twitch at the ends, and I almost lose my balance. I hold on behind me, happy no one seems to have noticed, because, let's face it, it's hard to look fearless when you're clutching the railing like a chicken.

"I, Theodore Finch, being of unsound mind, do hereby bequeath all my earthly possessions to Charlie Donahue, Brenda Shank-Kravitz, and my sisters. Everyone else can go f--- themselves." In my house, my mom taught us early to spell that word (if we *must* use it) or, better yet, not spell it, and, sadly, this has stuck.

Even though the bell has rung, some of my classmates are still milling around on the ground. It's the first week of the second semester of senior year, and already they're acting as if they're almost done and out of here. One of them looks up in my direction, as if he heard me, but the others don't, either because they haven't spotted me or because they know I'm there and *Oh well, it's just Theodore Freak.*

Then his head turns away from me and he points at the sky. At first I think he's pointing at me, but it's at that moment I see her, the girl. She stands a few feet away on the other side of the tower, also out on the ledge, dark-blond hair waving in the breeze, the hem of her skirt blowing up like a parachute. Even though it's January in Indiana, she is shoeless in tights, a pair of boots in her hand, and staring either at her feet or at the ground—it's hard to tell. She seems frozen in place.

In my regular, nonpreacher voice I say, as calmly as possible, "Take it from me, the worst thing you can do is look down."

Very slowly, she turns her head toward me, and I know this girl, or at least I've seen her in the hallways. I can't resist: "Come here often? Because this is kind of my spot and I don't remember seeing you here before."

She doesn't laugh or blink, just gazes out at me from behind these clunky glasses that almost cover her face. She tries to take a step back and her foot bumps the railing. She teeters a little, and before she can panic, I say, "I don't know what brings you up here, but to me the town looks prettier and the people look nicer and even the worst of them look almost kind. Except for Gabe Romero and Amanda Monk and that whole crowd you hang out with."

Her name is Violet Something. She is cheerleader popular—one of those girls you would never think of running into on a ledge six stories above the ground. Behind the ugly glasses she's pretty, almost like a china doll. Large eyes, sweet face shaped like a heart, a mouth that wants to curve into a perfect little smile. She's a girl who dates guys like Ryan Cross, baseball star, and sits with Amanda Monk and the other queen bees at lunch.

"But let's face it, we didn't come up here for the view. You're Violet, right?"

She blinks once, and I take this as a yes.

"Theodore Finch. I think we had pre-cal together last year."

She blinks again.

"I hate math, but that's not why I'm up here. No offense if that's why you are. You're probably better at math than I am, because pretty much everyone's better at math than I am, but it's okay, I'm fine with it. See, I excel at other, more important things—guitar, sex, and consistently disappointing my dad, to name a few. By the way, it's apparently true that you'll never use it in the real world. Math, I mean."

I keep talking, but I can tell I'm running out of steam. I need to take a piss, for one thing, and so my words aren't the only thing twitching. *(Note to self: Before attempting to take own life, remember to take a leak.)* And, two, it's starting to rain, which, in this temperature, will probably turn to sleet before it hits the ground.

"It's starting to rain," I say, as if she doesn't know this. "I guess there's an argument to be made that the rain will wash away the blood, leaving us a neater mess to clean up than otherwise. But it's the mess part that's got me thinking. I'm not a vain person, but I am human, and I don't know about you, but I don't want to look like I've been run through the wood chipper at my funeral."

She's shivering or shaking, I can't tell which, and so I slowly inch my way toward her, hoping I don't fall off before I get there, because the last thing I want to do is make a jackass out of myself in front of this girl. "I've made it clear I want cremation, but my mom doesn't believe in it." And my dad will do whatever she says so he won't upset her any more than he already has, and besides, *You're far too young to think about this, you know your Grandma Finch lived to be ninety-eight, we don't need to talk about that now, Theodore, don't upset your mother.*

"So it'll be an open coffin for me, which means if I jump, it ain't gonna be pretty. Besides, I kind of like my face intact like this, two eyes, one nose, one mouth, a full set of teeth, which, if I'm being honest, is one of my better features." I smile so she can see what I mean. Everything where it should be, on the outside at least.

When she doesn't say anything, I go on inching and talking. "Most of all, I feel bad for the undertaker. What a shitty job that must be anyway, but then to have to deal with an asshole like me?"

From down below, someone yells, "Violet? Is that Violet up there?"

"Oh God," she says, so low I barely hear it. "OhGodohGodohGod." The wind blows her skirt and hair, and it looks like she's going to fly away.

There is general buzzing from the ground, and I shout, "Don't try to save me! You'll only kill yourself!" Then I say, very low, just to her, "Here's what I think we should do." I'm about a foot away from her now. "I want you to throw your shoes toward the bell and then hold on to the rail, just grab right onto it, and once you've got it, lean against it and then lift your right foot up and over. Got that?"

She nods and almost loses her balance.

"Don't nod. And whatever you do, don't go the wrong way and step forward instead of back. I'll count you off. On three."

She throws her boots in the direction of the bell, and they fall with a *thud, thud* onto the concrete.

"One. Two. Three."

She grips the stone and kind of props herself against it and then lifts her leg up and over so that she's sitting on the railing. She stares down at the ground and I can see that she's frozen again, and so I say, "Good. Great. Just stop looking down."

She slowly looks at me and then reaches for the floor of the bell tower with her right foot, and once she's found it, I say, "Now get that left leg back over however you can. Don't let go of the wall." By now she's shaking so hard I can hear her teeth chatter, but I watch as her left foot joins her right, and she is safe.

So now it's just me out here. I gaze down at the ground one last time, past my size-thirteen feet that won't stop growing—today I'm wearing sneakers with fluorescent laces—past the open windows of the fourth floor, the third, the second, past Amanda Monk, who is cackling from the front steps and swishing her blond hair like a pony, books over her head, trying to flirt and protect herself from the rain at the same time.

I gaze past all of this at the ground itself, which is now slick and damp, and imagine myself lying there.

I could just step off. It would be over in seconds. No more "Theodore Freak." No more hurt. No more anything.

I try to get past the unexpected interruption of saving a life and return to the business at hand. For a minute, I can feel it: the sense of peace as my mind goes quiet, like I'm already dead. I am weightless and free. Nothing and no one to fear, not even myself.

Then a voice from behind me says, "I want you to hold on to the rail, and once you've got it, lean against it and lift your right foot up and over."

Like that, I can feel the moment passing, maybe already passed, and now it seems like a stupid idea, except for picturing the look on Amanda's face as I go sailing by her. I laugh at the thought. I laugh so hard I almost fall off, and this scares me—like, really scares me—and I catch myself and Violet catches me as Amanda looks up. "Weirdo!" someone shouts. Amanda's little group snickers. She cups her big mouth and aims it skyward. "You okay, V?"

Violet leans over the rail, still holding on to my legs. "I'm okay."

The door at the top of the tower stairs cracks open and my best friend, Charlie Donahue, appears. Charlie is black. Not CW black, but black-black. He also gets laid more than anyone else I know.

He says, "They're serving pizza today," as if I wasn't standing on a ledge six stories above the ground, my arms outstretched, a girl wrapped around my knees.

"Why don't you go ahead and get it over with, freak?" Gabe Romero, better known as Roamer, better known as Dumbass, yells from below. More laughter.

Because I've got a date with your mother later, I think but don't say because, let's face it, it's lame, and also he will come up here and beat my face in and then throw me off, and this defeats the point of just doing it myself.

Instead I shout, "Thanks for saving me, Violet. I don't know what I would've done if you hadn't come along. I guess I'd be dead right now."

The last face I see below belongs to my school counselor, Mr. Embry. As he glares up at me, I think, *Great. Just great.*

I let Violet help me over the wall and onto the concrete. From down below, there's a smattering of applause, not for me, but for Violet, the hero. Up close like this, I can see that her skin is smooth and clear except for two freckles on her right cheek, and her eyes are a gray-green that makes me think of fall. It's the eyes that get me. They are large and arresting, as if she sees everything. As warm as they are, they are busy, no-bullshit eyes, the kind that can look right into you, which I can tell even through the glasses. She's pretty and tall, but not too tall, with long, restless legs and curvy hips, which I like on a girl. Too many high school girls are built like boys.

"I was just sitting there," she says. "On the railing. I didn't come up here to—"

"Let me ask you something. Do you think there's such a thing as a perfect day?"

"What?"

"A perfect day. Start to finish. When nothing terrible or sad or ordinary happens. Do you think it's possible?"

"I don't know."

"Have you ever had one?"

"No."

"I've never had one either, but I'm looking for it."

She whispers, "Thank you, Theodore Finch." She reaches up and kisses me on the cheek, and I can smell her shampoo, which reminds me of flowers. She says into my ear, "If you ever tell anyone about this, I'll kill you." Carrying her boots, she hurries away and out of the rain, back through the door that leads to the flight of dark and rickety stairs that takes you down to one of the many too-bright and too-crowded school hallways.

Charlie watches her go and, as the door swings closed behind her, he turns back to me. "Man, why do you do that?"

"Because we all have to die someday. I just want to be prepared."

This isn't the reason, of course, but it will be enough for him. The truth is, there are a lot of reasons, most of which change daily, like the thirteen fourth graders killed earlier this week when some SOB opened fire in their school gym, or the girl two years behind me who just died of cancer, or the man I saw outside the Mall Cinema kicking his dog, or my father.

Charlie may think it, but at least he doesn't say "Weirdo," which is why he's my best friend. Other than the fact that I appreciate this about him, we don't have much in common.

Technically, I'm on probation this year. This is due to a small matter involving a desk and a chalkboard. (For the record, replacing a chalkboard is more expensive than you might think.) It's also due to a guitar-smashing incident during assembly, an illegal use of fire-works, and maybe a fight or two. As a result, I've agreed involuntarily to the following: weekly counseling; maintaining a high B average; and participation in at least one extracurricular. I chose macramé because I'm the only guy with twenty semihot girls, which I thought was pretty good odds for me. I also have to behave myself, play well with others, refrain from throwing desks, as well as refrain from any "violent physical altercations." And I must always, always, what-ever I do, hold my tongue, because not doing so, apparently, is how trouble starts. If I f--- anything up from here on out, it's expulsion for me.

Inside the counseling office, I check in with the secretary and take a seat in one of the hard wooden chairs until Mr. Embry is ready for me. If I know Embryo—as I call him to myself—like I know Embryo,

he'll want to know just what the hell I was doing in the bell tower. If I'm lucky, we won't have time to cover much more than that.

In a few minutes he waves me in, a short, thick man built like a bull. As he shuts the door, he drops the smile. He sits down, hunches over his desk, and fixes his eyes on me like I'm a suspect he needs to crack. "What in the hell were you doing in the bell tower?"

The thing I like about Embryo is that not only is he predictable, he gets to the point. I've known him since sophomore year.

"I wanted to see the view."

"Were you planning to jump off?"

"Not on pizza day. Never on pizza day, which is one of the better days of the week." I should mention that I am a brilliant deflector. So brilliant that I could get a full scholarship to college and major in it, except why bother? I've already mastered the art.

I wait for him to ask about Violet, but instead he says, "I need to know if you were or are planning to harm yourself. I am goddamn serious. If Principal Wertz hears about this, you're gone before you can say 'suspended,' or worse. Not to mention if I don't pay attention and you decide to go back up there and jump off, I'm looking at a lawsuit, and on the salary they pay me, believe me when I say I do not have the money to be sued. This holds true whether you jump off the bell tower or the Purina Tower, whether it's school property or not."

I stroke my chin like I'm deep in thought. "The Purina Tower. Now there's an idea."

He doesn't budge except to squint at me. Like most people in the Midwest, Embryo doesn't believe in humor, especially when it pertains to sensitive subjects. "Not funny, Mr. Finch. This is not a joking matter."

"No, sir. Sorry."

"The thing suicides don't focus on is their wake. Not just your parents and siblings, but your friends, your girlfriends, your classmates, your teachers." I like the way he seems to think I have many, many people depending on me, including not just one but multiple girlfriends.

"I was just messing around. I agree it was probably not the best way to spend first period."

He picks up a file and thumps it down in front of him and starts flipping through it. I wait as he reads, and then he looks at me again. I wonder if he's counting the days till summer.

He stands, just like a cop on TV, and walks around his desk until he's looming over me. He leans against it, arms folded, and I look past him, searching for the hidden two-way mirror.

"Do I need to call your mother?"

"No. And again no." And again: *no no no.* "Look, it was a stupid thing to do. I just wanted to see what it felt like to stand there and look down. I would never jump from the bell tower."

"If it happens again, if you so much as *think* about it again, I call her. And you're going to do a drug test."

"I appreciate your concern, sir." I try to sound my most sincere, because the last thing I want is a bigger, brighter spotlight directed at me, following me throughout the halls of school, throughout the other parts of my life, such as they are. And the thing is, I actually like Embryo. "As for the whole drug thing, there's no need to waste precious time. Really. Unless cigarettes count. Drugs and me? Not a good mix. Believe me, I've tried." I fold my hands like a good boy. "As for the whole bell tower thing, even though it

wasn't at all what you think, I can still promise that it won't happen again."

"That's right—it won't. I want you here twice a week instead of once. You come in Monday and Friday and talk to me, just so I can see how you're doing."

"I'm happy to, sir—I mean, I, like, really enjoy these conversations of ours—but I'm good."

"It's nonnegotiable. Now let's discuss the end of last semester. You missed four, almost five, weeks of school. Your mother says you were sick with the flu."

He's actually talking about my sister Kate, but he doesn't know that. She was the one who called the school while I was out, because Mom has enough to worry about.

"If that's what she says, who are we to argue?"

The fact is, I was sick, but not in an easily explained flu kind of way. It's my experience that people are a lot more sympathetic if they can *see* you hurting, and for the millionth time in my life I wish for measles or smallpox or some other recognizable disease just to make it simple for me and also for them. Anything would be better than the truth: *I shut down again. I went blank. One minute I was spinning, and the next minute my mind was dragging itself around in a circle, like an old, arthritic dog trying to lie down. And then I just turned off and went to sleep, but not sleep in the way you do every night. Think a long, dark sleep where you don't dream at all.*

Embryo once again narrows his eyes to a squint and stares at me hard, trying to induce a sweat. "And can we expect you to show up and stay out of trouble this semester?"

"Absolutely."

"And keep up with your classwork?"

"Yes, sir."

"I'll arrange the drug test with the nurse." He jabs the air with his finger, pointing at me. "Probation means 'period of testing somebody's suitability; period when student must improve.' Look it up if you don't believe me, and for Christ's sake, stay alive."

The thing I don't say is: I want to stay alive. The reason I don't say it is because, given that fat folder in front of him, he'd never believe it. And here's something else he'd never believe—I'm fighting to be here in this shitty, messed-up world. Standing on the ledge of the bell tower isn't about dying. It's about having control. It's about never going to sleep again.

Embryo stalks around his desk and gathers a stack of "Teens in Trouble" pamphlets. Then he tells me I'm not alone and I can always talk to him, his door is open, he's here, and he'll see me on Monday. I want to say no offense, but that's not much of a comfort. Instead, I thank him because of the dark circles under his eyes and the smoker's lines etched around his mouth. He'll probably light up a cigarette as soon as I go. I take a heaping pile of pamphlets and leave him to it. He never once mentioned Violet, and I'm relieved.

VIOLET

154 days till graduation

Friday morning. Office of Mrs. Marion Kresney, school counselor, who has small, kind eyes and a smile too big for her face. According to the certificate on the wall above her head, she's been at Bartlett High for fifteen years. This is our twelfth meeting.

My heart is still racing and my hands are still shaking from being up on that ledge. I have gone cold all over, and what I want is to lie down. I wait for Mrs. Kresney to say: *I know what you were doing first period, Violet Markey. Your parents are on their way. Doctors are standing by, ready to escort you to the nearest mental health facility.*

But we start as we always do.

"How are you, Violet?"

"I'm fine, and you?" I sit on my hands.

"I'm fine. Let's talk about you. I want to know how you're feeling."

"I'm good." Just because she hasn't brought it up does not mean she doesn't know. She almost never asks anything directly.

"How are you sleeping?"

The nightmares started a month after the accident. She asks about them every time I see her, because I made the mistake of mentioning them to my mom, who mentioned them to her. This is one of the main reasons why I'm here and why I've stopped telling my mom anything.

"I'm sleeping fine."

The thing about Mrs. Kresney is that she always, always smiles, no matter what. I like this about her.

"Any bad dreams?"

"No."

I used to write them down, but I don't anymore. I can remember every detail. Like this one I had four weeks ago where I was literally melting away. In the dream, my dad said, "You've come to the end, Violet. You've reached your limit. We all have them, and yours is now." *But I don't want it to be.* I watched as my feet turned into puddles and disappeared. Next were my hands. It didn't hurt, and I remember thinking: *I shouldn't mind this because there isn't any pain. It's just a slipping away.* But I did mind as, limb by limb, the rest of me went invisible before I woke up.

Mrs. Kresney shifts in her chair, her smile fixed on her face. I wonder if she smiles in her sleep.

"Let's talk about college."

This time last year, I would have loved to talk about college. Eleanor and I used to do this sometimes after Mom and Dad had gone to bed. We'd sit outside if it was warm enough, inside if it was too cold. We imagined the places we would go and the people we would meet, far away from Bartlett, Indiana, population 14,983, where we felt like aliens from some distant planet.

"You've applied to UCLA, Stanford, Berkeley, the University of Florida, the University of Buenos Aires, Northern Caribbean University, and the National University of Singapore. This is a very diverse list, but what happened to NYU?"

Since the summer before seventh grade, NYU's creative writing program has been my dream. This is thanks to visiting New York with my mother, who is a college professor and writer. She did her graduate work at NYU, and for three weeks the four of us stayed in what would be the point? It was a site about sisters. Besides, in that instant we went plowing through the guardrail, my words died too.

"I don't want to talk about the website."

"I believe your mother is an author. She must be very helpful in giving advice."

"Jessamyn West said, 'Writing is so difficult that writers, having had their hell on earth, will escape all punishment hereafter.'"

She lights up at this. "Do you feel you're being punished?" She is talking about the accident. Or maybe she is referring to being here in this office, this school, this town.

"No." *Do I feel I should be punished?* Yes. Why else would I have given myself bangs?

"Do you believe you're responsible for what happened?"

I tug on the bangs now. They are lopsided. "No."

the city and socialized with her former teachers and classmates—novelists, playwrights, screenwriters, poets. My plan was to apply for early admission in October. But then the accident happened and I changed my mind.

"I missed the application deadline." The deadline for regular admission was one week ago today. I filled everything out, even wrote my essay, but didn't send it in.

"Let's talk about the writing. Let's talk about the website."

She means EleanorandViolet.com. Eleanor and I started it after we moved to Indiana. We wanted to create an online magazine that offered two (very) different perspectives on fashion, beauty, boys, books, life. Last year, Eleanor's friend Gemma Sterling (star of the hit Web series *Rant*) mentioned us in an interview, and our following tripled. But I haven't touched the site since Eleanor died, because

She sits back. Her smile slips a fraction of an inch. We both know I'm lying. I wonder what she would say if I told her that an hour ago I was being talked off the ledge of the bell tower. By now, I'm pretty sure she doesn't know.

"Have you driven yet?"

"No."

"Have you allowed yourself to ride in the car with your parents?"

"No."

"But they want you to." This isn't a question. She says this like she's talked to one or both of them, which she probably has.

"I'm not ready." These are the three magic words. I've discovered they can get you out of almost anything.

She leans forward. "Have you thought about returning to cheer-leading?"

"No."

"Student council?"

"No."

"You still play flute in the orchestra?"

"I'm last chair." That's something that hasn't changed since the accident. I was always last chair because I'm not very good at flute.

She sits back again. For a moment I think she's given up. Then she says, "I'm concerned about your progress, Violet. Frankly, you should be further along than you are right now. You can't avoid cars forever, especially now that we're in winter. You can't keep standing still. You need to remember that you're a survivor, and that means . . ."

I will never know what that means because as soon as I hear the word "survivor," I get up and walk out.

On my way to fourth period. School hallway.

At least fifteen people—some I know, some I don't, some who haven't talked to me in months—stop me on my way to class to tell me how courageous I was to save Theodore Finch from killing himself. One of the girls from the school paper wants to do an interview.

Of all the people I could have "saved," Theodore Finch is the worst possible choice because he's a Bartlett legend. I don't know him that well, but I know *of* him. Everyone knows *of* him. Some people hate him because they think he's weird and he gets into fights and gets kicked out of school and does what he wants. Some people worship him because he's weird and he gets into fights and gets kicked out of school and does what he wants. He plays guitar in five or six different bands, and last year he cut a record. But he's kind of . . . extreme. Like he came to school one day painted head-to-toe red, and it wasn't even Spirit Week. He told some people he was protesting racism and others he was protesting the consumption of meat. Junior year he wore a cape every day for an entire month, cracked a chalkboard in half with a desk, and stole all the dissecting frogs from the science wing and gave them a funeral before burying them in the baseball field. The great Anna Faris once said that the secret of surviving high school is to "lay low." Finch does the opposite of this.

I'm five minutes late to Russian literature, where Mrs. Mahone and her wig assign us a ten-page paper on *The Brothers Karamazov.* Groans follow from everyone but me, because no matter what Mrs. Kresney seems to think, I have Extenuating Circumstances.

I don't even listen as Mrs. Mahone goes over what she wants. Instead I pick at a thread on my skirt. I have a headache. Probably from the glasses. Eleanor's eyes were worse than mine. I take the glasses off and set them on the desk. They were stylish on her. They're ugly on me. Especially with the bangs. But maybe, if I wear the glasses long enough, I can be like her. I can see what she saw. I can be both of us at once so no one will have to miss her, most of all me.

The thing is, there are good days and bad days. I feel almost guilty saying they aren't all bad. Something catches me off guard—a TV show, a funny one-liner from my dad, a comment in class—and I laugh like nothing ever happened. I feel normal again, whatever that is. Some mornings I wake up and I sing while I'm getting ready. Or maybe I turn up the music and dance. On most days, I walk to school. Other days I take my bike, and every now and then my mind tricks me into thinking I'm just a regular girl out for a ride.

Emily Ward pokes me in the back and hands me a note. Because Mrs. Mahone collects our phones at the start of every class, it's the old-fashioned kind, written on notebook paper.

Is it true you saved Finch from killing himself? x Ryan. There is only one Ryan in this room—some would argue there's only one Ryan in the whole school, maybe even the world—and that's Ryan Cross. I look up and catch his eye, two rows over. He is too good-looking. Broad shoulders, warm gold-brown hair, green eyes, and enough freckles to make him seem approachable. Until December, he was my boyfriend, but now we're taking a break.

I let the note sit on my desk for five minutes before answering it. Finally, I write: *I just happened to be there. x V.* Less than a minute later, it's passed back to me, but this time I don't open it. I think of how many girls would love to receive a note like this from Ryan Cross.

The Violet Markey of last spring would have been one of them.

When the bell rings, I hang back. Ryan lingers for a minute, waiting to see what I do, but when I just sit there, he collects his phone and goes on.

Mrs. Mahone says, "Yes, Violet?"

Ten pages used to be no big deal. A teacher would ask for ten and I would write twenty. If they wanted twenty, I'd give them thirty. Writing was what I did best, better than being a daughter or girlfriend or sister. Writing was me. But now writing is one of the things I can't do.

I barely have to say anything, not even "I'm not ready." It's in the unwritten rulebook of life, under How to React When a Student Loses a Loved One and Is, Nine Months Later, Still Having a Very Hard Time.

Mrs. Mahone sighs and hands me my phone. "Give me a page or a paragraph, Violet. Just do your best." My Extenuating Circumstances save the day.

Outside the classroom, Ryan is waiting. I can see him trying to figure out the puzzle so he can put me back together again and turn me into the fun girlfriend he used to know. He says, "You look really pretty today." He is nice enough not to stare at my hair.

"Thanks."

Over Ryan's shoulder, I see Theodore Finch strutting by. He nods at me like he knows something I don't, and he keeps on going.

FINCH

By lunch, it's all over school that Violet Markey saved Theodore
Finch from jumping off the bell tower. On my way to U.S. Geography, I walk behind a group of girls in the hallway who are going
on and on about it, no idea that I'm the one and only Theodore
Finch.

They talk over each other in these high voices that always end
in question marks, so that it sounds like *I heard he had a gun? I heard
she had to wrestle it out of his hands? My cousin Stacey, who goes to New
Castle, says she and a friend were in Chicago and he was playing this club
and he totally hooked up with both of them? Well, my brother was there*

when he set off the firecrackers, and he said before the police took him away, he was all "Unless you want to reimburse me, I'll wait for the finale"?

Apparently, I'm tragic and dangerous. *Oh yeah*, I think. *That's right. I am here and now and not just awake, but Awake, and everyone can just deal with it because I am the second freakin' coming.* I lean in and say to them, "I heard he did it over a girl," and then I swagger all the way to class.

Inside the classroom, I take my seat, feeling infamous and invincible and twitchy and strangely exhilarated, as if I just escaped, well, death. I look around, but no one is paying any attention to me or Mr. Black, our teacher, who is literally the largest man I have ever seen. He has a red, red face that always makes him look like he's on the verge of heatstroke or a heart attack, and he wheezes when he talks.

The whole time I've been in Indiana, which is all my life—the purgatory years, I call them—we've apparently lived just eleven miles away from the highest point in the state. No one ever told me, not my parents or my sisters or my teachers, until now, right this minute, in the "Wander Indiana" section of U.S. Geography—the one that was implemented by the school board this year in an effort to "enlighten students as to the rich history available in their own home state and inspire Hoosier pride."

No joke.

Mr. Black settles into his chair and clears his throat. "What better and more . . . . appropriate way to start off . . . the semester than by beginning . . . with the highest point?" Because of the wheezing, it's hard to tell if Mr. Black is all that impressed by the information he's relaying. "Hoosier Hill is . . . 1,257 feet above sea level . . . and it's in the backyard . . . of a family home. . . . In 2005, an Eagle . . . Scout from Kentucky . . . got permission to . . . build a trail and picnic area . . . and put up a sign. . . ."

I raise my hand, which Mr. Black ignores.

As he talks, I leave my hand in the air and think, *What if I went there and stood on that point? Would things look different from 1,257 feet? It doesn't seem very high, but they're proud of it, and who am I to say 1,257 feet isn't something to be impressed by?*

Finally, he nods at me, his lips so tight, it looks like he's swallowed them. "Yes, Mr. Finch?" He sighs the sigh of a one-hundred-year-old man and gives me an apprehensive, distrustful look.

"I suggest a field trip. We need to see the wondrous sights of Indiana while we still can, because at least three of us in this room are going to graduate and leave our great state at the end of this year, and what will we have to show for it except a subpar public school education from one of the worst school systems in the nation? Besides, a place like this is going to be hard to take in unless we see it. Kind of like the Grand Canyon or Yosemite. You need to be there to really appreciate its splendor."

I'm only being about twenty percent sarcastic, but Mr. Black says, "Thank you, Mr. Finch," in a way that means the direct opposite of thank you. I start drawing hills on my notebook in tribute to our state's highest point, but they look more like formless lumps or airborne snakes—I can't decide.

"Theodore is correct that some . . . of you will leave . . . here at the end of . . . this school year to go . . . somewhere else. You'll be departing our . . . great state, and before . . . you do, you should . . . see it. You should . . . wander. . . ."

A noise from across the room interrupts him. Someone has come in late and dropped a book and then, in picking up the book, has upset all her other books so that everything has gone tumbling. This is followed by laughter because we're in high school, which means we're predictable and almost anything is funny, especially if it's someone else's public humiliation. The girl who dropped everything is Violet Markey, the same Violet Markey from the bell tower. She turns beet red and I can tell she wants to die. Not in a jumping-from-a-great-height kind of way, but more along the lines of *Please, earth, swallow me whole.*

I know this feeling better than I know my mom or my sisters or Charlie Donahue. This feeling and I have been together all my life. Like the time I gave myself a concussion during kickball in front of Suze Haines; or the time I laughed so hard that something flew out of my nose and landed on Gabe Romero; or the entire eighth grade.

And so, because I'm used to it and because this Violet girl is about three dropped pencils away from crying, I knock one of my own books onto the floor. All eyes shift to me. I bend to pick it up and purposely send the others flying—boomeranging into walls, windows, heads—and just for good measure, I tilt my chair over so I go crashing. This is followed by snickers and applause and a "freak" or two, and Mr. Black wheezing, "If you're done . . . Theodore . . . I'd like to continue."

I right myself, right the chair, take a bow, collect my books, bow again, settle in, and smile at Violet, who is looking at me with what can only be described as surprise and relief and something else— worry, maybe. I'd like to think there's a little lust mixed in too, but that could be wishful thinking. The smile I give her is the best smile I have, the one that makes my mother forgive me for staying out too late or for just generally being weird. (Other times, I see my mom looking at me—when she looks at me at all—like she's thinking: *Where in the hell did you come from? You must get it from your father's side.*)

Violet smiles back. Immediately, I feel better, because she feels better and because of the way she smiles at me, as if I'm not something to be avoided. This makes twice in one day that I've saved her. *Tenderhearted Theodore*, my mother always says. *Too tenderhearted for his own good.* It's meant as a criticism and I take it as one.

Mr. Black fixes his eyes on Violet and then me. "As I was saying . . . your project for this . . . class is to report on . . . at least two, preferably three . . . wonders of Indiana." I want to ask, *Wonders or wanders?* But I'm busy watching Violet as she concentrates on the chalkboard, the corner of her mouth still turned up.

Mr. Black goes on about how he wants us to feel free to choose the places that strike our fancy, no matter how obscure or far away. Our mission is to go there and see each one, take pictures, shoot video, delve deep into their history, and tell him just what it is about these places that makes us proud to be a Hoosier. If it's possible to link them in some way, all the better. We have the rest of the semester to complete the project, and we need to take it seriously.

"You will work . . . in teams of . . . two. This will count . . . for thirty-five percent . . . of your final grade. . . ."

I raise my hand again. "Can we choose our partners?"

"Yes."

"I choose Violet Markey."

"You may work that out . . . with her after class."

I shift in my seat so I can see her, elbow on the back of my chair. "Violet Markey, I'd like to be your partner on this project."

Her face turns pink as everyone looks at her. Violet says to Mr. Black, "I thought if there was something else I could do—maybe research and write a short report." Her voice is low, but she sounds a little pissed. "I'm not ready to . . ."

He interrupts her. "Miss Markey, I'm going . . . to do you the biggest . . . favor of your life. . . . I'm going to say . . . no."

"No?"

"No. It is a new year. . . . It is time to get . . . back on the camel."

A few people laugh at this. Violet looks at me and I can see that, yes, she is pissed, and it's then I remember the accident. Violet and her sister, sometime last spring. Violet lived, the sister died. This is why she doesn't want attention.

The rest of class time is spent telling us about places Mr. Black thinks we might enjoy and that, no matter what, we must see before we graduate—the usual humdrum tourist spots like Conner Prairie, the Levi Coffin House, the Lincoln Museum, and James Whitcomb Riley's boyhood home—even though I know that most of us will stay right here in this town until we die.

I try to catch Violet's eye again, but she doesn't look up. Instead, she shrinks low in her seat and stares straight ahead.

Outside of class, Gabe Romero blocks my way. As usual, he's not alone. Amanda Monk waits just behind, hip jutted out, Joe Wyatt and Ryan Cross on either side of her. Good, easygoing, decent, nice-guy Ryan, athlete, A student, vice president of the class. The worst thing about him is that since kindergarten he's known exactly who he is.

Roamer says, "I better not catch you looking at me again."

"I wasn't looking at you. Believe me, there are at least a hundred other things in that room I'd look at before you, including Mr. Black's large, naked ass."

"Faggot."

Because Roamer and I have been sworn enemies since middle school, he shoves the books out of my hands, and even though this is right out of Fifth-Grade Bullying 101, I feel a familiar black grenade of anger—like an old friend—go off in my stomach, the thick, toxic smoke from it rising up and spreading through my chest. It's the same feeling I had last year in that instant before I picked up a desk and hurled it—not at Roamer, like he wants everyone to believe, but at the chalkboard in Mr. Geary's room.

"Pick 'em up, bitch." Roamer walks past me, knocking me in the chest—hard—with his shoulder. I want to slam his head into a locker and then reach down his throat and pull his heart out through his mouth, because the thing about being Awake is that everything in you is alive and aching and making up for lost time.

But instead I count all the way to sixty, a stupid smile plastered on my stupid face. *I will not get detention. I will not get expelled. I will be good. I will be quiet. I will be still.*

Mr. Black watches from the doorway, and I try to give him a casual nod to show him everything's cool, everything's under control, everything's fine, nothing to see, palms aren't itching, skin isn't burning, blood isn't pumping, please move along. I've made a promise to myself that this year will be different. If I keep ahead of everything, and that includes me, I should be able to stay awake and here, and not just semi-here but here as in present as in now.

The rain has stopped, and in the parking lot Charlie Donahue and I lean against his car under the washed-out January sun as he talks about the thing he most loves talking about other than himself—sex. Our friend Brenda stands listening, books clutched against her broad, broad chest, hair shining pink and red.

Charlie spent winter break working at the Mall Cinema, where he apparently let all the hot girls sneak in without paying. This got him more action than even he knew what to do with, mostly in the handicapped row in the back, the one missing armrests.

He nods at me. "What about you?"

"What about me?"

"Where were you?"

"Around. I didn't feel like coming to school, so I hit the interstate and didn't look back." There's no way of explaining the Asleep to my friends, and even if there was, there's no need. One of the things I like best about Charlie and Bren is that I don't have to explain myself. I come, I go, and *Oh well, it's just Finch.*

Charlie nods again. "What we need to do is get you laid." It's an indirect reference to the bell tower incident. If I get laid, I won't try to kill myself. According to Charlie, getting laid fixes everything. If only world leaders would get laid well and regularly, the world's problems might disappear.

Brenda frowns at him. "You're a pig, Charlie."

"You love me."

"You wish I'd love you. Why don't you be more like Finch? He's a gentleman." There aren't many people who would say this about me, but the great thing about this life of ours is that you can be someone different to everybody.

I say, "You can leave me out of it."

Bren shakes her head. "No, I'm serious. Gentlemen are rare. They're like virgins or leprechauns. If I ever get married, I'm going to marry one."

I can't resist saying, "A virgin or a leprechaun?" She slugs me in the arm.

"There's a difference between a gentleman and a guy with no play." Charlie nods at me. "No offense, man."

"None taken." It's true, after all, at least compared to him, and actually what he means is that I have bad luck with women. Something about going for the bitchy ones or the crazy ones or the ones who pretend not to know me when other people are around.

Anyway, I'm barely listening, because over Bren's shoulder I see her again—Violet. I can already feel myself falling hard, something I've been known to do. (Suze Haines, Laila Collman, Annalise Lemke, the three Brianas—Briana Harley, Briana Bailey, Briana Boudreau . . .) All because she smiled at me. But it was a damn good smile. A genuine one, which is hard to come by these days. Especially when you're me, Theodore Freak, Resident Aberration.

Bren turns around to see what I'm looking at. She shakes her head at me, her mouth all smirked up in a way that makes me protect my arm. "God, you guys are all the same."

At home, my mother is talking on the phone and defrosting one of the casseroles my sister Kate prepares at the start of each week.

Mom waves and then keeps right on. Kate runs down the stairs, swipes her car keys from the counter, and says, "Later, loser." I have two sisters—Kate, just one year older than I am, and Decca, who's eight. Clearly, she was a mistake, which she figured out at the age of six. But we all know if anyone is the mistake here, it's me.

I go upstairs, wet shoes squeaking against the floor, and shut the door to my room. I pull out something old on vinyl without checking what it is and slap it onto the turntable I found in the basement. The record bumps and scratches, sounding like something from the 1920s. I'm in a Split Enz kind of phase right now, hence the sneakers. I'm trying out Theodore Finch, '80s kid, and seeing how he fits.

I fish through my desk for a cigarette, stick it in my mouth, and remember as I'm reaching for my lighter that Theodore Finch, '80s kid, doesn't smoke. God, I hate him, the clean-cut, eager little prick. I leave the cigarette in my mouth unlit, trying to chew the nicotine out, and pick up the guitar, play along, then give it up and sit down at the computer, swinging my chair around so it's backward, the only way I can compose.

I type: **January 5. Method: Bell tower of school. On a scale of one to ten on the how-close-did-I-come scale: five. Facts: Jumping increases on full moons and holidays. One of the more famous jumpers was Roy Raymond, founder of Victoria's Secret. Related fact: In 1912, a man named Franz Reichelt jumped off the Eiffel Tower wearing a parachute suit he designed himself. He jumped to test his invention—he expected to fly— but instead he fell straight down, hitting the ground like a meteor and leaving a 5.9-inch-deep crater from the impact. Did he mean to kill himself? Doubtful. I think he was just cocky, and also stupid.**

A quick internet search turns up the information that only five to ten percent of all suicides are committed by jumping (so says Johns Hopkins). Apparently, jumping as a means of killing oneself is usually chosen for convenience, which is why places like San Francisco, with its Golden Gate Bridge (the world's top suicide destination), are so popular. Here, all we have is the Purina Tower and a 1,257-foot hill.

I write: **Reason for not jumping: Too messy. Too public. Too crowded.**

I switch off Google and hop onto Facebook. I find Amanda Monk's page because she's friends with everyone, even the people she's not friends with, and I pull up her friend list, typing in "Violet."

Just like that, there she is. I click on her photo and there she is, even bigger, wearing the same smile she gave me earlier. You have to be her friend to read her profile and view the rest of her pictures. I sit staring at the screen, suddenly desperate to know more. Who is this Violet Markey? I try a Google search, because maybe there's a secret back entrance to her Facebook page, one that requires a special knock or a three-digit code, something easily figured out.

What I pull up instead is a site called EleanorandViolet.com, which lists Violet Markey as cocreator/editor/writer. It's got all the usual boys-and-beauty-type blog posts, the most recent from April 3 of last year. The other thing I pull up is a news article.

> **Eleanor Markey, 18, a senior at Bartlett High School and member of the student congress, lost control of her car on A Street Bridge at approximately 12:45 a.m. April 5. Icy conditions and speed may have caused the crash. Eleanor was killed on impact. Her 16-year-old sister, Violet, a passenger in the vehicle, sustained only minor injuries.**

I sit reading and rereading this, a black feeling settling in the pit of my stomach. And then I do something I swore I'd never do. I sign up for Facebook just so I can send her a friend request. Having an account will make me look sociable and normal, and maybe work to offset the whole meeting-on-the-verge-of-suicide situation, so that she'll feel it's safe to know me. I take a picture of myself with my phone, decide I look too serious, take another one—too goofy—and settle on the third, which is somewhere in between.

I sleep the computer so I don't check every five minutes, and then I play the guitar, read a few pages of *Macbeth* for homework, and eat dinner with Decca and my mom, a tradition that started last year, after the divorce. Even though I'm not much into eating, dinner is one of the most enjoyable parts of my day because I get to turn my brain off.

Mom says, "Decca, tell me what you learned today." She makes sure to ask us about school so that she feels she's done her duty. This is her favorite way to start.

Dec says, "I learned that Jacob Barry is a jackass." She has been swearing more often lately, trying to get a reaction out of Mom, to see if she's really listening.

"Decca," Mom says mildly, but she is only half paying attention.

Decca goes on to tell us about how this boy named Jacob glued his hands to his desk just to get out of a science quiz, but when they tried to separate skin from wood, his palms came off with the glue. Decca's eyes gleam like the eyes of a small, rabid animal. She clearly thinks he deserved it, and then she says so.

Mom is suddenly listening. "Decca." She shakes her head. This is the extent of her parenting. Ever since my dad left, she's tried really hard to be the cool parent. Still, I feel bad for her because she loves him, even though, at his core, he's selfish and rotten, and even though he left her for a woman named Rosemarie with an accent over one of the letters—no one can ever remember which—and because of something she said to me the day he left: "I never expected to be single at forty." It was the way she said it more than the words themselves. She made it sound so *final*.

Ever since then, I've done what I could to be pleasant and quiet, making myself as small and unseen as possible—which includes pretending to go to school when I'm asleep, as in *the Asleep*—so that I don't add to the burden. I am not always successful.

"How was your day, Theodore?"

"Grand." I push my food around my plate, trying to create a pattern. The thing about eating is that there are so many other more interesting things to do. I feel the same way about sleeping. Complete wastes of time.

Interesting fact: A Chinese man died from lack of sleep when he stayed awake for eleven days straight as he attempted to watch every game in the European Championship (that's soccer, for those, like me, who have no clue). On the eleventh night, he watched Italy beat Ireland 2–0, took a shower, and fell asleep around five a.m. And died. No offense to the dead, but soccer is a really stupid thing to stay awake for.

Mom has stopped eating to study my face. When she does pay attention, which isn't often, she tries hard to be understanding about my "sadness," just like she tries hard to be patient when Kate stays out all night and Decca spends time in the principal's office. My mother blames our bad behavior on the divorce and my dad. She says we just need time to work through it.

Less sarcastically, I add, "It was okay. Uneventful. Boring. Typical." We move on to easier topics, like the house my mother is trying to sell for her clients and the weather.

When dinner is over, Mom lays a hand on my arm, fingertips barely touching the skin, and says, "Isn't it nice to have your brother back, Decca?" She says it as if I'm in danger of disappearing again, right in front of their eyes. The slightly blaming note in her voice makes me cringe, and I get the urge to go back to my room again and stay there. Even though she tries to forgive my sadness, she wants to count on me as man of the house, and even though she thinks I was in school for most of that four-almost-five-week period, I did miss a lot of family dinners. She takes her fingers back and then we're free, which is exactly how we act, the three of us running off in three different directions.

Around ten o'clock, after everyone else has gone to bed and Kate still isn't home, I turn on the computer again and check my Facebook account.

Violet Markey accepted your friend request, it says.

And now we are friends.

I want to shout and jog around the house, maybe climb up onto the roof and spread my arms wide but not jump off, not even think about it. But instead I hunch closer to the screen and browse through her photos—Violet smiling with two people who must be her parents, Violet smiling with friends, Violet smiling at a pep rally, Violet smiling cheek to cheek with another girl, Violet smiling all alone.

I remember the picture of Violet and the girl from the newspaper. This is her sister, Eleanor. She wears the same clunky glasses Violet had on today.

Suddenly a message appears in my inbox.

Violet: **You ambushed me. In front of everyone.**

Me: **Would you have worked with me if I hadn't?**

Violet: **I would have gotten out of it so I didn't have to do it to begin with. Why do you want me to do this project with you anyway?**

Me: **Because our mountain is waiting.**

Violet: **What's that supposed to mean?**

Me: **It means maybe you never dreamed of seeing Indiana, but, in addition to the fact that we're required to do this for school, and I've volunteered—okay, ambushed—you into being my partner, here's what I think: I think I've got a map in my car that wants to be used, and I think there are places we can go that need to be seen. Maybe no one else will ever visit them and appreciate them or take the time to think they're important, but maybe even the smallest places mean something. And if not,** maybe they can mean something to us. At the very least, by the time we leave, we know we will have seen it, this great state of ours. So come on. Let's go. Let's count for something. Let's get off that ledge.

When she doesn't respond, I write: I'm here if you want to talk.

Silence.

I imagine Violet at home right now, on the other side of the computer, her perfect mouth with its perfect corners turned up, smiling at the screen, in spite of everything, no matter what. *Violet smiling.* With one eye on my computer, I pick up the guitar, start making up words, the tune not far behind.

I'm still here, and I'm grateful, because otherwise I would be missing this. Sometimes it's good to be awake.

"So not today," I sing. "Because she smiled at me."

FINCH'S RULES FOR WANDERING

1. There are no rules, because life is made up of too many rules as it is.

2. But there are three "guidelines" (which sounds less rigid than "rules"):

   a) No using our phones to get us there. We have to do this strictly old-school, which means learning to read actual maps.

   b) We alternate choosing places to go, but we also have to be willing to go where the road takes us.

This means the grand, the small, the bizarre, the poetic, the beautiful, the ugly, the surprising. Just like life. But absolutely, unconditionally, resolutely *nothing ordinary*.

c) At each site, we leave something, almost like an offering. It can be our own private game of geocaching ("the recreational activity of hunting for and finding a hidden object by means of GPS coordinates posted on a website"), only not a game, and just for us. The rules of geocaching say "take something, leave something." The way I figure it, we stand to get something out of each place, so why not give something back? Also, it's a way to prove we've been there, and a way to leave a part of us behind.

VIOLET

Saturday night. Amanda Monk's house.

I walk there because it's only three blocks away. Amanda says it will just be us and Ashley Dunston and Shelby Padgett because Amanda's not talking to Suze right now. Again. Amanda used to be one of my closest friends, but ever since April, I've drifted away from her. Since I quit cheering, we don't have much in common. I wonder if we ever did.

I made the mistake of mentioning the whole sleepover thing to my parents, which is why I'm going. "Amanda is making an effort, and you should too, Violet. You can't use your sister's death as an excuse forever. You've got to get back to living." *I'm not ready* doesn't work on my mom and dad anymore.

As I cut across the Wyatts' yard and turn the corner, I hear the party. Amanda's house is lit up like Christmas. People are hanging out the windows. They are standing on the lawn. Amanda's father owns a chain of liquor stores, which is one of the reasons she's popular. That and the fact that she puts out.

I wait on the street, my bag across my shoulder, pillow under my arm. I feel like a sixth grader. Like a goody-good. Eleanor would laugh at me and push me up the walk. She'd already be inside. I get mad at her just picturing it.

I make myself go in. Joe Wyatt hands me something in a red plastic cup. "Beer's in the basement," he shouts. Roamer has taken over the kitchen with random other baseball players and football players.

"Did you score?" Roamer asks Troy Satterfield.

"No, man."

"Did you even kiss her?"

"No."

"Did you get any ass?"

"Yeah, but I think that was by mistake."

They laugh, including Troy. Everyone is talking too loud.

I make my way to the basement. Amanda and Suze Haines, best friends again, are lounging on a couch. I don't see Ashley or Shelby anywhere, but fifteen or twenty guys are sprawled on the floor playing a drinking game. Girls are dancing all around them, including the three Brianas and Brenda Shank-Kravitz, who is friends with Theodore Finch. Couples are making out.

Amanda waves her beer at me. "Oh my God, we need to fix your hair." She is talking about the bangs I gave myself. "And why are you still wearing those glasses? I get wanting to remember your sister, but didn't she have, like, a cute sweater you could wear instead?"

I set my cup down. I'm still carrying my pillow. I say, "My stomach's bugging me. I think I'm going home."

Suze turns her big blue eyes on me. "Is it true you pulled Theodore Finch off a ledge?" (She was "Suzie" until ninth grade, when she dropped the *i*. It's now pronounced "Sooze.")

"Yes." Please, God, I want that whole day to just go away.

Amanda looks at Suze. "I told you it was true." She looks at me and rolls her eyes. "That's just the kind of thing he does. I've known him since, like, kindergarten, and he's only gotten weirder."

Suze takes a drink. "I know him even better than that." Her voice goes slutty. Amanda slaps her arm and Suze slaps her back. When they're done, Suze says to me, "We hooked up sophomore year. He may be weird, but I'll say this for him, that's one guy who knows what he's doing." Her voice goes sluttier. "Unlike most of these boring-ass boys around here." A couple of those boring-ass boys yell from the floor: "Why don't you come and try this on for size, bitch?" Amanda slaps Suze again. And on they go.

I shift my bag over my shoulder. "I'm just glad I was there."

To be more accurate, I'm just glad he was there before I fell off the ledge and killed myself in front of everyone. I can't even think about my parents, forced to deal with the death of their only remaining child. Not even an accidental death, but an intentional one. That's one reason I came tonight without a fight. I feel ashamed of what I almost put them through.

"Glad you were where?" Roamer stumbles up with a bucket of beers. He slams it down, ice sloshing everywhere.

Suze looks at him through cat eyes. "The bell tower."

Roamer stares at her chest. He forces himself to look at me. "Why were you up there, anyway?"

"I was on my way to Humanities and saw him go through the door at the end of the hall, the one that goes to the tower."

Amanda says, "Humanities? I thought that was second period."

"It is, but I had to talk to Mr. Feldman about something."

Roamer says, "They keep that door locked and barricaded. That place is harder to get into than your pants, from what I hear." He laughs and laughs.

"He must have picked the lock." Or maybe that was me. One of the benefits of looking innocent is you're able to get away with things. People almost never suspect you.

Roamer pops the top off a beer and chugs it down. "Asshole. You should have let him jump. Prick almost took my head off last year." He's referring to the chalkboard incident.

"Do you think he likes you?" Amanda makes a face at me.

"Of course not."

"I hope not. I'd be careful around him if I were you."

Ten months ago, I would have sat beside them, drinking beer and fitting in, and writing witty commentary in my head: *She puts the words out there on purpose, like a lawyer trying to lead the jury.* "Objection, Miss Monk." "So sorry. Please disregard." *But it's too late because the jury has heard the words and latched onto them—if he likes her, she must like him in return. . . .*

But now I stand there, feeling dull and out of place and wondering how I was ever friends with Amanda to begin with. The air is too close. The music is too loud. The smell of beer is everywhere. I feel like I'm going to be sick. Then I see Leticia Lopez, the reporter from the school paper, on her way over to me.

"I've gotta go, Amanda. I'll talk to you tomorrow."

Before anyone can say anything, I walk upstairs and out of the house.

The last party I went to was April 4, the night Eleanor was killed. The music and the lights and the yelling bring it back. Just in time, I pull my hair out of my face, bend over, and throw up onto the curb. Tomorrow they'll think it was just another drunk kid.

I search for my phone and text Amanda. **Really sorry. Not feeling great.** ☹ **xx V.**

I turn around toward home and slam right into Ryan Cross. He is damp and tousled. His eyes are large and beautiful and bloodshot. Like all hot guys, he has a crooked smile. When he does smile with more than one corner of his mouth, there are dimples. He is perfect and I have memorized him.

I am not perfect. I have secrets. I am messy. Not just my bedroom but me. No one likes messy. They like smiling Violet. I wonder what Ryan would do if he knew Finch was the one who talked me down and not the other way around. I wonder what any of them would do.

Ryan picks me up and twirls me, pillow, bag, and all. He tries to kiss me and I turn my head.

The first time he kissed me was in the snow. Snow in April. Welcome to the Midwest. Eleanor wore white, I wore black, a kind of Freaky Friday, switched-up bad sister–good sister thing that we did sometimes. Ryan's older brother, Eli, threw the party. While Eleanor went upstairs with Eli, I danced. It was Amanda, Suze, Shelby, Ashley, and me. Ryan was at the window. He was the one who said, "It's snowing!"

I danced over, through the crowd, and he looked at me. "Let's go." Just like that.

He took my hand and we ran outside. The flakes were as heavy as rain, large and white and glittering. We tried to catch them with our tongues, and then Ryan's tongue found its way into my mouth, and I closed my eyes as the flakes landed on my cheeks.

From inside, there was the noise of shouting and something breaking. Party sounds. Ryan's hands found their way under my shirt. I remember how warm they were, and even as I kissed him, I was thinking, I'm kissing Ryan Cross. Things like this didn't happen to me before we moved to Indi-

ana. I slipped my own hands under his sweatshirt, and the skin there was hot but smooth. It was exactly what I imagined it would feel like.

There was more shouting, more breaking. Ryan pulled away, and I looked up at him, at the smear of my lipstick on his mouth. I could only stand there and think, That's my lipstick on Ryan Cross's lips. Oh. My. God.

I wish I had a photograph of my face in that exact instant so I could remember myself the way I used to be. That instant was the last good moment before everything turned bad and changed forever.

Now Ryan holds me against him, my feet off the ground. "You're headed in the wrong direction, V." He starts to carry me toward the house.

"I've already been in there. I have to go home. I'm sick. Put me down." I rap at him with my fists, and he sets me down because Ryan's a nice boy who does what he's told.

"What's up?"

"I'm sick. I just threw up. I have to go." I pat his arm like it's a dog. I turn away from him and hurry across the lawn, down the street, around the corner to home. I hear him calling after me, but I don't look back.

"You're home early." My mom is on the sofa, her nose deep in a book. My father is stretched out at the other end, eyes closed, headphones on.

"Not early enough." I pause at the bottom of the stairs. "Just so you know, that was a bad idea. I knew it was a bad idea, but I went anyway so you could see I'm trying. But it wasn't a sleepover. It was a party. A full-on let's-get-wasted orgiastic free-for-all." I say this *at* them, as if it's their fault.

My mom nudges my dad, who pulls off the headphones. They both sit up. Mom says, "Do you want to talk about anything? I know that must have been hard, and surprising. Why don't you hang out with us for a while?"

Like Ryan, my parents are perfect. They are strong and brave and caring, and even though I know they must cry and get angry and maybe even throw things when they're alone, they rarely show it to me. Instead, they encourage me to get out of the house and into the car and back on the road, so to speak. They listen and ask and worry, and they're there for me. If anything, they're a little *too* there for me now. They need to know where I'm going, what I'm doing, who I'm seeing, and when I'll be back. *Text us on the way there, text us on your way home.*

I almost sit down with them now, just to give them something, after all they've been through—after what I almost put them through yesterday. But I can't.

"I'm just tired. I think I'll go to bed."

Ten thirty p.m. My bedroom. I am wearing my Freud slippers, the fuzzy ones made to look like his face, and Target pajamas, the ones with the purple monkeys. This is the clothing equivalent of my happy place. I cross off this day with a black "X" on the calendar that covers my closet door, and then I curl up on my bed, propped against my pillows, books spread across the comforter. Since I stopped writing, I read more than ever. *Other people's words, not my own—my words are gone.* Right now, I'm into the Brontë sisters.

I love the world that is my room. It's nicer in here than out there, because in here I'm whatever I want to be. I am a brilliant writer. I can write fifty pages a day and I never run out of words. I am an accepted future student of the NYU creative writing program. I am the creator of a popular Web magazine—not the one I did with Eleanor, but a new one. I am fearless. I am free. I am safe.

I can't decide which of the Brontë sisters I like best. Not Charlotte, because she looks like my fifth-grade teacher. Emily is fierce and reckless, but Anne is the one who gets ignored. I root for Anne. I read, and then I lie for a long time on top of my comforter and stare at the ceiling. I have this feeling, ever since April, like I'm waiting for something. But I have no idea what.

At some point, I get up. A little over two hours ago, at 7:58 p.m., Theodore Finch posted a video on his Facebook wall. It's him with a guitar, sitting in what I guess is his room. His voice is good but raw, like he's smoked too many cigarettes. He's bent over the guitar, black hair falling in his eyes. He looks blurry, like he filmed this on his phone. The words of the song are about a guy who jumps off his school roof.

When he's done, he says into the camera, "Violet Markey, if you're watching this, you must still be alive. Please confirm."

I click the video off like he can see me. I want yesterday and Theodore Finch and the bell tower to go away. As far as I'm concerned, the whole thing was a bad dream. The worst dream. The worst nightmare EVER.

I write him a private message: **Please take that off your wall or edit out what you say at the end so no one else sees/hears it.**

He writes back immediately: **Congratulations! I deduce by your message that you're alive! With that out of the way, I was thinking we** should probably talk about what happened, especially now that we're partners on this project. (No one will see the video but us.)

Me: I'm fine. I'd really like to drop it and forget the whole thing ever happened. (How do you know that?)

Finch: (Because I only started this page as an excuse to talk to you. Besides, now that you've seen it, the video will self-destruct in five seconds. Five, four, three, two ...)

Finch: Please refresh the page.

The video is gone.

Finch: If you don't want to talk on Facebook, I can just come over.

Me: Now?

Finch: Well, technically in, like, five or ten minutes. I should get dressed first, unless you prefer me naked, and we have to allow for driving time.

Me: It's late.

Finch: That depends on who you ask. See, I don't necessarily think it's late. I think it's early. Early in our lives. Early in the night. Early in the new year. If you're counting, you'll notice the *early*s outnumber the *late*s. It's just to talk. Nothing more. It's not like I'm hitting on you.

Finch: Unless you want me to. Hit on you, I mean.

Me: No.

Finch: "No" you don't want me to come over? Or "no" you don't want me hitting on you?

Me: Both. Either. All of the above.

Finch: Okay. We can just talk at school. Maybe across the room during geography, or I can find you at lunch. You eat with Amanda and Roamer, am I right?

Oh my God. Make it stop. Make him go away.

Me: **If you come over tonight, do you promise to drop it once and for all?**

Finch: **Scout's honor.**

Me: **Just to talk. Nothing more. And you don't stay long.**

As soon as I write it, I want to take it back. Amanda and her party are just around the corner. Anyone might come by and see him here.

Me: **Are you still there?**

He doesn't answer.

Me: **Finch?**

FINCH

I climb into my mom's old Saturn VUE, better known as Little Bastard, and head to Violet Markey's on the farm road that runs parallel to National Road, the main artery that cuts through town. I slam my foot against the gas pedal, and there's the rush as the speedometer climbs to sixty, seventy, eighty, ninety, the needle shaking the higher it gets, the Saturn doing its best in that moment to be a sports car instead of a five-year-old minivan.

On March 23, 1950, Italian poet Cesare Pavese wrote: *"Love is truly the great manifesto; the urge to be, to count for something, and, if death must come, to die valiantly, with acclamation—in short, to remain a memory."* Five months later, he walked into a newspaper office and chose his obituary photograph from the photo archive. He checked himself into a hotel, and days later an employee found him stretched out on the bed, dead. He was fully dressed except for his shoes. On the bedside table were sixteen empty packets of sleeping pills and a note: *"I forgive everyone and ask forgiveness of everyone. OK? Not too much gossip, please."*

Cesare Pavese has nothing to do with driving fast on an Indiana farm road, but I understand the urge to be and to count for something. While I'm not sure taking off your shoes in a strange hotel room and swallowing too many sleeping pills is what I would call dying valiantly and with acclamation, it's the thought that counts.

I push the Saturn to ninety-five. I will ease off only when I reach

one hundred. Not ninety-seven. Not ninety-eight. It's one hundred or nothing.

I lean forward, like I'm a rocket, like I. Am. The. Car. And I start yelling because I'm getting more awake by the second. I feel the rush and then some—I feel everything around me and in me, the road and my blood and my heart beating up into my throat, and I could end right now, in a valiant acclamation of crushed metal and explosive fire. I slam the gas harder, and now I can't stop because I am faster than anything on earth. The only thing that matters is the forward thrust and the way I feel as I hurtle toward the Great Manifesto.

Then, in that exact, precise fraction of a moment before my heart might explode or the engine might explode, I lift my foot up and off and go sailing across the old, rutted pavement, Little Bastard carrying me on its own as we fly up over the ground and land hard, several feet

away, half in, half out of the ditch, where I sit catching my breath. I hold up my hands and they aren't shaking at all. They're steady as can be, and I look around me, at the starry sky and the fields, and the dark, sleeping houses, and I'm here, motherf-----s. I am here.

Violet lives one street away from Suze Haines in a large white house with a red chimney in a neighborhood on the opposite side of town. I roll up in Little Bastard, and she's sitting on the front step, wrapped in a giant coat, looking small and alone. She jumps up and meets me halfway down the sidewalk, then immediately glances past me like she's looking for someone or something. "You didn't need to come all the way over here." She's whispering, as if we might wake up the neighborhood.

I whisper back, "It's not like we live in L.A. or even Cincinnati. It took me, like, five minutes to get here. Nice house, by the way."

"Look, thanks for coming, but I don't need to talk about anything." Her hair is pulled back in a ponytail, and wisps of it are falling down around her face. She tucks a piece behind her ear. "I'm totally fine."

"Never bullshit a bullshitter. I know a cry for help when I see one, and I'd say being talked off a ledge overqualifies. Are your parents home?"

"Yes."

"Too bad. Want to walk?" I start walking.

"Not that way." She pulls on my arm and drags me in the other direction.

"Are we avoiding something?"

"No. It's just, uh—nicer over here."

I put on my best Embryo voice. "So, how long have you been having these suicidal feelings?"

"God, don't talk so loud. And I'm not . . . I'm not . . ."

"Suicidal. You can say it."

"Well, anyway, I'm not."

"Unlike me."

"That's not what I meant."

"You were up on the ledge because you didn't know where else to turn and what else to do. You'd lost all hope. And then, like a gallant knight, I saved your life. By the way, you look totally different without makeup. Not bad necessarily, but different. Maybe even better. So what's up with this website of yours? Have you always

wanted to write? Tell me about yourself, Violet Markey."

She answers like a robot: *There's not much to say. I guess so. There's nothing to tell.*

"So, California. That must have been a change for you. Do you like it?"

"Like what?"

"Bartlett."

"It's all right."

"What about this neighborhood?"

"It's all right too."

"These are not the words of someone who just had her life handed back to her. You should be on top of the f---ing world right now. I'm here. You're here. Not only that, you're here with me. I can think of at least one girl who'd want to trade places with you."

She makes this frustrated (and strangely hot) *arrrrrr* sound. "What do you want?"

I stop under a streetlight. I drop the fast talk and the charm. "I want to know why you were up there. And I want to know that you're okay."

"If I tell you, will you go home?"

"Yes."

"And never bring it up again?"

"That depends on your answers."

She sighs and starts to walk. For a while she doesn't say anything, so I stay quiet, waiting her out. The only sounds are someone's television and a party somewhere in the distance.

After several blocks of this, I say, "Anything you tell me stays between us. You might not have noticed, but I'm not exactly swimming in friends. And even if I was, it wouldn't matter. Those assholes have enough to gossip about."

She takes a breath. "When I went to the tower, I wasn't really thinking. It was more like my legs were walking up the stairs and I just went where they took me. I've never done anything like that before. I mean, that's not me. But then it was like I woke up and I was on that ledge. I didn't know what to do, so I started to freak out."

"Have you told anyone what happened?"

"No." She stops walking, and I resist the urge to touch her hair, which blows across her face. She pushes it out of the way.

"Not your parents?"

"Especially not my parents."

"You still didn't tell me *what* you were doing up there."

I don't actually expect her to answer, but she says, "It was my sister's birthday. She would have been nineteen."

"Shit. I'm sorry."

"But that isn't why. The why is that none of it matters. Not school, not cheerleading, not boyfriends or friends or parties or creative writing programs or . . ." She waves her arms at the world. "It's all just time filler until we die."

"Maybe. Maybe not. Whether it's filler or not, I'm pretty glad to be here." If there's anything I've learned, it's that you need to make the most of it. "It mattered enough for you not to jump."

"Can I ask you something?" She is studying the ground.

"Sure."

"Why do they call you Theodore Freak?"

Now I'm studying the ground like it's the most interesting thing

I've ever seen. It takes me a while to answer because I'm trying to decide how much to say. *Honestly, Violet, I don't know why the kids don't like me.* Lie. I mean, I know but I don't. I've always been different, but to me different is normal. I decide on a version of the truth.

"In eighth grade, I was a lot smaller than I am now. That was before your time, before you got here." I look up long enough to see her nod her head. "Ears stuck out. Elbows stuck out. My voice didn't drop till the summer before high school, when I shot up fourteen inches."

"That's all?"

"That and sometimes I say and do things without thinking. People don't like that."

She's quiet as we round a corner, and I can see her house in the distance. I walk slower, buying us more time. "I know the band playing down at the Quarry. We could head over there, get warm, listen to music, forget about everything. I also know a place with a pretty awesome view of the town." I shoot her one of my better grins.

"I'm going inside and going to sleep."

I'm always amazed by people and their sleep. I wouldn't ever sleep if I didn't have to.

"Or we can make out."

"That's okay."

A minute or so later, we're at my car. "How'd you get up there, anyway? The door was open when I tried it, but it's usually sealed tight."

She smiles for the first time. "I might have picked the lock."

I whistle. "Violet Markey. There's more to you than meets the eye."

In a flash, she is up the walk and inside her house. I stand watching until a light flicks on in an upstairs window. A shadow moves in front of it so that I can see the outline of her, as if she's watching me through the curtain. I lean back against the car, waiting to see who gives in first. I stay there until the shadow moves away and the light goes off.

At home, I park Little Bastard in the garage and start my nightly run. Run in winter, swim the rest of the year. My regular route is down National Road, out past the hospital and Friendship Campground to this old steel bridge that seems forgotten by everyone but me. I sprint across the tops of its walls—the ones that act as guardrails—and when I make it without falling, I know I'm alive.

Worthless. Stupid. These are the words I grew up hearing. They're the words I try to outrun, because if I let them in, they might stay there and grow and fill me up and in, until the only thing left of me is *worthless stupid worthless stupid worthless stupid freak.* And then there's nothing to do but run harder and fill myself with other words: *This time will be different. This time, I will stay awake.*

I run for miles but don't count them, passing dark house after dark house. I feel sorry for everyone in this town who's sleeping.

I take a different route home, over the A Street Bridge. This bridge has more traffic because it links downtown with the west side of Bartlett, where the high school is and the local college is and all these neighborhoods are, growing up in between.

I run past what's left of the stone guardrail. There is still an angry hole in the middle where the rest of the wall used to be, and someone has placed a cross beside it. The cross lies on its side, white paint faded gray from the Indiana weather, and I wonder who put it there—Violet? Her parents? Someone from school? I run to the end of the bridge and cut onto the grass, down the embankment to the bottom, which is an old dried-up riverbed full of cigarette butts and beer bottles.

I kick through the trash and the rocks and the dirt. Something shines silver in the dark, and then I see other shining things—pieces of glass and metal. There is the red plastic eye of a taillight. The shattered lump of a side mirror. A license plate, dented and nearly folded in half.

All of this makes it suddenly real. I could sink like a stone into the earth and be swallowed whole by the weight of what happened here.

I leave everything as it was, except for the license plate, which I take with me. Leaving it there seems wrong, as if it's too personal a thing to sit out in the open where someone who doesn't know Violet or her sister might take it and think it's cool, or collect it as a souvenir. I run toward home, feeling both heavy and hollowed out. *This time will be different. This time, I will stay awake.*

I run until time stops. Until my mind stops. Until the only thing I feel is the cold metal of the license plate in my hand and the pounding of my blood.

VIOLET

152 days till graduation

Sunday morning. My bedroom.

The EleanorandViolet.com domain name is expiring. I know this because the hosting company has sent me an email with a warning that says I must renew now or let it go forever. On my laptop, I open our folders of notes and sort through all the ideas we were working on before last April. But they're only fragments that don't make sense without Eleanor here to help me decipher her shorthand.

The two of us had different views on what we wanted the magazine to be. Eleanor was older (and bossier), which meant she was usually in charge and usually got her way. I can try to salvage the site, maybe revamp it and turn it into something else—a place where writers can share their work. A place that isn't about just nail polish and boys and music, but other things too, like how to change a tire or how to speak French or what to expect once you get out into the world.

I write these things down. Then I go onto the site itself and read the last post, written the day before the party—two opposite takes on the book *Julie Plum, Girl Exorcist*. Not even *The Bell Jar* or *Catcher in the Rye*. Nothing important or earth-shattering. Nothing that says: *This is the last thing you will ever write before the world changes.*

I delete her notes and mine. I delete the hosting company email. And then I empty my trash so that the email is as dead and gone as Eleanor.

FINCH

On Sunday evening, Kate and Decca and I drive to my dad's new house in the more expensive part of town for Weekly Obligatory Family Dinner. I'm wearing the same plain navy shirt and khakis I always wear when I see my father.

We are silent on the way over, each of us staring out the window. We don't even play the radio. "Have fun over there," Mom said before we left, trying to be cheerful, when I know that the second the car hit the street, she was on the phone to a girlfriend and opening a bottle of wine. It'll be my first time seeing my dad since before

Thanksgiving and my first time in his new home, the one he shares with Rosemarie and her son.

They live in one of these colossal brand-new houses that look like every other house up and down the street. As we pull up out front, Kate says, "Can you imagine trying to find this place drunk?"

The three of us march up the clean white sidewalk. Two matching SUVs are parked in the drive, shining as if their pretentious mechanical lives depend on it.

Rosemarie answers the door. She is maybe thirty, with red-blond hair and a worried smile. Rosemarie is what's known as a caretaker, according to my mother, which—also according to my mother—is exactly what my father needs. She came with a $200,000 settlement from her ex-husband and a gap-toothed seven-year-old named Josh

Raymond, who may or may not be my real brother.

My dad comes booming toward us from the backyard, where he's grilling thirty-five pounds of meat even though it's January, not July. His T-shirt says SUCK IT, SENATORS. Twelve years ago, he was a professional hockey player better known as the Slammer, until he shattered his femur against another player's head. He looks the same as he did the last time I saw him—too handsome and too fit for a guy his age, like he expects to be called back to duty at any moment—but his dark hair is flecked with gray, which is new.

He hugs my sisters and slaps me on the back. Unlike most hockey players, he somehow managed to keep his teeth, and he flashes them at us now like we're groupies. He wants to know how our week was, how was school, did we learn anything he might not know. This is a challenge—his equivalent of throwing down the gauntlet. It's a way for us to try to stump wise old Pops, which is no fun for anyone, and so we all say no.

Dad asks about the November/December study-away program, and it takes me a minute to realize he's talking to me. "Uh, it was okay." Good one, Kate. I make a note to thank her. He doesn't know about the shutting down or the trouble at school beyond sophomore year because last year, after the guitar-smashing episode, I told Principal Wertz my dad was killed in a hunting accident. He never bothered to check up on it, and now he calls my mother whenever there's a problem, which means he actually calls Kate because Mom never bothers to check voicemail.

I pick a leaf off the grill. "They invited me to stay on, but I turned them down. I mean, as much as I enjoy figure skating, and as good as I am at it—I guess I get that from you—I'm not sure I want to make a career of it." One of the great pleasures of my life is making comments like this, because having a gay son is my bigoted prick of a father's worst nightmare.

His only response is to pop open another beer and attack the thirty-five pounds of meat with his tongs like it's in danger of rising up and devouring us all. I wish it would.

When it's actually time to eat, we sit in the white-and-gold dining room with the natural-wool carpet, the most expensive money can buy. This is apparently a huge improvement over the shitty nylon carpet that was in the house when they moved in.

Josh Raymond barely clears the table, because his mother is small and her ex-husband is small, unlike my dad, who is a giant. My step-brother is a different sort of small than I was at his age—the neat and tidy sort, no elbows or ears jutting out, everything in proportion.

This is one thing that leads me to believe he may not be genetically linked to my father after all.

Right now, Josh Raymond kicks at the table leg and stares at us over his plate with the enormous, unblinking eyes of an owl. I say, "How's it hanging, little man?"

He squeaks a reply, and my father the Slammer strokes his perfectly stubbled jaw and says in the soft, patient voice of a nun, "Josh Raymond, we've discussed kicking the table." It is a tone he has never once used with me or my sisters.

Decca, who has already filled her plate, begins eating as Rosemarie serves everyone else one by one. When she gets to me, I say, "I'm good without, unless you've got a veggie burger on there." She only blinks at me, her hand still hovering in midair. Without turning her face, she swivels her eyes in my father's direction.

"Veggie burger?" His voice isn't soft or patient. "I was raised on meat and potatoes, and I've made it to thirty-five." (He was forty-three in October.) "I figured my parents were the ones putting the food on the table, so it wasn't my job to question it." He pulls up his shirt and pats his stomach—still flat, but no longer a six-pack—shakes his head, and smiles at me, the smile of a man who has a new wife and a new son and a new house and two new cars and who only has to put up with his old, original kids for another hour or two.

"I don't eat red meat, Dad." Actually, to be technical, it's '80s Finch who's the vegetarian.

"Since when?"

"Since last week."

"Oh, for Christ's . . ." Dad sits back and stares at me as Decca takes a big, bloody bite of her burger, the juice dripping down her chin.

Kate says, "Don't be an asshole, Dad. He doesn't have to eat it if he doesn't want to."

Before I can stop him, '80s Finch says, "There are different ways to die. There's jumping off a roof and there's slowly poisoning yourself with the flesh of another every single day."

"I am so sorry, Theo. I didn't know." Rosemarie darts a look at my father, who's still staring at me. "How about I make you a potato salad sandwich?" She sounds so hopeful that I let her, even though the potato salad has bacon in it.

"He can't eat that. The potato salad has bacon." This is from Kate.

My dad says, "Well, he can goddamn pick it out." The "out" sounds like "oot," a relic of Dad's Canadian upbringing. He's starting to get annoyed, and so we shut up because the faster we eat, the faster we leave.

⋆　⋆　⋆

At home, I give Mom a kiss on the cheek because she needs it, and I inhale the scent of red wine. "Did you kids have fun?" she asks, and we know she's hoping we'll beg for permission to never go there again.

Decca says, "We most certainly did not," and goes stomping up the stairs.

My mother sighs in relief before taking another drink and going after her. She does her best parenting on Sundays.

Kate opens a bag of chips and says, "This is so stupid." And I know what she means. "This" equals our parents and Sundays and maybe our whole screwed-up lives. "I don't even see why we have to go over there and pretend to like each other when everyone knows that's exactly what we're doing. Pretending." She hands me the bag.

"Because people like you to pretend, Kate. They prefer it."

She flicks her hair over her shoulder and scrunches up her face in a way that means she's thinking. "You know, I've decided to go to college in the fall after all." Kate offered to stay home when the divorce happened. *Someone needs to look after Mom,* she said.

Suddenly I'm hungry, and the two of us pass the bag back and forth, back and forth. I say, "I thought you liked having time off from school." I love her enough to pretend along with her that this is the other reason she stayed home, that it had nothing to do with her cheating high school boyfriend, the same one she'd planned her future around.

She shrugs. "I don't know. Maybe it's not quite as 'time off' as I expected. I'm thinking about going to Denver, maybe seeing what's to see out there."

"Like Logan?" Better known as the cheating high school boyfriend.

"This has nothing to do with him."

"I hope not."

I want to repeat the things I've been telling her for months: *You're better than him. You've already wasted too much time on that asshole.* But her jaw has gone rigid and she is frowning into the chips bag. "It beats living at home."

I can't argue with her there, so instead I ask, "Do you remember Eleanor Markey?"

"Sure. She was in my class. Why?"

"She's got a sister." I met her on the bell tower when we were both thinking about jumping. We could have held hands and leaped off together. They would have thought we were star-crossed lovers. They'd write songs about us. We'd be legends.

Kate shrugs. "Eleanor was okay. A little full of herself. She could be fun. I didn't know her all that well. I don't remember her sister." She finishes the wine from Mom's glass and grabs the car keys. "Later."

Upstairs, I bypass Split Enz, Depeche Mode, and the Talking Heads for Johnny Cash. I throw *At Folsom Prison* onto the turntable, fish through my desk for a cigarette, and tell '80s Finch to get over it. After all, I created him, and I can take him away. As I light the cigarette, though, I can suddenly picture my lungs turning as black as a newly paved road, and I think of what I said to my dad earlier: *There are different ways to die. There's jumping off a roof and there's slowly poisoning yourself with the flesh of another every single day.*

No animals died to make this cigarette, but for once I don't like the way it makes me feel, like I'm being polluted, like I'm being poisoned. I stub it out and, before I can change my mind, break all the others in half. Then I cut the halves with scissors and sweep them into the trash, sign onto the computer, and start typing.

January 11. According to the New York Times, nearly 20 percent of suicides are committed by poison, but among doctors who kill themselves, that number is 57 percent. My thoughts on the method: Seems like kind of a coward's way out, if you ask me. I think I'd rather feel something. That said, if someone held a gun to my head (haha—sorry, suicide humor) and made me use poison, I'd choose cyanide. In gaseous form, death can be instant, which I realize defeats the purpose of feeling something. But come to think of it, after a lifetime of feeling too much, maybe there's actually something to be said for fast and sudden.

When I finish, I walk into the bathroom to dig through the medicine cabinet. Advil, aspirin, some kind of over-the-counter sleeping pills I stole from Kate and then stored in an old prescription bottle of Mom's. I meant what I said to Embryo about drugs. We don't mix. What it comes down to for me is I have a hard enough time keeping control over my brain without something else getting in the way.

But you never know when you might need a good sleeping pill. I open the bottle now, dump the blue tablets into my palm, and count them. Thirty. Back at my desk, I line the pills up one by one by one, like a little blue army.

I sign onto Facebook, and over on Violet's page someone from school has posted about her being a hero for saving me. There are 146 comments and 289 likes, and while I'd like to think there are this many people grateful that I'm still alive, I know better. I go to my own page, which is empty except for Violet's friend picture.

I set my fingers on the keyboard, looking at the way they rest there, the nails broad and round. I run my hands along the keys, as if I'm playing piano. And then I type, **Obligatory family meals suck, especially when meat and denial are involved. "I feel we can't go through another of those terrible times." Especially when there is so much else to do.** The quote is from Virginia Woolf's suicide note to her husband, but I think it fits the occasion.

I send the message and wait around the computer, organizing the pills into groups of three, then ten, when really I'm hoping for something from Violet. I work at banging the license plate flat again, scribble down *Another of those terrible times,* and add it to the wall of my room, which is already covered in notes just like this. The wall has various names: Wall of Thoughts, Wall of Ideas, Wall of My Mind, or just The Wall, not to be confused with Pink Floyd. The wall is a place to keep track of thoughts, as fast as they come, and remember them when they go away. Anything interesting or weird or even halfway inspired goes up there.

An hour later, I check my Facebook page. Violet has written: **"Arrange whatever pieces come your way."**

My skin starts to burn. She's quoting Virginia Woolf back to me. My pulse has tripled its pace. *Shit,* I think. That's all the Virginia Woolf I know. I do a quick internet search, looking for just the right response. Suddenly I wish I'd paid more attention to Virginia Woolf, a writer I've never had much use for until now. Suddenly I wish I'd done nothing but study her for all of my seventeen years.

I type back: **"My own brain is to me the most unaccountable of machinery—always buzzing, humming, soaring roaring diving, and then buried in mud. And why? What's this passion for?"**

This goes to what Violet said about time filler and how none of it matters, but it's also me exactly—buzzing, humming, soaring roaring diving, and then falling deep into mud, so deep I can't breathe. The Asleeps and Awakes, no in-betweens.

It's a damn good quote, so good it gives me chills. I study the hairs standing up on my arm, and by the time I look back at the screen, Violet has responded. **"When you consider things like the stars, our affairs don't seem to matter very much, do they?"**

I'm full-on cheating now, pulling up every Virginia Woolf site I can find. I wonder if she's cheating too. I write: **"I am rooted, but I flow."**

I nearly change my mind. I think about deleting the line, but then she writes back. **I like that one. Where is it from?**

The Waves. I cheat again and find the passage. **Here's more: "I feel a thousand capacities spring up in me. I am arch, gay, languid, melancholy by turns. I am rooted, but I flow. All gold, flowing . . ."**

I decide to end there, mostly because I'm in a hurry to see if she'll write back.

It takes her three minutes. **I like: "This is the most exciting moment I have ever known. I flutter. I ripple. I stream like a plant in the river, flowing this way, flowing that way, but rooted, so that he may come to me.**

'Come,' I say, 'come.'"

My pulse isn't the only part of my body stirring now. I adjust myself and think how weirdly, stupidly sexy this is.

I write, **You make me feel gold, flowing.** I post it without thinking. I can go on quoting Virginia Woolf—believe me, the passage gets even hotter—but I decide I want to quote myself instead.

I wait for her response. I wait for three minutes. Five minutes. Ten. Fifteen. I open up her website, the one she ran with her sister, and check the date of the last post, which hasn't changed since the last time I looked.

I get it, I think. *Not gold, not flowing. Standing still.*

Then another message appears: **I got your rules for wandering and I have an addition: We don't travel in bad weather. We walk, jog, or ride bikes. No driving. We don't go far from Bartlett.**

She is all business now. I reply: **If we're walking, jogging, or riding bikes, that's not going to be a problem.** Thinking of her website sitting dead and empty, I add: **We should write about our wanderings so we have something to show for them besides pictures. Actually, you should do the writing. I'll just smile and look pretty.**

I am still sitting there an hour later, but she's gone. Like that, I've either irritated her or scared her away. So I make up song after song. Most nights, these are Songs That Will Change the World because they are that good and that deep and that damn amazing. But tonight I'm telling myself I don't have anything in common with this Violet girl, no matter how much I want to, and asking myself if the words between us were really that hot or if maybe it was just me imagining, me in over-drive for a girl I barely know, all because she's the first person I've met who seems to speak my language. A few words of it anyway.

I scoop up the sleeping pills and hold them in my palm. I can swallow them right now, lie down on my bed, close my eyes, drift away. But who's going to check on Violet Markey to make sure she's not back up on that ledge? I drop the pills into the toilet and flush them down. And then I go back to EleanorandViolet.com, search the archives till I get to the first post, and move forward through all of them until I've read every single one.

I stay up as long as I can, finally falling asleep sometime around four a.m. I dream that I'm naked and standing in the bell tower at school, in the cold and the rain. I look below me and everyone is there, teachers and students, and my dad eating a hamburger raw, holding it up to the sky like he's toasting me. I hear a noise over my shoulder and turn to see Violet, on the opposite end of the ledge and naked too except for a pair of black boots. It's stupefying—the very best thing I've ever seen with these two eyes—but before I can unhook myself from the stone railing and go to her, she opens her mouth, leaps into the air, and starts to scream.

It's the alarm, of course, and I slam it once with my fist before throwing it against the wall, where it lies, bleating like a lost sheep.

VIOLET

Monday morning. First period.

Everyone is talking about the newest post in the *Bartlett Dirt*, the school gossip rag that not only has its own website but seems to be taking over the entire internet. "Senior Hero Saves Crazy Classmate from Bell Tower Jump." We aren't named, but there is a picture of my face, eyes startled behind Eleanor's glasses, bangs crooked. I look like a makeover "before." There's also a picture of Theodore Finch.

Jordan Gripenwaldt, editor of our school paper, is reading the article to her friends Brittany and Priscilla in a low, disgusted voice. Now and then they glance in my direction and shake their heads, not at me but at this perfect example of journalism at its worst.

These are smart girls who speak their minds. I should be friends with them instead of Amanda. This time last year, I would have spoken up and agreed with them and then written a scathing blog post about high school gossip. Instead I pick up my bag and tell the teacher I have cramps. I bypass the nurse and climb the stairs to the top floor. I pick the lock to the bell tower. I go only as far as the stairs, where I sit down and, by the light of my phone, read two chapters of *Wuthering Heights*. I've given up on Anne Brontë and decided there's only Emily—unruly Emily, angry at the world.

"*If all else perished, and he remained, I should still continue to be; and if all else remained, and he were annihilated, the universe would turn to a mighty stranger.*"

"A mighty stranger," I say to no one. "You got that right."

FINCH

By Monday morning, it's clear that '80s Finch has to go. For one thing, the picture of him in the *Bartlett Dirt* is not flattering. He looks unnervingly wholesome—I suspect he's a goody-good, what with all the not smoking and vegetarianism and turned-up collars. And, for two, he just doesn't feel right to me. He's the kind of guy who's probably great with teachers and pop quizzes and who actually doesn't mind driving his mom's Saturn, but I don't trust him not to screw things up with girls. More specifically, I don't trust him to get anywhere with Violet Markey.

I meet Charlie at Goodwill during third period. There's one down by the train station, in an area that used to be nothing but abandoned, burned-out factories and graffiti. Now it's been "regentrified," which means it got a new coat of paint and someone decided to pay attention to it.

Charlie brings Brenda for fashion backup, even though nothing she wears ever matches, something she swears she does on purpose. While Charlie talks up one of the salesgirls, Bren follows me from rack to rack yawning. She flips halfheartedly through hangers of leather jackets. "What exactly are we looking for?"

I say, "I need to be regentrified." She yawns again without covering her mouth, and I can see her fillings. "Late night?"

She grins, bright-pink lips spreading wide. "Amanda Monk had a party Saturday night. I made out with Gabe Romero." In addition to being Amanda's boyfriend, Roamer is the biggest prick in school. For some reason, Bren has had a thing for him since freshman year.

"Will he remember it?"

Her grin fades a little. "He was pretty wasted, but I left one of these in his pocket." She holds up a hand and waves her fingers. One of her blue plastic fingernails is missing. "And, just in case, my nose ring."

"I thought you looked different today."

"That's just the glow." She's more awake now. She claps her hands together and rubs them all mad-scientist-like. "So what are we looking for?"

"I don't know. Something a little less squeaky clean, maybe a little sexier. I'm done with the eighties."

She frowns. "Is this about what's-her-name? The skinny chick?"

"Violet Markey, and she's not skinny. She has hips."

"And a sweet, sweet ass." Charlie has joined us now.

"No." Bren is shaking her head so hard and fast, it looks as if she's having a seizure. "You don't dress to please a girl—especially not a girl like that. You dress to please yourself. If she doesn't like you for you, then you don't need her." All of this would be fine if I knew exactly who *me* for *me* was. She goes on: "This is the girl with the blog, the one that actress Gemma Sterling likes? The one who saved her 'crazy classmate' from jumping? Well, screw her and her skinny, skinny ass." Bren hates all girls who aren't at least a size twelve.

As she rattles on, about Violet, about Gemma Sterling, about the *Bartlett Dirt,* I don't say anything else. I suddenly don't want Bren or Charlie to talk about Violet, because I want to keep her to myself, like the Christmas I was eight—back when Christmases were still good—and got my first guitar, which I named No Trespassing, as in no one could touch it but me.

Finally, though, I have no choice but to interrupt Bren. "She was in that accident last April with her sister, the one where they drove off the A Street Bridge."

"Oh my God. That was her?"

"Her sister was a senior."

"Shit." Bren cradles her chin in her hand and taps it. "You know, maybe you should play it a little safer." Her voice is softer. "Think Ryan Cross. You see how he dresses. We should go to Old Navy or American Eagle, or better yet, to Abercrombie over in Dayton."

Charlie says to Brenda, "She's never gonna go for him. Doesn't matter what he wears. No offense, man."

"None taken. And fuck Ryan Cross." I use that word for the first time in my life. It feels so liberating that I suddenly feel like running around the store. "Fuck him." I decide the new Finch swears whenever and however he wants to. He's the kind of Finch who would stand on a building and think about jumping just because nothing scares him. He is seriously badass.

"In that case." Charlie yanks a jacket off its hanger and holds it up. It's pretty badass too. All scuffed, worn-out leather, like something Keith Richards might have worn way, way back in the day.

It's pretty much the coolest jacket I've ever seen. I'm pulling it on as Bren sighs, walks away, and comes strolling back with a giant pair of black Beatles boots. "They're size fourteen," she says. "But the way you grow, you'll fill them out by Friday."

By lunch, I'm starting to dig Badass Finch. For one thing, girls seem to like him. A cute underclassman actually stops me in the hall and asks if I need help finding my way. She must be a freshman, because it's clear she has no idea who I am. When she wants to know if I'm from London, I say *cheers* and *aye up* and *bangers and mash,* in what I think is a pretty convincing accent. She alternately giggles and flips her hair as she guides me to the cafeteria.

Because BHS has some two thousand students, they have us divided into three different lunch periods. Brenda skips class today to eat with Charlie and me, and I greet them with a *cheerio* and *'ello, mates,* and *you're the dog's bollocks,* and such. Bren just blinks at me, then blinks at Charlie. "Please tell me he's not British." He shrugs and keeps eating.

I spend the rest of lunch hour talking to them about my favorite spots back home—Honest Jon's, Rough Trade East, and Out on the Floor, the record shops I hang out in. I tell them about my mean but sexy Irish girlfriend, Fiona, and my best blokes, Tam and Natz. By the time lunch is through, I've created a universe I can see down to the last detail—the Sex Pistols and Joy Division posters on my wall, the fags I smoke out the window of the flat Fiona and I share, the nights spent playing music at the Hope and Anchor and the Half-moon, the days devoted to cutting records at Abbey Road studios. When the bell rings and Charlie says, "Let's go, you todger," I feel homesick for this London I left behind.

Yes, sir. As I walk through the halls, there's no telling what Badass British Finch might do. Take over the school, take over the town, take over the world. It will be a world of compassion, of neighbor loving neighbor, of student loving student or at least treating one another with respect. No judgments. No name-calling. No more, no more, no more.

By the time I get to U.S. Geography, I've almost convinced myself this world exists. Until I see Ryan Cross, all gold, flowing, his hand on the back of Violet's chair as if he's the host at the Macaroni Grill. He is smiling at her and talking, and she is smiling at him with her mouth closed, gray-green eyes wide and serious behind her glasses, and just like that, I am Indiana-born Theodore Finch in a pair of secondhand boots. Guys like Ryan Cross have a way of reminding you who you are, even when you don't want to remember.

As I try to catch Violet's eye, she's too busy nodding and listening to Ryan, and then Roamer is there and Amanda Monk, who fixes me with a death glare and snaps, "What are you looking at?" Then Violet is swallowed by them, so all I can do is stare in the direction of where she once was.

Mr. Black wheezes to the front of the room as the bell rings and asks if anyone has questions about the project. Hands go up, and one by one he addresses the concerns. "Get out there and see . . . your state. Go to museums . . . and parks . . . and historic sites. Get yourselves . . . some culture . . . so that when you do leave . . . you can take it with you."

In my very best British, I say, "But I thought you can't take it with you."

Violet laughs. She is the only one. As soon as she does, she turns away from everyone and stares at the wall beside her right shoulder.

When the bell rings, I walk past Ryan Cross and Roamer and Amanda until I'm standing so close to Violet that I can smell her flower shampoo. The thing about Badass Finch is that guys like Ryan Cross don't intimidate him for long.

Amanda says, "Can we help you?" in her nasally little-girl voice.

In my regular, non-British accent I say to Violet, "It's time to start wandering."

"Where?" Her eyes are cold and a little wary, as if she's afraid I might out her right here, right now.

"Have you been to Hoosier Hill?"

"No."

"It's the highest point in the state."

"I've heard."

"I thought you might like it. Unless you have a fear of heights." I cock my head.

Her face goes blank and then she recovers, the corners of her perfect mouth turning up in a perfect fake smile. "No. I'm okay with them."

"She saved you from jumping off that ledge, didn't she?" This is from Amanda. She waves her phone, where I can just make out the headline from the *Bartlett Dirt*.

Roamer mumbles, "Maybe you should go back up there and try again."

"And miss the opportunity to see Indiana? No thanks." Their eyes bore into me as I look at Violet. "Let's go."

"Right now?"

"No time like the present, and all that. You of all people should know we're only guaranteed right now."

Roamer says, "Hey, asshole, why don't you ask her boyfriend?"

I say to Roamer, "Because I'm not interested in Ryan, I'm interested in Violet." I say to Ryan, "It's not a date, man. It's a project."

"He's not my boyfriend," Violet says, and Ryan looks so hurt that I almost feel bad for him, except that it's impossible to feel bad for a guy like him. "I can't skip class."

"Why not?"

"Because I'm not a delinquent." Her tone is clear—*not like you*—and I tell myself she's only putting it on for the crowd.

"I'll wait for you in the parking lot after school." On the way out, I pause. "'Come,' I say, 'come.'"

It might be my imagination, but she almost smiles.

"Freak," I hear Amanda mutter as I walk out. I accidentally whack my elbow against the doorframe, and, for good luck, whack the other.

VIOLET

151 days till graduation

Three thirty. School parking lot.

I stand in the sun, shading my eyes. At first I don't see him. Maybe he left without me. Or maybe I went out the wrong door. Our town is small but our school is large. We have over two thousand students because we're the only high school for miles. He could be anywhere.

I am holding on to the handles of my bike, an old orange ten-speed inherited from Eleanor. She named it Leroy because she liked being able to say to our parents, "I was out riding Leroy," and "I'm just going to ride Leroy for a while."

Brenda Shank-Kravitz stalks by, a bright-pink storm cloud. Charlie Donahue saunters behind. "He's over there," Brenda says. She points a blue-nailed finger at me. "If you break his heart, I will kick that skinny ass all the way to Kentucky. I mean it. The last thing he needs is you playing with his head. Understood?"

"Understood."

"And I'm sorry. You know. About your sister."

I look in the direction Brenda pointed and there he is. Theodore Finch leans against an SUV, hands in pockets, like he has all the time in the world and he expects me. I think of the Virginia Woolf lines, the ones from *The Waves*: "*Pale, with dark hair, the one who is coming is melancholy, romantic. And I am arch and fluent and capricious; for he is melancholy, he is romantic. He is here.*"

I wheel the bike over to him. His dark hair is kind of wild and messy like he's been at the beach, even though there's no beach in Bartlett, and shines blue-black in the light. His pale skin is so white, I can see the veins in his arms.

He opens the passenger door to his car. "After you."

"I told you no driving."

"I forgot my bike, so we'll have to go to my house and get it."

"Then I'll follow you."

He drives slower than he needs to, and ten minutes later we reach his house. It's a two-story brick colonial with shrubs crowding under the windows, black shutters, and a red door. There's a matching red mailbox that says FINCH. I wait in the driveway while he sorts through the mess of a garage, searching for a bicycle. Finally he lifts it up and out, and I watch the muscles in his arms flex.

"You can leave your bag in my room." He's wiping the dust off the bike seat with his shirt.

"But my stuff's in there. . . ." A book on the history of Indiana, checked out from the library after last period, and plastic bags of various sizes—courtesy of one of the lunch ladies—for any souvenirs we might collect.

"I've got it covered." He unlocks the door and holds it open for me. Inside, it looks like a regular, ordinary house, not one I'd expect Theodore Finch to live in. I follow him upstairs. The walls are lined with framed school photos. Finch in kindergarten. Finch in middle school. He looks different every year, not just agewise but personwise. Class-clown Finch. Awkward Finch. Cocky Finch. Jock Finch.

At the end of the hall, he pushes open a door.

The walls are a dark, deep red, and everything else is black—desk, chair, bookcase, bedspread, guitars. One entire wall is covered in pictures and Post-it notes and napkins and torn pieces of paper. On the other walls there are concert posters and a large black-and-white photo of him onstage somewhere, guitar in hand.

I stand in front of the wall of notes and say, "What's all this?"

"Plans," he says. "Songs. Ideas. Visions." He throws my bag onto his bed and digs something out of a drawer.

Most look like fragments of things, single words or phrases that don't make sense on their own: *Night flowers. I do it so it feels real. Let us fall. My decision totally. Obelisk. Is today a good day to?*

Is today a good day to what? I want to ask. But instead I say, "Obelisk?"

"It's my favorite word."

"Really?"

"One of them, at least. Look at it." I look. "That is one straight-up, upstanding, powerful word. Unique, original, and kind of stealthy because it doesn't really sound like what it is. It's a word that surprises you and makes you think, *Oh. All right then.* It commands respect, but it's also modest. Not like 'monument' or 'tower.'" He shakes his head. "Pretentious bastards."

I don't say anything because I used to love words. I loved them and was good at arranging them. Because of this, I felt protective of all the best ones. But now all of them, good and bad, frustrate me.

He says, "Have you ever heard the phrase 'get back on the camel' before?"

"Not until Mr. Black used it."

He leans over his desk, tears a piece of paper in half, and writes it down. He slaps it on the wall as we leave.

Outside, I climb onto Leroy, resting one foot on the ground. Theodore Finch pulls on a backpack, his T-shirt riding up across his stomach where an ugly red scar cuts across the middle.

I push Eleanor's glasses up onto my head. "Where did you get the scar?"

"I drew it on. It's been my experience that girls like scars even better than tattoos." He straddles the bike, resting back on the seat, both feet firmly planted. "Have you been in a car since the accident?"

"No."

"That's gotta be some sort of record. We're talking, what, eight, nine months? How do you get to school?"

"I ride my bike or walk. We don't live that far."

"What about when it rains or snows?"

"I ride my bike or walk."

"So you're afraid to ride in a car but you'll climb up on a bell tower ledge?"

"I'm going home."

He laughs and reaches out for my bike, holding on to it before I can take off. "I won't bring it up again."

"I don't believe you."

"Look, you're already here, and we're already committed to this project, so the way I see it, the faster we get to Hoosier Hill, the faster you get this over with."

★　★　★

We pass cornfield after cornfield. Hoosier Hill is only eleven miles from town, so we don't have far to go. The day is cold but bright, and it feels good to be out. I close my eyes and tip my head upward. It's a remnant of the Violet who came Before. Normal teenage Violet. Violet Unremarkey-able.

Finch rides along beside me. "You know what I like about driving? The forward motion of it, the propulsion of it, like you might go anywhere."

I open my eyes and frown at him. "This isn't driving."

"You're telling me." He weaves across the road in figure eights, then around me in circles, then rides beside me again. "I'm surprised you don't wear a helmet or full-on body armor, just to be extra safe. What if the apocalypse happened and everyone but you turned into zombies, and the only way you could save yourself was to get the hell out of town? No airplanes, no trains, no buses. Public transportation is completely broken down. The bike's too exposed, too dangerous. What then?"

"How do I know I'll be safe out of town?"

"Bartlett's the only place that's been affected."

"And I know this for sure?"

"It's public knowledge. The government has confirmed it."

I don't answer.

He figure-eights around me. "Where would you go if you could go anywhere?"

"Is it still the apocalypse?"

"No."

New York, I think.

"Back to California," I say. What I mean is the California of four years ago, before we moved here, when Eleanor was a sophomore and I was going into ninth grade.

"But you've already been there. Don't you want to see places you've never been?" He pedals along, hands in his armpits now.

"It's warm there and it never snows." I hate snow and will always hate snow. And then I hear Mrs. Kresney and my parents telling me to make an effort. So I say, "I might go to Argentina or Singapore for school. I'm not applying any place less than two thousand miles away." Or any place with an annual snowfall greater than one inch, which is why NYU is out. "I might stay here though. I haven't decided."

"Don't you want to know where I'd go if I could?"

Not really, I think. "Where would you go if you could go anywhere?" It comes out bitchier than I mean for it to.

He leans forward over the handlebars, eyes on me. "I'd go to Hoosier Hill with a beautiful girl."

A grove of trees stands on one side. Flat farmland spreads out on the other, dusted with snow. Finch says, "I think it's down that way."

We leave our bikes by the tree line, and then we cross the road and follow this dirt path, only a few yards long. My legs are aching from the ride. I feel strangely breathless.

There are some kids hanging out in the field, swaying back and forth on the fence. When they see us coming, one of them bumps another and straightens. "You can go on ahead," he says. "People come from all over the world to see it and you ain't the first."

"There used to be a paper sign," one of the other kids adds. She sounds bored.

With an Australian accent Finch tells them, "We're here from Perth. We've come all this way to see the highest peak in Indiana. Is it all right if we scale the summit?"

They don't ask where Perth is. They just shrug.

We turn off into the grove of brown winter trees, brushing branches out of our faces. We duck onto a narrower dirt path and keep going, no longer side by side. Finch is in front, and I pay more attention to the shine of his hair and the way he ambles, loose-jointed and fluid, than I do to the scenery.

Suddenly we're there, in the middle of a brown circle. A wooden bench sits underneath a tree, a picnic table just past it. The sign is to our right—INDIANA HIGHPOINT, HOOSIER HILL, ELEV. 1257 FT. The marker is straight ahead—a wooden stake poking up out of the ground in the middle of a pile of stones, no wider or higher than a pitcher's mound.

"This is it?" I can't help saying.

Some high point. It's amazingly underwhelming. But then what did I expect?

He takes my hand and pulls me up after him so that we're standing on the stones.

In that instant his skin touches mine, I feel a little shock.

I tell myself it's nothing more than the understandable jolt of actual physical contact when you aren't used to it from someone new. But then these electric currents start shooting up my arm, and he is rubbing my palm with his thumb, which makes the currents go shooting through the rest of me. *Uh-oh.*

In the Australian accent he says, "What do we think?" His hand is firm and warm, and somehow, big as it is, it fits with mine.

"If we're here from Perth?" I'm distracted by the electric currents and trying not to show it. If I do, I know he will never let me hear the end of it.

"Or maybe we've come from Moscow." He has a good Russian accent too.

"We are seriously pissed."

In his own voice he says, "Not as pissed as the folks over at Sand Hill, the second-highest spot in Indiana. It's only 1,076 feet, and they don't even have a picnic area."

"If they're second, they don't really need one."

"An excellent point. As far as I'm concerned, it's not even worth looking at. Not when you've got Hoosier Hill." He smiles at me, and for the first time I notice how blue his eyes are—like, bright-sky blue. "At least it feels that way standing here with you." He closes his blue eyes and breathes in. When he opens them again, he says, "Actually, standing next to you makes it feel as high as Everest."

I yank my hand back. Even after I let go, I can feel the stupid current. "Shouldn't we be collecting things? Writing stuff down? Shooting video? How do we organize this?"

"We don't. When we're in the act of wandering, we need to be present, not watching it through a lens."

Together, we look out over the circle of brown and the bench and the trees and the flat, white landscape beyond. Ten months ago, I would have stood here writing this place in my head. *There is this sign, which is a good thing, because otherwise you would never know you're looking at the highest point in Indiana. . . .* I would have thought up an entire backstory for the kids, something epic and exciting. Now they're just Indiana farm kids hanging on a fence.

I say, "I think this is the ugliest place I've ever seen. Not just here. The whole state." I hear my parents telling me not to be negative, which is funny because I've always been the happy one. It's Eleanor who was moody.

"I used to think that. But then I realized, believe it or not, it's actually beautiful to some people. It must be, because enough people live here, and they can't all think it's ugly." He smiles out at the ugly trees and the ugly farmland and the ugly kids as if he can see Oz. As if he can really, truly see the beauty that's there. In that moment I wish I could see it through his eyes. I wish he had glasses to give me. "Also, I figure while I'm here, I might as well get to know it, you know—see what there is to see."

"Wander Indiana?"

"Yeah."

"You look different than you did the other day."

He glances at me sideways, eyes half closed. "It's the altitude."

I laugh and then stop myself.

"It's okay to laugh, you know. The earth's not going to split open. You're not going to hell. Believe me. If there's a hell, I'll be there ahead of you, and they'll be too busy with me to even check you in."

I want to ask what happened to him. Is it true he had a breakdown? Is it true he OD'd? Where was he at the end of last semester?

"I've heard a lot of stories."

"About me?"

"Are they true?"

"Probably."

And then he says, "Let's jump."

"Are you sure? It is the high point of Indiana."

"I'm sure. It's now or never, but I need to know if you're with me."

"Okay."

"Ready?"

"Ready."

"On three."

We jump just as the kids ramble up. We land, dusty and laughing. In the Australian accent Finch says to them, "We're professionals. Whatever you do, don't try this at home."

The things we leave behind are some British coins, a red guitar pick, and a Bartlett High keychain. We store them in this hide-a-key fake rock that Finch found in his garage. He wedges it in among the stones that surround the high point. He brushes the dirt off his

He shakes the hair out of his eyes and stares at me good and hard. His gaze trails slowly down my face to my mouth. For a second, I think he's going to kiss me. For a second, I want him to.

"So we can cross this one off, right? One down, one to go. Where to next?" I sound like my dad's secretary.

"I've got a map in my backpack." He doesn't make a move to get it. Instead he stands there, breathing it in, looking all around. I want to get to the map because that's how I am, or used to be, ready for the next thing once I've got it in my mind. But he's not going anywhere, and then his hand finds mine again. Instead of snatching it back, I make myself stand here too, and actually it's nice. The electric currents are racing. My body is humming. The breeze is blowing, rustling the leaves on the trees. It's almost like music. We stand side by side, looking out and up and around.

hands as he stands. "Whether you want to or not, now we'll always be a part of here. Unless those kids get in there and rob us blind."

My hand feels cold without his. I pull out my phone and say, "We need to document this somehow." I start taking pictures before he nods okay, and we take turns posing on the high point.

Then he gets the map out of his backpack along with a college-ruled notebook. He hands me the notebook and a pen, and when I say, "That's okay," he tells me his handwriting is like chicken scratch and it's up to me to keep the notes. The thing I can't say is I'd rather drive all the way to Indianapolis than write in this notebook.

But because he's watching me, I scrawl down a few things— location, date, time, a brief description of the place itself and the kids by the fence—and afterward, we spread the map out on the picnic table.

Finch traces the red highway lines with his index finger. "I know Black mentioned picking two wonders and running with them, but I don't think that's enough. I think we need to see all of them."

"All of what?"

"Every place of interest in the state. As many as we can cram into the semester."

"Only two. That's the deal."

He studies the map, shakes his head. His hand moves over the paper. By the time he's done, he's made pen marks across the entire state, circling every town he knows of where there's a wonder— Dune State Park, the World's Largest Egg, Home of Dan Patch the racehorse, the Market Street Catacombs, and the Seven Pillars, which are a series of enormous limestone columns, carved by nature, that overlook the Mississinewa River. Some of the circles are close to Bartlett, some are far away.

"That's too many," I say.

"Maybe. Maybe not."

Early evening. Finch's driveway. I stand with Leroy as Finch shoves his bike into the garage. He opens the door to go inside, and when I don't move, he says, "We have to get your bag."

"I'll wait here."

He just laughs and goes away. While he's gone, I text my mom to tell her I'll be heading home soon. I picture her waiting at the window, watching for me, even though she would never let me catch her at it.

In a few minutes, Finch is back and standing too close, looking down at me with blue-blue eyes. With one hand, he brushes the hair out of them. It's been a long time since I've been this close to a boy other than Ryan, and I suddenly remember what Suze said about Finch knowing what to do with a girl. Theodore "Freak" or no freak, he is lean and good-looking and trouble.

Like that, I feel myself pulling back in. I drop Eleanor's glasses onto my face so that Finch looks warped and strange, like I'm seeing him in a fun-house mirror.

"Because you smiled at me."

"What?"

"You asked why I wanted to do this with you. It's not because you were up on the ledge too, even though, okay, that's part of it. It's not because I feel this weird responsibility to keep an eye on you, which is also part of it. It's because you smiled at me that day in class. A real smile, not the bullshit one I see you give everyone all the time where your eyes are doing one thing and your mouth is doing another."

"It was just a smile."

"Maybe to you."

"You know I'm going out with Ryan Cross."

"I thought you said he wasn't your boyfriend." Before I can recover, he laughs. "Relax. I don't like you like that."

Dinnertime. My house. My father makes chicken piccata, which means the kitchen is a mess. I set the table as Mom ties her hair back and takes the plates from Dad. In my house, eating is an event accompanied by the right music and the right wine.

My mom takes a bite of chicken, gives my dad a thumbs-up, and looks at me. "So tell me more about this project."

"We're supposed to wander Indiana, as if there's anything interesting to see. We have to have partners, so I'm working with this boy in my class."

My dad raises an eyebrow at my mother and then me. "You know, I was terrific at geography back in the day. If you need any help with that project—"

Mom and I cut him off at the same time, telling him how good the food is, asking if we can have more. He gets up, pleased and distracted, and my mother mouths to me, "Close one." My dad lives to help with school projects. The problem is he ends up taking them over completely.

He comes back in saying, "So, this project . . ." just as my mom is saying, "So this boy . . ."

Except for wanting to know my every move, my parents act

pretty much like they always did. It throws me when they're the parents of Before, because nothing about me is like it used to be.

"Dad, I was just wondering," I begin, my mouth full of chicken. "Where did this dish begin? I mean, how did they come up with it?"

If there's anything my dad likes more than projects, it's explaining the history of things. For the rest of the meal, he talks nonstop about ancient Italy and the Italians' love for clean, simple cooking, which means my project and this boy are forgotten.

Upstairs, I scroll around Finch's Facebook page. I'm still his only friend. Suddenly a new message appears. **I feel like I just walked through the back of the wardrobe and into Narnia.**

I immediately research Narnia quotes. The one that stands out is: *"I have come home at last! This is my real country! I belong here. This is the land I have been looking for all my life, though I never knew it till now. . . . Come further up, come further in!"*

But instead of copying it down and sending it, I get up and mark the day off on the calendar. I stand looking at the word "Graduation," all the way in June, as I think about Hoosier Hill, Finch's blue-blue eyes, and the way he made me feel. Like everything else that doesn't last, today is gone now, but it was a pretty good day. The best I've had in months.

FINCH

The night of the day my life changed

My mother stares at me over her plate. Decca, as usual, is eating like a small, ravenous horse, and for once I'm doing my share of shoveling it in.

Mom says, "Decca, tell me what you learned today."

Before she can answer, I say, "Actually, I'd like to go first."

Dec stops eating long enough to gape at me, her mouth full of partially chewed casserole. Mom smiles nervously and holds on to her glass and plate, as if I might get up and start throwing things.

"Of course, Theodore. Tell me what you learned."

"I learned that there is good in this world, if you look hard enough for it. I learned that not everyone is disappointing, including me, and that a 1,257-foot bump in the ground can feel higher than a bell tower if you're standing next to the right person."

Mom waits politely, and when I don't say anything else, she starts nodding. "This is great. That's really good, Theodore. Isn't that interesting, Decca?"

As we clear the plates, my mother looks as dazed and disconcerted as she always does, only more so because she doesn't have the first clue what to do with my sisters and me.

Since I feel happy about my day and also bad for her because my father not only broke her heart, he pretty much shat all over her pride and self-worth, I tell her, "Mum, why don't you let me do the dishes tonight? You should put your feet up." When my dad left us this last and final time, my mom earned her Realtor's license, but because the housing market is less than booming, she part-times at a bookstore. She is always tired.

Her face crumples, and for one awful moment I'm afraid she's going to cry, but then she kisses me on the cheek and says, "Thank you," in such a world-weary way that I almost want to cry myself, except that I'm feeling much too good for that.

Then she says, "Did you just call me 'Mum'?"

I'm putting on my shoes at the very moment the sky opens up and it starts to pour. By the looks of it we're talking cold, blinding sleet, so instead of going out for a run, I take a bath. I strip, climb in, water splashing onto the floor, leaving little pools that shake like beached fish. The whole operation doesn't work well at first because I am twice as long as the bathtub, but the tub is full of water and I've come this far, and I have to see it through. My feet rest halfway up the tile of the wall as I go under, eyes open, staring up at the shower-head and the black curtain and plastic liner and the ceiling, and then I close my eyes and pretend I'm in a lake.

Water is peaceful. I am at rest. In the water, I am safe and pulled in where I can't get out. Everything slows down—the noise and the racing of my thoughts. I wonder if I could sleep like this, here on the bottom of the bathtub, if I wanted to sleep, which I don't. I let my mind drift. I hear words forming as if I'm sitting at the computer already.

In March of 1941, after three serious breakdowns, Virginia Woolf wrote a note to her husband and walked to a nearby river. She shoved heavy stones into her pocket and dove into the water. *"Dearest,"* the note began, *"I feel certain that I am going mad again. I feel we can't go through another of those terrible times. . . . So I am doing what seems the best thing to do."*

How long has it been? Four minutes? Five? Longer? My lungs are starting to burn. *Stay calm,* I tell myself. *Stay relaxed. The worst thing you can do is panic.*

Six minutes? Seven? The longest I've held my breath is six and a half minutes. The world record is twenty-two minutes and twenty-two seconds, and this belongs to a German competitive breath holder. He says it's all about control and endurance, but I suspect it has more to do with the fact that his lung capacity is 20 percent larger than the average person's. I wonder if there's something to this competitive breath holding, if there's really a living to be made at it.

"You have been in every way all that anyone could be. . . . If anybody could have saved me it would have been you."

I open my eyes and sit straight up, gasping, filling my lungs. I'm happy no one's here to see me, because I'm sputtering and splashing and coughing up water. There's no rush of having survived, only emptiness, and lungs that need air, and wet hair sticking to my face.

VIOLET

148 days till graduation

Thursday. U.S. Geography.

The *Bartlett Dirt* has named the top ten suicidal students in school, and my phone is buzzing because Theodore Finch is number one on the list. Jordan Gripenwaldt has covered the front page of the school paper with resources and information about teen suicide and what to do if you're thinking of killing yourself, but no one is paying attention to this.

I turn off my phone and put it away. To distract myself and him, I ask Ryan about the "Wander Indiana" project. He is partners with Joe Wyatt. Their theme is baseball. They're planning to visit the county baseball museum and the Indiana Baseball Hall of Fame in Jasper.

"That sounds really great," I say. He is playing with my hair, and to make him stop, I lean over and pretend to search for something in my bag.

For their wanderings, Amanda and Roamer are planning to focus on the James Whitcomb Riley Museum and our local farm and history museum, which is right here in Bartlett and features an actual Egyptian mummy. I can't think of anything more depressing than to be an Egyptian high priest on display next to a set of vintage wagon wheels and a two-headed chicken.

Amanda examines the ends of her ponytail. She is the only person besides me who is ignoring her phone. "So how is it? Is it awful?" She stops examining long enough to look at me.

"What?"

"Finch?"

I shrug. "It's okay."

"Oh my God, you like him!"

"No I don't." But I can feel my face turning pink because everyone is looking at me. Amanda has such a loud mouth.

Thankfully, the bell rings, and Mr. Black wants eyes on him, people. At some point, Ryan slips me a note because my phone is off. I see it under his arm, waving at me, and I take it. *Drive-in double feature Saturday night? Just you and me?*

I write: *Can I let you know?*

I tap Ryan's arm and hand him the note. Mr. Black walks to the chalkboard and writes POP QUIZ and then a list of questions. Everybody groans and there's the sound of ripping paper.

Five minutes later, Finch breezes in, same black shirt, same black jeans, backpack over one shoulder, books and notebooks and thrashed leather jacket under his arm. Things are spilling everywhere, and he retrieves keys and pens and cigarettes before giving Mr. Black a little salute. I look at him and think: *This is the person who knows your worst secret.*

Finch pauses to read the board. "Pop quiz? Sorry, sir. Just a second." He's using his Australian accent. Before he takes his seat, he heads right for me. He sets something on my notebook.

He slaps Ryan on the back, drops an apple on the teacher's desk with another apology to Mr. Black, and falls into his chair across the room. The thing he set in front of me is an ugly gray rock.

Ryan looks down at it and up at me, and then past me at Roamer, who narrows his eyes in Finch's direction. "Freak," he says loudly.

He mimes hanging himself.

Amanda punches me a little too hard in the arm. "Let me see it."

Mr. Black raps on the desk. "In five more seconds . . . I will give each and . . . every one of you an F . . . on this quiz." He picks up the apple and looks as if he's going to throw it.

We all go quiet. He sets the apple down. Ryan turns around and now I can see the freckles on the base of his neck. The quiz is made up of five easy questions. After Mr. Black collects the papers and starts to lecture, I pick up the rock and flip it over.

Your turn, it says.

After class, Finch is out the door before I can talk to him. I drop the rock into my bag. Ryan walks me to Spanish, and we don't hold hands. "So what's up with that? Why's he giving you things? Is it, what, a thank-you for saving his life?"

"It's a rock. If it was a thank-you for saving him, I'd hope for something a little better than that."

"I don't care what it is."

"Don't be that guy, Ryan."

"What guy?" As we walk, he nods at people going by, everyone smiling and calling out, "Hey, Ryan," "What's up, Cross?" They do everything but bow and throw confetti. A few of them are good enough to call out to me too, now that I'm a hero.

"The guy who's jealous of the guy his ex-girlfriend's doing a project with."

"I'm not jealous." We stop outside my classroom. "I'm just crazy about you. And I think we should get back together."

"I don't know if I'm ready."

"I'm going to keep asking."

"I guess I can't stop you."

"If he gets out of line, let me know."

The corner of his mouth goes up. When he smiles like that, there's a single dimple. It was the thing that got me the very first time I saw him. Without thinking, I reach up and kiss the dimple when what I mean to do is kiss his cheek. I don't know which of us is more surprised. I say, "You don't need to worry. It's only a project."

At dinner that night, the thing I fear most happens. My mom turns to me and asks, "Were you in the bell tower of school last week?"

She and my dad are staring at me from opposite ends of the table. I immediately choke on my food, so noisily and violently that my mother gets up to pat me on the back.

My dad says, "Too spicy?"

"No, Dad, it's great." I barely get the words out because I'm still coughing. I cover my mouth with my napkin and cough and cough like some tubercular old uncle.

Mom pats me until I quiet down and then takes her seat again. "I got a call from a reporter at the local paper who wants to do a story on our heroic daughter. Why didn't you tell us?"

"I don't know. They're making a bigger deal of it than it is. I'm not a hero. I just happened to be up there. I don't think he really would have jumped." I drink my entire glass of water because my mouth is suddenly dry.

"Who's this boy you saved?" my dad wants to know.

"He's just a boy I go to school with. He's okay now."

My mother and father glance at each other, and in that one shared look, I can see what they're thinking: our daughter isn't as hopelessly lost as we thought. They will start expecting things, beginning with a newer, braver Violet who isn't afraid of her own shadow.

Mom picks up her fork again. "The reporter left her name and number and asked that you call her when you have a chance."

"Great," I say. "Thanks. I will."

"By the way . . . ." My mom's voice turns casual, but there's something in it that makes me want to hurry and finish so I can get out of there fast. "How does New York sound for spring break? We haven't taken a family trip in a while."

We haven't taken one since before the accident. This would be our first trip without Eleanor, but then there have been lots of firsts—first Thanksgiving, first Christmas, first New Year's Eve. This is the first calendar year of my life that she hasn't been in.

"We can take in some shows, do a little shopping. We can always stop by NYU and see if there are any interesting lectures." She smiles too brightly. Even worse, my dad is smiling too.

"It sounds great," I say, but we all know I don't mean it.

That night, I have the same nightmare I've been having for months—the one where someone comes at me from behind and tries to strangle me. I feel the hands on my throat, pressing tighter and tighter, but I can't see who's doing it. Sometimes the person doesn't get as far as touching me, but I know he's there. Other times, I can feel the breath going out of me. My head goes light, my body floats away, and I start to fall.

I wake up, and for a few seconds I don't know where I am. I sit up and turn on a light and look around my room, as if the man might be lurking behind the desk or in the closet. I reach for my laptop. In the days Before, I would have written something—a short story or a blog post or just random thoughts. I would have written till it was out of me and on the page. But now I open a new document and stare at the screen. I write a couple words, erase them. Write, erase. I was the writer, not Eleanor, but there is something about the act of writing that makes me feel as if I'm cheating on her. Maybe because I'm here and she's not, and the whole thing—every big or small moment I've lived since last April—feels like cheating in some way.

Finally, I sign onto Facebook. There's a new message from Finch, 1:04 a.m. **Did you know the world's tallest woman and one of the world's tallest men were from Indiana? What does that say about our state?**

I check the current time: 1:44 a.m. I write, **We have greater nutritional resources than other states?**

I watch the page, the house quiet around me. I tell myself he's probably asleep by now, that it's just me who's awake. I should read or turn out the light and try to get some rest before I have to get up for school.

Finch writes: **Also the world's largest man. I'm worried that our nutritional resources are actually damaged. Maybe this is one reason I'm so tall. What if I don't stop growing? Will you want me just as much when I'm fifteen feet nine inches?**

Me: **How can I want you then when I don't want you now?**

Finch: **Give it time. The thing I'm most concerned with is how I'm going to ride a bike. I don't think they make them that big.**

Me: **Look on the bright side—your legs will be so long that one of** your steps will be the same as thirty or forty of a regular person's.

Finch: **So you're saying I can carry you when we wander.**

Me: **Yes.**

Finch: **After all, you're famous.**

Me: **You're the hero, not me.**

Finch: **Believe me, I'm no hero. What are you doing up, anyway?**

Me: **Bad dreams.**

Finch: **Regular occurrence?**

Me: **More than I'd like.**

Finch: **Since the accident or before?**

Me: **Since. You?**

Finch: **Too much to do and write and think. Besides, who would keep you company?**

I want to say I'm sorry about the *Bartlett Dirt*—no one really believes the lies they print; it'll all die down eventually—but then he writes: **Meet me at the Quarry.**

Me: **I can't.**

Finch: **Don't keep me waiting. On second thought, I'll meet you at your house.**

Me: **I can't.**

No answer.

Me: **Finch?**

FINCH

Day 13

I throw rocks at her window but she doesn't come down. I think about ringing the doorbell, but that would only wake the parents. I try waiting her out, but the curtain doesn't move, and the door doesn't open, and it is really fucking cold, so finally I climb into Little Bastard and go home.

I'm up the rest of the night making a list called "How to Stay Awake." There's the obvious—Red Bull, caffeine, NoDoz and other drugs—but this isn't about skipping a couple hours' sleep, it's about staying up and staying here for the long haul.

1. Run.
2. Write (this includes any thoughts I don't want to have—write them out fast so they're out of me and on the paper).
3. Along those lines, accept any and all thoughts (don't be afraid of them no matter what they are).
4. Surround myself with water.
5. Plan.
6. Drive anywhere and everywhere, even when there's nowhere to go. (Note: There's always somewhere to go.)
7. Play guitar.
8. Organize room, notes, thoughts. (This is different from planning.)

9. Do whatever it takes to remind myself that I'm still here and have a say.
10. Violet.

VIOLET

The next morning. My house. I walk out the door to find Finch lying on the front lawn, eyes closed, black boots crossed at the ankle. His bike rests on its side, half in and half off the street.

I kick the sole of his shoe. "Were you out here all night?"

He opens his eyes. "So you did know I was here. Hard to tell when a person's being ignored while standing, I may add, in the freezing arctic cold." He pulls himself to his feet, shoulders his backpack, picks up his bike. "Any more nightmares?"

"No."

While I get Leroy from the garage, Finch rides up and down the driveway. "So where are we headed?"

"School."

"I mean tomorrow when we wander. Unless you've got big plans."

He says this as if he knows I don't. I think about Ryan and the drive-in. I still haven't told him yes or no. "I'm not sure I'm free tomorrow." We push off toward school, Finch sprinting forward, doubling back, sprinting forward, doubling back.

The ride is almost peaceful, until he says, "I was thinking that, as your partner and the guy who saved your life, I should know what happened the night of the accident."

Leroy wobbles and Finch reaches out and steadies the bike and me. The electric currents start shooting through me, just like before, and there goes my balance again. We ride for a minute with his hand on the back of the seat. I keep my eyes open for Amanda or Suze because I know exactly how this will look.

"So what happened?" I hate the way he brings up the accident just like that, like it's okay to talk about. "I'll tell you how I got my scar if you tell me about that night."

"Why do you want to know?"

"Because I like you. Not in a romantic, let's-get-it-on way, but as a fellow student of U.S. geography. And because it might help you to talk about it."

"You first."

"I was playing this show over in Chicago with these guys I met at a bar. They were like, 'Hey, man, our guitar player just walked out, and you look like you know your way around a stage.' I got up there, no clue what I was doing, what they were doing, but we threw it down. I mean, threw. It. Down. I was hotter than Hendrix—they knew it, and the original guitar player knew it. So the sonuvabitch climbed up after me and cut me open with his guitar pick."

"Did that really happen?" The school's in sight. Kids are getting out of their cars and hanging around on the lawn.

"There may have also been a girl involved." I can't tell by the look on his face if he's bullshitting me or not, but I'm pretty sure he is. "Your turn."

"Only after you tell me what really happened." I take off and fly toward the parking lot and the bike rack. When I come to a stop, Finch is right behind me, laughing his head off. In my pocket, my phone is buzzing and buzzing. I pull it out and there are five texts from Suze, all with the same message: **Theodore Freak?!! WTF?!** I look around but she isn't anywhere.

"See you tomorrow," he's saying.

"Actually, I've got plans."

He glances at my phone and then at me, giving me a look that's hard to read. "All right. That's cool. Later then, Ultraviolet."

"What did you call me?"

"You heard me."

"School's that way." I point toward the building.

"I know." And away he goes in the other direction.

Saturday. My house. I am on the phone with Jerri Sparks, the reporter from the local paper, who wants to send someone out to take my picture. She says, "How does it feel to know you've saved someone's life? I know, of course, about the terrible tragedy you suffered last year. Does this in any way give you closure?"

"How would this give me closure?"

"The fact that you couldn't save your sister's life, but you were able to save the life of this boy, Theodore Finch . . ."

I hang up on her. *As if they are one and the same, and besides, I'm not the one who saved a life.* Finch is the hero, not me. I'm just a girl pretending to be a hero.

I am still seething by the time Ryan shows up, five minutes early. We walk to the drive-in because it's only a mile from my house. I keep my hands in the pockets of my coat, but we walk with our arms bumping. It's like a first date all over again.

At the drive-in, we find Amanda and Roamer, who are parked in

Roamer's car. He drives an enormous old Chevy Impala, which is as large as a city block. He calls it the Party Car because it can fit about sixty-five people at once.

Ryan opens the back door for me and I get in. Because the Impala is parked, I'm fine being in there, even though it smells like smoke and old fast food and, faintly, of pot. I'm probably incurring years of secondhand smoke damage just sitting here.

The movie is a Japanese monster movie double feature, and before it starts, Ryan, Roamer, and Amanda talk about how awesome college will be—they're all going to Indiana University. I sit thinking about Jerri Sparks and New York and spring break and how bad I feel about blowing off Finch and for being rude to him when he *saved my life.* Wandering with him would be more fun than this. Anything would be more fun than this.

The car is hot and fumy, even though the windows are open, and when the second movie starts, Roamer and Amanda lie down flat in the enormous front seat and go almost completely quiet. Almost. Every now and then I hear a slurping, smacking sound as if they're two hungry dogs lapping at the food bowl.

I try watching the movie, and when that doesn't work, I try writing the scene in my mind. *Amanda's head pops up over the seat, her shirt hanging open so that I can see her bra, which is baby blue with yellow flowers. Like that, I can feel the image burning into my retinas, where it will remain forever. . . .*

There are too many distractions, and so I talk over the noise to Ryan, but he's more interested in sneaking his hand up my shirt. I've managed to make it seventeen years, eight months, two weeks, and one day without having sex in the backseat of an Impala (or anywhere, for that matter), so I tell him I'm dying to see the view, and I push open the door and stand there. We are surrounded by cars and, beyond that, cornfields. There is no view except up. I tilt my head back, suddenly fascinated by the stars. Ryan scrambles after me, and I pretend to know the constellations, pointing them out and making up stories about each one.

I wonder what Finch is doing right now. Maybe he's playing guitar somewhere. Maybe he's with a girl. I owe him a wander and, actually, a lot more than that. I don't want him to think I blew him off today because of my so-called friends. I make a note to research where we should go next as soon as I get home. (Search terms: *unusual Indiana attractions, nothing ordinary Indiana, unique Indiana, ec-*

centric Indiana.) I should also have a copy of the map so I make sure I don't duplicate anything.

Ryan puts his arm around me and kisses me, and for a minute I kiss him. I'm transported back in time, and instead of the Impala, it's Ryan's brother's Jeep, and instead of Roamer and Amanda, it's Eli Cross and Eleanor, and we're here at the drive-in seeing a double feature of *Die Hard.*

Then Ryan's hand is snaking its way up my shirt again, and I pull away. The Impala is back. Roamer and Amanda are back. The monster movie is back.

I say, "I hate to do this, but I have a curfew."

"Since when?" Then he seems to remember something. "Sorry, V." And I know he's thinking it's because of the accident.

Ryan offers to walk me home. I tell him no, I'm good, I got this, but he does it anyway.

"I had a great time," he says on my front step.

"Me too."

"I'll call you."

"Great."

He leans in to kiss me good night and I turn just slightly so he'll get my cheek instead. He's still standing there as I let myself inside the house.

FINCH

I go to Violet's early and catch her parents as they're eating breakfast. He is bearded and serious with deep worry lines around his mouth and eyes, and she looks like Violet will look in about twenty-five years, dark-blond hair falling in waves, face shaped like a heart, everything etched a little more sharply. Her eyes are warm, but her mouth is sad.

They invite me to breakfast, and I ask them about Violet before the accident since I've only known her after. By the time she comes downstairs, they are remembering the time she and her sister were supposed to go to New York for spring break two years ago but instead decided to follow Boy Parade from Cincinnati to Indianapolis to Chicago to try to get an interview.

When Violet sees me, she goes, "Finch?" like I might be a dream, and I say, *"Boy Parade?"*

"Oh my God. Why would you tell him that?"

I can't help it, I start laughing, and this gets her mom laughing and then her dad too, until the three of us are laughing like old friends while Violet stares at us as if we've lost our minds.

Afterward, Violet and I stand in front of her house and, because it's her turn to pick the place, she gives me a rough idea of the route and tells me to follow her there. Then she takes off across the lawn and toward her driveway.

"I didn't bring my bike." Before she can say anything, I hold up my hand like I'm taking an oath. "I, Theodore Finch, being of unsound mind, hereby swear not to drive faster than thirty miles per hour through town, fifty on the interstate. If at any time you want to stop, we stop. I just ask that you give it a chance."

"It's snowing."

She's exaggerating. It's barely even coming down.

"Not the kind that sticks. Look, we've wandered all we can wander within a reachable-by-bike radius. We can see a lot more if we drive. I mean, the possibilities are pretty much endless. At least sit inside. Humor me. Sit in there and I'll stand way, way over here, nowhere near the car, so you know I can't ambush you and start driving."

She is frozen to the sidewalk. "You can't keep pushing people to do things they don't want to do. You just barge in and help yourself and say we're doing this, we're doing that, but you don't listen. You don't think about anyone else other than yourself."

"Actually, I'm thinking about you holed up in that room of yours or on that stupid orange bike. Must go here. Must go there. Here. There. Back and forth, but nowhere new or outside those three or four miles."

"Maybe I like those three or four miles."

"I don't think you do. This morning, your parents painted a pretty good picture of the *you* you used to be. That other Violet sounds fun and kind of badass, even if she had horrible taste in music. Now all I see is someone who's too afraid to get back out there. Everyone around you is going to give you a gentle push now and then, but never hard enough because they don't want to upset Poor Violet. You need shoving, not pushing. You need to jump back on that camel. Otherwise you're going to stay up on the ledge you've made for yourself."

Suddenly she brushes past me. She climbs into the car and sits looking all around. Even though I tried to clean up a little, the center console is stuffed with pencil stubs and pieces of paper, cigarette butts, a lighter, guitar picks. There's a blanket in the back, and a pillow, and I can tell she's noticed these by the look she gives me.

"Oh, relax. The plan is not to seduce you. If it was, you'd know it. Seat belt." She snaps it into place. "Now close the door." I stand on the lawn, arms crossed as she pulls the door shut.

Then I walk to the driver's side, open the door, and lean in as she's reading the back of a napkin from a place called the Harlem Avenue Lounge.

"What do you say, Ultraviolet?"

She takes a breath. Lets it out. "Okay."

I go slow at first, barely twenty miles per hour, as I roll through her neighborhood. We take it block by block. At each stop sign and stoplight, I say, "How're we doing over there?"

"Good. Just fine."

I pull out onto National Road and pick it up to thirty-five. "How's this?"

"Great."

"How about now?"

"Stop asking me."

We go so slow that cars and trucks are speeding past and honking. One guy yells at us out his window and flips us off. It's taking all I have not to slam my foot against the gas pedal, but then I'm used to slowing down so that everyone else can catch up.

To distract myself and her, I talk to her like we're on the bell tower ledge. "My whole life I've run either three times faster than everyone else or three times slower. When I was little, I used to race in circles around the living room, over and over, until I wore this ring into the carpet. It got so I started following the ring, until my dad tore up the rug himself, just ripped it right out with his bare hands. Instead of replacing the carpet, he left the concrete exposed so there were these little patches of glue everywhere, with bits of rug stuck to it."

"So do it. Go fast."

"Oh no. Forty all the way, baby." But I bring it up to fifty. Right about now, I'm feeling pretty damn good because I got Violet into the car and my dad is headed out of town on business, which means no Obligatory Family Dinner tonight. "Your parents are awesome, by the way. You lucked out in the parental lottery, Ultraviolet."

"Thanks."

"So . . . Boy Parade. Did you ever get that interview?"

She gives me a look.

"Okay, tell me about the accident." I don't expect her to, but she gazes out the window, then starts talking.

"I don't remember much of it. I remember getting in the car as we were leaving the party. She and Eli had a fight—"

"Eli Cross?"

"They'd been going out for most of last year. She was upset, but she wouldn't let me drive. I was the one who told her to take the A Street Bridge." She goes very, very quiet. "I remember the sign that said 'Bridge ices before road.' I remember sliding and Eleanor saying, 'I can't hold on.' I remember the air as we went through it, and Eleanor screaming. After that, everything went black. I woke up three hours later in the hospital."

"Tell me about her."

She stares out the window. "She was smart, stubborn, moody, funny, mean when she lost her temper, sweet, protective of the people she loved. Her favorite color was yellow. She always had my back, even if we fought sometimes. I could tell her anything, because the thing about Eleanor was that she didn't judge. She was my best friend."

"I've never had one. What's it like?"

"I don't know. I guess you can be yourself, whatever that means—the best and the worst of you. And they love you anyway. You can fight, but even when you're mad at them, you know they're not going to stop being your friend."

"I might need to get one of those."

"Listen, I wanted to say I'm sorry about Roamer and those guys."

The speed limit is seventy, but I make myself stay at sixty. "It's not your fault. And sorry wastes time. You have to live your life like you'll never be sorry. It's easier just to do the right thing from the start so there's nothing to apologize for." Not that I'm one to talk.

The Bookmobile Park is just outside Bartlett on a country road lined with cornfields. Because the earth is flat and there are hardly any trees, the trailers rise out of the landscape like skyscrapers. I lean forward over the wheel. "What the hell . . . ?"

Violet is leaning forward too, hands on the dashboard. As I turn off the pavement onto gravel, she says, "We used to do this thing in California where sometimes my parents and Eleanor and I would get in the car and go on a bookstore hunt. We each chose a book we wanted to find, and we couldn't go home till we'd found copies of all of them. We might hit up eight or ten stores in a day."

She's out of the car before I am and heading toward the first bookmobile—an Airstream trailer from the 1950s—which is across the gravel and across the field. There are seven trailers in all, different makes and models and years, and they sit in a line with the corn growing up around them. Each one advertises a specific category of books.

"This is one of the coolest fucking things I've ever seen." I don't know if Violet even hears me because she's already climbing up into the first trailer.

"Watch that mouth, young man." A hand is being extended, and now I'm shaking that hand, and it belongs to a short, round woman with bleached yellow hair, warm eyes, and a crinkled-up face. "Faye Carnes."

"Theodore Finch. Are you the mastermind behind this?" I nod at the line of bookmobiles.

"I am." She walks, and I follow. "The county discontinued bookmobile service in the eighties, and I told my husband, 'Now, that's a shame. I mean, a true-blue shame. What's going to happen to those trailers? Someone ought to buy them and keep them going.' So we did. At first we drove them around town ourselves, but my husband, Franklin, he's got a bad back, so we decided to plant them, just like corn, and let folks come to us."

Mrs. Carnes leads me from trailer to trailer, and at each one I go up and in and explore. I pick through stacks of hardcovers and paperbacks, all of them well used and well read. I'm looking for something in particular, but so far I don't see it.

Mrs. Carnes follows along, straightening the books, dusting off the shelves, and tells me about husband Franklin and daughter Sara, and son Franklin Jr., who made the mistake of marrying a girl from Kentucky, which means they never see him except at Christmas. She's a talker, but I like her.

Violet finds us in trailer six (children's), her arms full of classics. She says hello to Mrs. Carnes and asks, "How does this work? Do I need my library card?"

"You got the choice of buying or borrowing, but either way you don't need a card. If you borrow, we trust you to bring them back. If you buy, we only take cash."

"I'd like to buy." Violet nods at me. "Can you reach the money in my bag?"

Instead, I pull out my wallet and hand Mrs. Carnes a twenty, which is the smallest I have, and she counts off the books. "That's a dollar a book, times ten. I'm going to have to go up to the house to get change." She's gone before I can tell her to keep the money.

Violet sets the books down, and now I go with her to explore each trailer. We add a few more books to the pile, and at some point I catch her eye and she's smiling at me. It's the kind of smile you smile when you're thinking someone over and trying to decide how you feel about them. I smile at her and she looks away.

Then Mrs. Carnes is back, and we argue about the change— I want her to keep it, she wants me to keep it, and finally I do because she absolutely won't take no. I jog the books to the car while she talks to Violet. In my wallet I find one more twenty, and when I get back to the trailers, I duck into the first one and drop the twenty and the change into the old register that sits on a kind of makeshift counter.

A group of kids arrives, and we tell Mrs. Carnes good-bye. As we walk away, Violet says, "That was awesome."

"It was, but it doesn't count as a wandering."

"It's technically one more place, and that's all we needed."

"Sorry. Awesome as it is, it's practically in our backyard, in the middle of your three-to-four-mile safe zone. Besides, it's not about crossing things off a list."

She is now walking several feet ahead, pretending I don't exist, but that's okay, I'm used to it, and what she doesn't know is that it doesn't faze me. People either see me or they don't. I wonder what it's like to walk down the street, safe and easy in your skin, and just blend right in. No one turning away, no one staring, no one waiting and expecting, wondering what stupid, crazy thing you'll do next.

Then I can't hold back anymore, and I take off running, and it feels good to break free from the slow, regular pace of everyone else. I break free from my mind, which is, for some reason, picturing myself as dead as the authors of the books Violet collected, asleep for good this time, buried deep in the ground under layers and layers of dirt and cornfields. I can almost feel the earth closing in, the air going stale and damp, the dark pressing down on top of me, and I have to open my mouth to breathe.

In a blur, Violet passes me, hair sailing behind her like a kite, the sun catching it and turning it gold at the ends. I'm so deep in my own head, accepting the thoughts, letting them come, that at first I'm not sure it's her, and then I sprint to catch up, and run along beside her, matching my pace to hers. She's off again, and we push ourselves so hard and fast, I expect to go flying off the earth. This is my secret—that any moment I might fly away. Everyone on earth but me—and now Violet—moves in slow motion, like they're filled with mud. We are faster than all of them.

And then we're at the car, and Violet is giving me a "so there, take that" look. I tell myself I let her win, but she's beat me fair and square.

After we're in and the engine is running, I toss her our notebook, the one we're using to record our wanderings, and say, "Write it all down before we forget anything."

"I thought this one didn't count." But she's flipping through the pages.

"Humor me. Oh, and we're hitting one more place on the way home."

We've left the gravel and are cruising along on pavement again when she looks up from the notebook she's now writing in. "I was so busy with the books, I forgot to leave something behind."

"It's okay. I did."

He misses the turnoff, goes right over the grassy center to the other side, and climbs back onto the interstate, heading in the opposite direction. At some point, we exit onto a quiet country road.

We take this for a mile or so, and Finch has turned up the music and is singing along. He drums the beat on the steering wheel, and then we turn into this little town that is just a couple blocks long. Finch hunches over the dash and slows down to a crawl. "Do you see any street signs?"

"That one says 'Church.'"

"Good. Brilliant." He turns and, just a block later, pulls over to the curb and parks. "We're here." He's out of the car and at my door, opening it, offering his hand. We're walking toward this big old factory building that looks abandoned. I can see something along the wall, stretching for the entire length of it. Finch keeps going and comes to a sudden stop at the far end.

Before I die . . . it says on what looks like a giant chalkboard. And there below these giant white letters are column after column, line after line, that say *Before I die I want to* _____. And the blanks have been filled in with different colors of chalk, smudged and half melted from the rain and snow, in all different handwriting.

We walk along reading. *Before I die I want to have kids. Live in London. Own a pet giraffe. Skydive. Divide by zero. Play the piano. Speak French.*

Write a book. Travel to a different planet. Be a better dad than mine was. Feel good about myself. Go to New York City. Know equality. Live.

Finch bumps my arm and hands me a piece of blue chalk.

I say, "There's no space left."

"So we make some."

He writes *Before I die I want to* and draws a line. He writes it again. Then he writes it a dozen more times. "After we fill these up, we can keep going on the front of the building and down the other side. It's a good way to figure out just why we're here." And I know by "here" he doesn't mean this sidewalk.

He starts writing: *Play guitar like Jimmy Page. Come up with a song that will change the world. Find the Great Manifesto. Count for something. Be the person I'm meant to be and have that be enough. Know what it's like to have a best friend. Matter.*

For a long time, I just stand there reading, and then I write: *Stop being afraid. Stop thinking too much. Fill the holes left behind. Drive again. Write. Breathe.*

Finch stands over my shoulder. He is so close, I can feel his breath. He leans forward and adds: *Before I die I want to know a perfect day.* He steps back, reading it over, and steps forward again. *And meet Boy Parade.* Before I can say anything, he laughs, rubs it out, and replaces it with: *And kiss Violet Markey.*

I wait for him to erase this too, but he drops the chalk and brushes the dust off his hands, wiping them on his jeans. He gives me a crooked grin, and then he stares at my mouth. I wait for him to make a move. I tell myself, *Just let him try.* And then I think, *I hope he does,* and the thought alone sets off the electric currents and sends them shooting through me. I wonder if kissing Finch would be that different from kissing Ryan. I've only kissed a handful of boys in my life, and they were pretty much all the same.

He shakes his head. "Not here. Not now." And then he jogs toward the car. I jog after him, and once we're inside, and the engine and the music are on, he says, "Before you get any ideas, that doesn't mean I like you."

"Why do you keep saying that?"

"Because I see the way you look at me."

"Oh my God. You are unbelievable."

He laughs.

Back on the road, my mind is racing. Just because I wanted him to kiss me for, like, one second doesn't mean I like Theodore Finch. It's just that it's been a while since I've kissed someone who isn't Ryan.

In our notebook, I write *Before I die I want to* . . . but that's as far as I get, because all I see is Finch's line floating on the page: *And kiss Violet Markey.*

Before Finch takes me home, he drives straight to the Quarry in downtown Bartlett, where they don't even check our IDs. We walk right in, and the place is crowded and smoky, and the band is loud. Everyone seems to know him, but instead of joining the band on-stage, he grabs my hand and we dance. One minute he acts like he's in a mosh pit and the next we're doing the tango.

I shout over the noise, "I don't like you either." But he just laughs again.

yours?" Her voice sounds kind of drifting and far off, like she's somewhere else.

I don't even have to think about it. "Theodore Finch, in search of the Great Manifesto."

She gives me a sharp look, and I can see she's present and accounted for again. "I don't know what that means."

"It means 'the urge to be, to count for something, and, if death must come, to die valiantly, with acclamation—in short, to remain a memory.'"

She goes quiet, as if she's thinking this over. "So where were you Friday? Why didn't you go to school?"

"I get these headaches sometimes. No big deal." This isn't an out-and-out lie, because the headaches are a part of it. It's like my brain is firing so fast that it can't keep up with itself. Words. Colors.

FINCH

On the way back to Violet's house, I think up epitaphs for the people we know: Amanda Monk (*I was as shallow as the dry creek bed that branches off the Whitewater River*), Roamer (*My plan was to be the biggest asshole I could be—and I was*), Mr. Black (*In my next life, I want to rest, avoid children, and be paid well*).

So far she's been quiet, but I know she's listening, mostly because there's no one else around but me. "What would yours say, Ultraviolet?"

"I'm not sure." She tilts her head and gazes out over the dash at some distant point as if she'll see the answer there. "What about

I take a good long look at her. I know life well enough to know you can't count on things staying around or standing still, no matter how much you want them to. You can't stop people from dying. You can't stop them from going away. You can't stop yourself from going away either. I know myself well enough to know that no one else can keep you awake or keep you from sleeping. That's all on me too. But man, I like this girl.

"Yeah," I say. "I think I am."

At home, I access voicemail on the landline, the one Kate and I get around to checking when we remember, and there's a message from Embryo. *Shit*. Shit. Shit. Shit. He called Friday because I missed our counseling session and he wants to know where in

Sounds. Sometimes everything else fades into the background and all I'm left with is sound. I can hear everything, but not just hear it—I can feel it too. But then it can come on all at once—the sounds turn into light, and the light goes too bright, and it's like it's slicing me in two, and then comes the headache. But it's not just a headache I *feel*, I can *see* it, like it's made up of a million colors, all of them blinding. When I tried to describe it to Kate once, she said, "You can thank Dad for that. Maybe if he hadn't used your head as a punching bag."

But that's not it. I like to think that the colors and sounds and words have nothing to do with him, that they're all me and my own brilliant, complicated, buzzing, humming, soaring roaring diving, godlike brain.

Violet says, "Are you okay now?" Her hair is windblown and her cheeks are flushed. Whether she likes it or not, she seems happy.

the hell I am, especially because he seems to have read the *Bartlett Dirt*, and he knows—or thinks he knows—what I was doing on that ledge. On the bright side, I passed the drug test. I delete the message and tell myself to be early on Monday, just to make it up to him.

And then I go up to my room, climb onto a chair, and contemplate the mechanics of hanging. The problem is that I'm too tall and the ceiling is too low. There's always the basement, but no one ever goes down there, and it could be weeks, maybe even months, before Mom and my sisters would find me.

Interesting fact: Hanging is the most frequently used method of suicide in the United Kingdom because, researchers say, it's viewed as being both quick and easy. But the length of the rope has to be calibrated in proportion to the weight of the person; otherwise there is nothing quick or easy about it. Additional interesting fact: The modern method of judicial hanging is termed the Long Drop.

That is exactly what it feels like to go to Sleep. It is a long drop from the Awake and can happen all at once. Everything just . . . stops.

But sometimes there are warnings. Sound, of course, and headaches, but I've also learned to look out for things like changes in space, as in the way you see it, the way it feels. School hallways are a challenge—too many people going too many directions, like a crowded intersection. The school gym is worse than that because you're packed in and everyone is shouting, and you can become trapped.

I made the mistake of talking about it once. A few years ago, I asked my then good friend Gabe Romero if he could feel sound and see headaches, if the spaces around him ever grew or shrank, if he ever wondered what would happen if he jumped in front of a car or train or bus, if he thought that would be enough to make it stop. I asked him to try it with me, just to see, because I had this feeling, deep down, that I was make-believe, which meant invincible, and he went home and told his parents, and they told my teacher, who told the principal, who told my parents, who said to me, *Is this true, Theodore? Are you telling stories to your friends?* The next day it was all over school, and I was officially Theodore Freak. One year later, I grew out of my clothes because, it turns out, growing fourteen inches in a summer is easy. It's growing out of a label that's hard.

Which is why it pays to pretend you're just like everyone else, even if you've always known you're different. *It's your own fault, I* told myself then—my fault I can't be normal, my fault I can't be like Roamer or Ryan or Charlie or the others. *It's your own fault,* I tell myself now.

While I'm up on the chair, I try to imagine the Asleep is coming. When you're infamous and invincible, it's hard to picture being anything but awake, but I make myself concentrate because this is important—it's life or death.

Smaller spaces are better, and my room is big. But maybe I can cut it in half by moving my bookcase and dresser. I pick up the rug and start pushing things into place. No one comes up to ask what the hell I'm doing, although I know my mom and Decca and Kate, if she's home, must hear the pulling and scraping across the floor.

I wonder what would have to happen for them to come in here—a bomb blast? A nuclear explosion? I try to remember the last time any of them were in my room, and the only thing I can come up with is a time four years ago when I really did have the flu. Even then, Kate was the one who took care of me.

FINCH

In order to make up for missing Friday, I decide to tell Embryo about Violet. I don't mention her by name, but I've got to say something to someone other than Charlie or Brenda, who don't do more than ask me if I've gotten laid yet or remind me of the ass-kicking Ryan Cross will give me if I ever make a move on her.

First, though, Embryo has to ask me if I've tried to hurt myself. We run through this routine every week, and it goes something like this:

Embryo: Have you tried to hurt yourself since I saw you last?
Me: No, sir.

Embryo: Have you thought about hurting yourself?

Me: No, sir.

I've learned the hard way that the best thing to do is say nothing about what you're really thinking. If you say nothing, they'll assume you're thinking nothing, only what you let them see.

Embryo: Are you bullshitting me, son?

Me: Would I bullshit you, an authority figure?

Because he still hasn't acquired a sense of humor, he squints at me and says, "I certainly hope not."

Then he decides to break routine. "I know about the article in the *Bartlett Dirt*."

I actually sit speechless for a few seconds. Finally I say, "You can't always believe what you read, sir." It comes out snarky. I decide to drop the sarcasm and try again. Maybe it's because he's thrown me.

Or maybe it's because he's worried and he means well, and he is one of the few adults in my life who pay attention. "Really." My voice actually cracks, making it clear to both of us that the stupid article bothers me more than I let on.

After this exchange is over, I spend the rest of the time proving to him how much I have to live for. Today is the first day I've brought up Violet.

"So there's this girl. Let's call her Lizzy." Elizabeth Meade is head of the macramé club. She's so nice, I don't think she'd mind if I borrowed her name in the interest of guarding my privacy. "She and I have gotten to be kind of friendly, and that's making me very, very happy. Like stupidly happy. Like so-happy-my-friends-can't-stand-to-be-around-me happy."

He is studying me as if trying to figure out my angle. I go on about Lizzy and how happy we are, and how all I want to do is spend my days being happy about how happy I am, which is actually true, but finally he says, "Enough. I get it. Is this 'Lizzy' the girl from the paper?" He makes air quotes around her name. "The one who saved you from jumping off the ledge?"

"Possibly." I wonder if he'd believe me if I told him it was the other way around.

"Just be careful."

No, no, no, Embryo, I want to say. *You, of all people, should know better than to say something like this when someone is so happy.* "Just be careful" implies that there's an end to it all, maybe in an hour, maybe in three years, but an end just the same. Would it kill him to be, like, *I'm really glad for you, Theodore. Congratulations on finding someone who makes you feel so good?*

"You know, you could just say congratulations and stop there."

"Congratulations." But it's too late. He's already put it out there and now my brain has grabbed onto "Just be careful" and won't let go. I try to tell it he might have meant "Just be careful when you have sex. Use a condom," but instead, because, you know, it's a brain, and therefore has—is—a mind of its own, it starts thinking of every way in which Violet Markey might break my heart.

I pick at the arm of the chair where someone has sliced it in three places. I wonder who and how as I pick pick pick and try to silence my brain by thinking up Embryo's epitaph. When this doesn't work, I make up one for my mother (*I was a wife and am still a mother, although don't ask me where my children are*) and my father (*The only change I believe in is getting rid of your wife and children and starting over with someone else*).

Embryo says, "Let's talk about the SAT. You got a 2280." He sounds so surprised and impressed, I want to say, *Oh yeah? Screw you, Embryo.*

The truth is, I test well. I always have. I say, "Congratulations would be appropriate here as well."

He charges on ahead as if he hasn't heard me. "Where are you planning on going to college?"

"I'm not sure yet."

"Don't you think it's time to give some thought to the future?"

I do think about it. Like the fact that I'll see Violet later today.

"I do think about it," I say. "I'm thinking about it right now."

He sighs and closes my file. "I'll see you Friday. If you need anything, call me."

Because BHS is a giant school with a giant population of students, I don't see Violet as often as you might think. The only class we have together is U.S. Geography. I'm in the basement when she's on the third floor, I'm in the gym when she's all the way across the school in Orchestra Hall, I'm in the science wing when she's in Spanish.

On Tuesday, I say to hell with it and meet her outside every one of her classes so I can walk her to the next. This sometimes means running from one end of the building to the other, but it's worth every step. My legs are long, so I can cover a lot of ground, even if I have to dodge people left and right and sometimes leap over their heads. This is easy to do because they move in slow motion, like a herd of zombies or slugs.

"Hello, all of you!" I shout as I run. "It's a beautiful day! A perfect day! A day of possibility!" They're so listless, they barely look up to see me.

The first time I find Violet, she's walking with her friend Shelby Padgett. The second time, she says, "Finch, again?" It's hard to tell if she's happy to see me or embarrassed, or a combination. The third time, she says, "Aren't you going to be late?"

"What's the worst they can do?" I grab her hand and drag her bumping along. "Coming through, people! Clear the way!"

After seeing her to Russian literature, I jog back down the stairs and down more stairs and through the main hall, where I run directly into Principal Wertz, who wants to know what I think I'm doing out of class, young man, and why I'm running as if the enemy is on my heels.

"Just patrolling, sir. You can't be too safe these days. I'm sure you've read about the security breaches over at Rushville and New Castle. Computer equipment stolen, library books destroyed, money taken from the front office, and all in the light of day, right under their noses."

I'm making this up, but it's clear he doesn't know that. "Get to class," he tells me. "And don't let me catch you again. Do I need to remind you you're on probation?"

"No, sir." I make a show of walking calmly in the other direction, but when the next bell rings, I take off down the hall and up the stairs like I'm on fire.

The first people I see are Amanda, Roamer, and Ryan, and I make the mistake of accidentally ramming into Roamer, which sends him into Amanda. The contents of her purse go spiraling across the hall-way floor, and she starts screaming. Before Ryan and Roamer can beat me to a six-foot-three-inch bloody pulp, I sprint away, putting as much distance between them and me as I can. I'll pay for this later, but right now I don't care.

This time Violet is waiting. As I double over, catching my breath, she says, "Why are you doing this?" And I can tell she isn't happy or embarrassed, she's pissed.

"Let's run so you're not late to class."

"I'm not running anywhere."

"I can't help you then."

"Oh my God. You are driving me crazy, Finch."

I lean in, and she backs up into a locker. Her eyes are darting everywhere like she's terrified someone might see Violet Markey and Theodore Finch together. God forbid Ryan Cross walks by and gets the wrong idea. I wonder what she'd say to him—*It's not what it looks like. Theodore Freak is harassing me. He won't leave me alone.*

"Glad I can return the favor." Now *I'm* pissed. I rest one hand against the locker behind her. "You know, you're a lot friendlier when we're by ourselves and no one's around to see us together."

"Maybe if you didn't run through the halls and shout at everyone. I can't tell if you do all this because it's expected or because it's just the way you are."

"What do you think?" My mouth is an inch from hers, and I wait for her to slap me or push me away, but then she closes her eyes, and that's when I know—I'm in.

Okay, I think. *Interesting turn of events.* But before I can make a move, someone yanks me by the collar and jerks me back. Mr. Kappel, baseball coach, says, "Get to class, Finch. You too." He nods at Violet. "And that's detention for the both of you."

After school, she walks into Mr. Stohler's room and doesn't even look at me. Mr. Stohler says, "I guess there really is a first time for everything. We're honored to have your company, Miss Markey. To what do we owe the pleasure?"

"To him," she says, nodding in my direction. She takes a seat at the front of the room, as far away from me as she can get.

VIOLET

142 days to go

Two a.m. Wednesday. My bedroom.

I wake up to the sound of rocks at my window. At first I think I'm dreaming, but then I hear it again. I get up and peek through the blinds, and Theodore Finch is standing in my front yard dressed in pajama bottoms and a dark hoodie.

I open the window and lean out. "Go away." I'm still mad at him for getting me detention, first of my life. And I'm mad at Ryan for thinking we're going out again, and whose fault is that? I've been acting like a tease, kissing him on his dimple, kissing him at the drive-in. I'm mad at everyone, mostly myself. "Go away," I say again.

"Please don't make me climb this tree, because I'll probably fall and break my neck and we have too much to do for me to be hospitalized."

"We don't have anything else to do. We've already done it."

But I smooth my hair and roll on some lip gloss and pull on a bathrobe. If I don't go down, who knows what might happen?

By the time I get outside, Finch is sitting on the front porch, leaning back against the railing. "I thought you'd never come," he says.

I sit down beside him, and the step is cold through my layers. "Why are you here?"

"Were you awake?"

"No."

"Sorry. But now that you are, let's go."

"I'm not going anywhere."

He stands and starts walking to the car. He turns and says too loudly, "Come on."

"I can't just take off when I want to."

"You're not still mad, are you?"

"Actually, yes. But look at me. I'm not even dressed."

"Fine. Leave the ugly bathrobe. Get some shoes and a jacket. Do not take time to change anything else. Write a note to your parents so they won't worry if they wake up and find you gone. I'll give you three minutes before I come up after you."

We drive toward Bartlett's downtown. The blocks are bricked off into what we call the Boardwalk. Ever since the new mall opened, there's been no reason to come here except for the bakery, which has the best cupcakes for miles. The businesses here are hangers-on, relics from about twenty years ago—a sad and very old department store, a shoe store that smells like mothballs, a toy store, a candy shop, an ice cream parlor.

Finch parks the Saturn and says, "We're here."

All the storefronts are dark, of course, and there is no one out. It's easy to pretend that Finch and I are the only two people in the world.

He says, "I do my best thinking at night when everyone else is sleeping. No interruptions. No noise. I like the feeling of being awake when no one else is." I wonder if he sleeps at all.

I catch sight of us in the window of the bakery, and we look like two homeless kids. "Where are we going?"

"You'll see."

The air is crisp and clean and quiet. In the distance, the Purina

Tower, our tallest building, is lit up, and beyond it the bell tower of the high school.

Outside Bookmarks, Finch pulls out a set of keys and unlocks the door. "My mother works here when she's not selling houses."

The bookstore is narrow and dark, a wall of magazines on one side, shelves of books, a table and chairs, an empty counter where coffee and sweet things are sold during working hours.

He stoops behind the counter now and opens a refrigerator that's hidden behind it. He digs around until he comes up with two sodas and two muffins, and then we move over to the kids' area, which has beanbags and a worn blue rug. He lights a candle he found near the register, and the light flickers across his face as he carries it from shelf to shelf and trails his fingers along the spines of the books.

"Are you looking for something?"

"Yes."

Finally, he sinks down beside me and runs his hands through his hair, making it go off in all directions. "They didn't have it at the Bookmobile Park and they don't have it here." He picks up a stack of children's books and hands me a couple. "They do, thank goodness, have these."

He sits cross-legged, wild hair bent over one of the books, and immediately it's as if he's gone away and is somewhere else.

I say, "I'm still mad at you about getting me detention." I expect some fast reply, something flirty and flip, but instead he doesn't look up, just reaches for my hand and keeps reading. I can feel the apology in his fingers, and this takes the wind out of me, so I lean into him—just a little—and read over his shoulder. His hand is warm and I don't want to stop holding it.

We eat one-handed and read our way through the stack, and then we start reading aloud from Dr. Seuss—*Oh, the Places You'll Go!* We alternate stanzas, first Finch, then me, Finch, then me.

> *Today is your day.*
> *You're off to Great Places!*
> *You're off and away!*

At some point, Finch gets to his feet and starts acting it out. He doesn't need the book because he knows the words by heart, and I forget to read because it's more fun watching him, even when the words and his voice turn serious as he recites lines about dark places and useless places and waiting places, where people don't do anything but wait.

Then his voice turns light again and he is singing the words.

You'll find the bright places
where Boom Bands are playing.

He pulls me to my feet.

With banner flip-flapping,
once more you'll ride high!
Ready for anything under the sky.

The two of us are doing our own version of flip-flapping, which is a kind of leaping over things—the beanbags, the rug, the other books. We sing the last lines together—*Your mountain is waiting.*

So . . . get on your way!—and end in a heap on the floor, candlelight dancing across us, laughing like we've lost our minds.

The only way up the Purina Tower is the steel ladder built into the side, and there seem to be about twenty-five thousand steps. At the top, we stand—wheezing like Mr. Black—beside the Christmas tree, which sits planted all year. Up close, it's larger than it looks from the ground. Past it, there's a wedge of open space, and Finch spreads out the blanket and then we huddle on top of it, arm to arm, pulling the rest of the cover around us.

He says, "Look." On all sides of us, spread out below, are little white lights and black pockets of trees. Stars in the sky, stars on the ground. It's hard to tell where the sky ends and the earth begins. I hate to admit it, but it's beautiful. I feel the need to say something grand and poetic, but the only thing I come up with is "It's lovely."

"'Lovely' is a lovely word that should be used more often." He reaches down to cover my foot, which has found its way out of the blanket. "It's like it's ours," he says.

And at first I think he means the word, but then I know he means the town. And then I think, *Yes, that's it. Theodore Finch always knows what to say, better than I do. He should be the writer, not me.* I feel jealous, just for a second, of his brain. In this moment, mine feels so ordinary.

"The problem with people is they forget that most of the time it's the small things that count. Everyone's so busy waiting in the Waiting Place. If we stopped to remember that there's such a thing as a Purina Tower and a view like this, we'd all be happier."

For some reason I say, "I like writing, but I like a lot of things.

Maybe out of those things, I'm best at writing. Maybe it's what I like best of all. Maybe it's where I've always felt most at home. Or maybe the writing part of me is over. Maybe there's something else I'm supposed to do instead. I don't know."

"There's a built-in ending to everything in the world, right? I mean, a hundred-watt lightbulb is designed to last seven hundred and fifty hours. The sun will die in about five billion years. We all have a shelf life. Most cats can live to be fifteen, maybe longer. Most dogs make it to twelve. The average American is designed to last twenty-eight thousand days after birth, which means there's a specific year, day, and time to the minute when our lives will end. Your sister's happened to be eighteen. But if a human was to avoid all life-threatening diseases and infections and accidents, he—or she—should live to be a hundred and fifteen."

"So you're saying I may have reached my built-in ending to writing."

"I'm saying you have time to decide." He hands me our official wandering notebook and a pen. "For now, why not write things down where no one will see it? Write it on a piece of paper and stick it on the wall. Of course, for all I know, you may suck at it." He laughs as he dodges away from me, and then he pulls out an offering—the Bookmarks napkins, the half-burned candle, a matchbook, and a lopsided macramé bookmark. We lock them into a flat Tupperware container he's confiscated from his house and leave it sitting out in plain view for the next person who comes here. Then he's up and standing at the edge, where only a knee-high metal guardrail keeps him from falling to the ground.

He throws his arms out over his head, fists clenched, and shouts:

"Open your eyes and look at me! I'm right bloody here!" He shouts all the things he hates and wants to change until his voice is hoarse. Then he nods over at me. "Your turn."

I join him at the edge, but he's farther out than I am, as if he doesn't care whether he falls off. I take hold of his shirt without him noticing, as if that will save him, and instead of looking down, I look out and up. I think of all the things I want to shout: *I hate this town! I hate winter! Why did you die?* This last thought is directed at Eleanor. *Why did you leave me? Why did you do this to me?*

But instead I stand there holding on to Finch's shirt, and he looks down at me and shakes his head, and in a moment he starts singing Dr. Seuss again. This time I join him, and our voices drift together across the sleeping town.

When he drives me home, I want him to kiss me good night, but he doesn't. Instead, he strolls backward to the street, hands shoved in pockets, eyes on me. "Actually, Ultraviolet, I'm pretty sure you don't suck at writing." He says it loud enough for the entire neighborhood to hear.

FINCH

Day 22 and I'm still here

The minute we walk into my dad's house, I know something's wrong. Rosemarie greets us and invites us into the living room, where Josh Raymond sits on the floor playing with a battery-operated helicopter that flies and makes noise. Kate, Decca, and I all stare, and I know they're thinking what I'm thinking: toys with batteries are too loud. Growing up, we weren't allowed to have anything that talked or flew or made a sound.

"Where's Dad?" Kate asks. Looking through the back door, I can see the grill sitting closed. "He came home from the trip, didn't he?"

"He got back Friday. He's just in the basement." Rosemarie is busy handing us sodas to drink straight out of the can, which is another sure sign that something's wrong.

"I'll go," I tell Kate. If he's in the basement, it can only mean one thing. He's in one of his moods, as Mom calls them. *Don't mind your father, Theodore; he's just in one of his moods. Give him time to settle down, and he'll be fine.*

The basement is actually nice and carpeted and painted, with lights everywhere and my dad's old hockey trophies and framed jersey and bookshelves packed with books, even though he absolutely does not read. Along one entire wall is a giant flat screen, and my dad is planted in front of this now, enormous feet on the coffee table, watching some sort of game and shouting at the television. His face is purple, and the veins in his neck are hulking out. He's got a beer in one hand and a remote in the other.

I walk over to him so I'm in his line of sight. I stand there, hands in pockets, and stare at him until he looks up. "Christ," he says. "Don't go sneaking up on people."

"I'm not. Unless you've gone deaf in your old age, you had to hear me coming down those stairs. Dinner's ready."

"I'll be up in a while."

I move over so that I'm in front of the flat screen. "You should come up now. Your family's here—remember us? The originals? We're here and we're hungry, and we didn't come all this way to hang out with your new wife and child."

I can count on one hand the times I've talked to my father like this, but maybe it's the magic of Badass Finch, because I'm not one bit afraid of him.

He slams the beer so hard against the coffee table that the bottle shatters. "Don't you come into my house and tell me what to do." And then he's off the couch and lunging for me, and he catches me by the arm and *wham*, slams me into the wall. I hear the crack as my skull makes contact, and for a minute the room spins.

But then it rights itself, and I say, "I have you to thank for the fact that my skull is pretty tough now." Before he can grab me again, I'm up the stairs.

I'm already at the dinner table by the time he gets there, and the sight of his shiny new family makes him remember himself. He says, "Something smells good," gives Rosemarie a kiss on the cheek, and sits down across from me, unfolding his napkin. He doesn't look at me or speak to me the rest of the time we're there.

In the car afterward, Kate says, "You're stupid, you know that.

He could have put you in the hospital."

"Let him," I say.

At home, Mom looks up from her desk, where she is attempting to go over ledgers and bank statements. "How was dinner?"

Before anyone else can answer, I give her a hug and a kiss on the cheek, which—since we're not a family that likes to show affection—leaves her looking alarmed. "I'm going out."

"Be safe, Theodore."

"I love you too, Mom." This throws her even more, and before she can start crying, I am out the door to the garage, climbing into Little Bastard. I feel better once the engine has started. I hold up my hands and they're shaking, because my hands, like the rest of me, would like to kill my father. Ever since I was ten and he sent Mom to the hospital with a busted chin, and then a year later when it was my turn.

With the garage door still closed, I sit, hands on the wheel, thinking how easy it would be to just keep sitting here.

I close my eyes.

I lean back.

I rest my hands on my lap.

I don't feel much, except maybe a little sleepy. But that could just be me and the dark, slow-churning vortex that's always there, in me and around me, to some degree.

The rate of car exhaust suicides in the States has declined since the mid-sixties, when emission controls were introduced. In England, where emission controls barely exist, that rate has doubled.

I am very calm, as if I'm in science class conducting an experiment. The rumble of the engine is a kind of lullaby. I force my mind to go blank, like I do on the rare occasions I try to sleep.

Instead of thinking, I picture a body of water and me on my back floating, still and peaceful, no movement except my heart beating in my chest. When they find me, I'll just look like I'm sleeping.

In 2013, a man in Pennsylvania committed suicide via carbon monoxide, but when his family tried to rescue him, they were overcome by the fumes and every single one of them died before rescue crews could save them.

I think of my mom and Decca and Kate, and then I hit the opener, and up goes the door, and out I go into the wild blue yonder. For the first mile or so, I feel high and excited, like I just ran into a burning building and saved lives, like I'm some sort of hero.

But then a voice in me says, *You're no hero. You're a coward. You only saved them from yourself.*

When things got bad a couple months ago, I drove to French Lick, which sounds a helluva lot sexier than it is. The original name was Salt Spring, and it's famous for its casino, fancy spa and resort, basketball player Larry Bird, and healing springs.

In November I went to French Lick and drank the water and waited for it to fix the dark, slow churning of my mind, and for a few hours I actually felt better, but that might have been because I was so hydrated. I spent the night in Little Bastard, and when I woke the next morning, dull and dead feeling, I found one of the guys who worked there and said to him, "Maybe I drank the wrong water."

He looked over his right shoulder, then his left, like someone in a movie, and then he leaned in and said, "Where you want to go is Mudlavia."

At first I thought he was high. I mean, *Mudlavia*? But then he said, "That up there's the real deal. Al Capone and the Dillinger gang always went there after some sort of heist. Nothing much left of it now except ruins—it burned down in 1920—but them waters flow strong as ever. Whenever I get an ache in my joints, that's where I go."

I didn't go then, because by the time I returned from French Lick, I was tapped out and that was it, and there was no more traveling anywhere for a long while. But Mudlavia is where I'm headed now. Since this is serious personal business and not a wandering, I don't bring Violet.

It takes about two and a half hours to get to Kramer, Indiana, population thirty. The terrain is prettier here than in Bartlett—hills and valleys and miles of trees, everything snow covered, like something out of Norman Rockwell.

For the actual resort, I'm picturing a place along the lines of Middle Earth, but what I find is acres of thin brown trees and ruins. It's all crumbling buildings and graffiti-covered walls overgrown with weeds and ivy. Even in winter, you can tell nature is on a mission to take it back.

I pick my way through what used to be the hotel—the kitchen, hallways, guest rooms. The place is grim and creepy, and it leaves me sad. The walls still standing are tagged with paint.

Protect the penis.

Insanity please.

Fuck all you who may see this.

This does not feel like a healing place. Back outside, I tramp through leaves and dirt and snow to find the springs. I'm not sure exactly where they are, and it takes standing still and listening before I go in the right direction.

I prepare to be disappointed. Instead, I break through the trees to find myself on the banks of a rushing stream. The water is alive and not frozen over, the trees here fuller than the others, as if the water is feeding them. I follow the creek bed until the embankment grows into rock walls, and then I wade right into the middle, feeling the water push past my ankles. I crouch down and form a cup with my palms. I drink. It's cold and fresh and tastes faintly of mud. When it doesn't kill me, I drink again. I fill the water bottle I brought with me and then wedge it into the muddy bottom so it doesn't float away. I lie down flat on my back in the middle of the stream and let the water cover me.

As I walk into the house, Kate is on her way out, already lighting a cigarette. As direct as Kate is, she doesn't want either of my parents to know she smokes. Usually she waits till she's safely in her car and down the street.

She says, "Were you with that girl of yours?"

"How do you know there's a girl?"

"I can read the signs. Name?"

"Violet Markey."

"The sister."

"Yeah."

"Do we get to meet her?"

"Probably not."

"Smart." She takes a long drag on the cigarette. "Decca's upset. Sometimes I think this Josh Raymond situation is hardest on her since they're practically the same age." She blows three perfect smoke rings. "Do you ever wonder?"

"Wonder what?"

"If he's Dad's?"

"Yeah, except he's so small."

"You were small till ninth grade and look at you now, beanstalk."

Kate heads down the walk and I head in, and as I'm shutting the door, she calls, "Hey, Theo?" I turn and she's standing beside her car, nothing but an outline against the night. "Just be careful with that heart of yours."

Once again: *Just be careful.*

Upstairs, I brave Decca's chamber of horrors to make sure she's okay. Her room is enormous, and covered with her clothes and books and all the strange things she collects—lizards and beetles and flowers and bottle caps and stacks and stacks of candy wrappers and American Girl dolls, left over from when she was six and went through a phase. All the dolls have stitches on their chins, like the ones Decca got at the hospital after a playground accident. Her artwork covers every inch of wall space, along with a single poster of Boy Parade.

I find her on her floor, cutting words out of books she's collected from around the house, including some of Mom's romance novels. I ask if she has another pair of scissors, and without looking up, she points at her desk. There are about eighteen pairs of scissors there, ones that have gone missing over the years from the drawer in the kitchen. I choose a pair with purple handles and sit down opposite her, our knees bumping.

"Tell me the rules."

She hands me a book—*His Dark, Forbidden Love*—and says, "Take out the mean parts and the bad words."

We do this for half an hour or so, not talking, just cutting, and then I start giving her a big-brother pep talk about how life will get better, and it isn't only hard times and hard people, that there are bright spots too.

"Less talking," she says.

We work away silently, until I ask, "What about things that aren't categorically mean but just unpleasant?"

She stops cutting long enough to deliberate. She sucks in a stray chunk of hair and then blows it out. "Unpleasant works too."

I focus on the words. Here's one, and another. Here's a sentence. Here's a paragraph. Here's an entire page. Soon I have a pile of mean words and unpleasantness beside my shoe. Dec grabs them and adds them to her own pile. When she's finished with a book, she tosses it aside, and it's then I get it: it's the mean parts she wants. She is collecting all the unhappy, mad, bad, unpleasant words and keeping them for herself.

"Why are we doing this, Dec?"

"Because they shouldn't be in there mixed with the good. They like to trick you."

And somehow I know what she means. I think of the *Bartlett Dirt* and all its mean words, not just about me but about every student who's strange or different. Better to keep the unhappy, mad, bad, unpleasant words separate, where you can watch them and make sure they don't surprise you when you're not expecting them.

When we're done, and she goes off in search of other books, I pick up the discarded ones and hunt through the pages until I find the words I'm looking for. I leave them on her pillow: MAKE IT LOVELY. Then I take the unwanted, cut-up books with me down the hall.

Where something is different about my room.

I stand in the doorway trying to figure out exactly what it is. The red walls are there. The black bedspread, dresser, desk, and chair are in place. The bookshelf may be too full. I study the room from where I stand because I don't want to go inside until I know what's wrong. My guitars are where I left them. The windows are bare because I don't like curtains.

The room looks like it did earlier today. But it feels different, as if someone has been in here and moved things around. I cross the floor slowly, as if that same someone might jump out, and open the door to my closet, half expecting it to lead into the real version of my room, the right one.

Everything is fine.

You are fine.

I walk into the bathroom and strip off my clothes and step under the hot-hot water, standing there until my skin turns red and the water heater gives out. I wrap myself in a towel and write *Just be careful* across the fogged-up mirror. I walk back into the room to give it another look from another angle. The room is just as I left it, and I think maybe it isn't the room that's different. Maybe it's me.

In the bathroom again, I hang up my towel, throw on a T-shirt and boxers, and catch sight of myself in the mirror over the sink as the steam starts to clear and the writing fades away, leaving an oval just large enough for two blue eyes, wet black hair, white skin. I lean in and look at myself, and it's not my face but someone else's.

On my bed, I sit down and flip through the cut-up books one by one, reading all the cut-up passages. They are happy and sweet, funny and warm. I want to be surrounded by them, and so I clip out some of the best lines and the very best words—like "symphony," "limit-less," "gold," "morning"—and stick them on the wall, where they overlap with others, a combination of colors and shapes and moods.

I pull the comforter up around me, as tight as I can—so that I can't even see the room anymore—and lie back on my bed like a mummy. It's a way to keep in the warmth and the light so that it can't get out again. I reach one hand through the opening and pick up another book and then another. What if life could be this way? Only the happy parts, none of the terrible, not even the mildly unpleasant. What if we could just cut out the bad and keep the good? This is what I want to do with Violet—give her only the good, keep away the bad, so that good is all we ever have around us.

VIOLET

Sunday night. My bedroom. I flip through our notebook, Finch's and mine. I pick up the pen he gave me and find a blank page. Bookmarks and the Purina Tower aren't official wanderings, but this doesn't mean they shouldn't be remembered too.

Stars in the sky, stars on the ground. It's hard to tell where the sky ends and the earth begins. I feel the need to say something grand and poetic, but the only thing I come up with is "It's lovely."

He says, "'Lovely' is a lovely word that should be used more often."

Then I get an idea. Over my desk, I've got this enormous bulletin board, and on it I've tacked black-and-white photographs of writers at work. I take these down and dig through my desk until I come up with a stack of brightly colored Post-its. On one of them, I write: *lovely.*

Half an hour later, I stand back and look at the board. It is covered in fragments—some are words or sentences that may or may not become story ideas. Others are lines I like from books. In the last column, I have a section for *New Nameless Web Magazine.* On three separate Post-its I've tacked beneath it: *Lit. Love. Life.* I'm not sure what these are supposed to be—categories or articles or just nice-sounding words.

Even though it isn't much yet, I take a picture and send it to Finch. I write: **Look what you've got me doing.** Every half hour, I check for a response, but by the time I go to bed, I still haven't heard from him.

FINCH

Last night is like a puzzle—only not put together: all the pieces are scattered everywhere and some are missing. I wish my heart wouldn't beat so *fast*.

I get out the books again and read the good words Decca left behind, but they blur on the page so that they don't make sense. I can't concentrate.

And then I start to clean and organize. I take down every single note until the wall is blank. I shove them into a trash bag, but this isn't enough, so I decide to paint. I'm sick of the red walls of my room. The color is too dark and depressing. *This is what I need*, I think. *A change of scenery. This is why the room feels off.*

I get into Little Bastard and drive to the nearest hardware store and buy primer and ten gallons of blue paint because I'm not sure how much it will take.

It takes many, many coats to cover the red. No matter what I do, it seeps right through, like the walls are bleeding.

By midnight, the paint still isn't dry, and so I gather up the black comforter and shove it into the back of the linen closet in the hall, and I dig around until I find an old blue comforter of Kate's. I spread this on my bed. I open the windows and move my bed into the middle of the room, and then I climb under the blanket and go to sleep.

The next day, I paint the walls again. It takes two days for them to hold the color, which is the clear, bright blue of a swimming pool. I lie on my bed feeling easier, like I can catch my breath. *Now we're talking*, I think. *Yes.*

The only thing I leave alone is the ceiling, because white contains all the wavelengths of the visible spectrum at full brightness. Okay, this is technically true of white light and not white paint, but I don't care. I tell myself that all the colors are there anyway, and this gives me an idea. I think of writing it as a song, but instead I sign onto the computer and send a message to Violet. **You are all the colors in one, at full brightness.**

VIOLET

135, 134, 133 days to go

Finch doesn't show up at school for a week. Someone says he's been suspended, others say he overdosed and was carted off to rehab. The rumors spread the old-fashioned way—in whispers and texts—because Principal Wertz has found out about the *Bartlett Dirt* and shut it down.

Wednesday. First period. In honor of the *Dirt*'s demise, Jordan Gripenwaldt is passing out celebration candy. Troy Satterfield sticks two suckers in his mouth and says around them, "Where's your boyfriend, Violet? Shouldn't you be on suicide watch?" He and his friends laugh. Before I can say anything, Jordan yanks the suckers out of his mouth and throws them in the garbage.

On Thursday, I find Charlie Donahue in the parking lot after last period. I tell him I'm working with Finch on a class project and that I haven't heard from him for a few days. I don't ask if the rumors are true, even though I want to.

Charlie tosses his books into the backseat of his car. "That's just his thing. He comes and goes when he wants." He takes off his jacket and throws this on top of the books. "One thing you'll learn is he is one moody old todger."

Brenda Shank-Kravitz walks up and past us and opens the passenger door. Before she gets in, she says to me, "I like your glasses." I can tell she actually means it.

"Thanks. They were my sister's."

She looks like she's thinking this over, and then she nods okay.

The next morning, on my way to third period, I see him in the hallway—Theodore Finch—only he's different. For one thing, he's wearing a ratty red knit cap, loose black sweater, jeans, sneakers, and these fingerless black gloves. *Homeless Finch,* I think. *Slacker Finch.* He's leaning against a locker, one knee bent, talking to Chameli Belk-Gupta, one of the junior-year drama girls. He doesn't seem to notice me as I walk by.

In third period, I hook my bag over my chair and take out my calculus book. Mr. Heaton says, "Let's start by going over the homework," but he barely gets the words out before the fire alarm starts blaring. I gather my stuff and follow everyone outside.

A voice behind me says, "Meet me in the student parking lot." I turn, and Finch is standing there, hands shoved into pockets. He walks away as if he's invisible and we aren't surrounded by teachers and faculty, including Principal Wertz, braying into his phone.

I hesitate and then start to run, bag slapping against my hip. I'm scared to death someone will come after me, but it's too late to go back because I'm already running. I run until I catch up with Finch, and then we run faster, and no one has shouted at us to stop, come back here. I feel terrified but free.

We race across the boulevard that cuts in front of the school, and alongside the trees that separate the main parking lot from the river that splits the town in half. When we come to a break in the trees, Finch takes my hand.

"Where are we going?" I'm breathing hard.

"Down there. But be quiet. First one to make a noise has to streak back to school." He is talking fast, moving fast.

"Streak how?"

"Streak naked. That's what 'streaking' means. It is, I believe, the very definition of the word."

I slip and slide down the embankment while Finch leads the way soundlessly, making it look easy. When we get to the edge of the river, he points across it, and at first I can't see what he's showing me. Then something moves and catches my eye. The bird is about three feet tall, with a red crown on a white head, and a charcoal-gray body. It splashes in the water and then pecks around the opposite bank, strutting like a man.

"What is it?"

"A hooded crane. The only one in Indiana. Maybe the only one in the United States. They winter in Asia, which means he's about seven thousand miles from home."

"How did you know he was here?"

"Sometimes when I can't stand it over there"—he nods in the direction of the high school—"I come down here. Sometimes I go for a swim, and other times I just sit. This guy's been hanging around about a week now. I was afraid he was hurt."

"He's lost."

"Uh-uh. Look at him." The bird stands in the shallows, pecking at the water, then wades deeper and starts splashing around. He reminds me of a kid in a swimming pool. "See, Ultraviolet? He's wandering."

Finch steps back, shielding his eyes because the sun is peeking through the branches, and there is a crack as his foot comes down on a twig. "Bollocks," he whispers.

"Oh my God. Does that mean you have to streak back to school now?" The look on his face is so funny that I can't help laughing.

He sighs, drops his head in defeat, and then pulls off his sweater, his shoes, his hat, his gloves, and his jeans, even though it's freezing out. He hands each item to me until he's wearing only his boxers, and I say, "Off with them, Theodore Finch. You were the one who said 'streaking,' and I believe 'streaking' implies full-on nakedness. I believe, in fact, it is the very definition of the word."

He smiles, his eyes never leaving mine, and, just like that, he drops his boxers. I'm surprised because I only half thought he would do it. He stands, the first real-live naked boy I've ever seen, and doesn't seem one bit self-conscious. He is long and lean. My eyes trace the thin, blue veins of his arms and the outline of muscle in his shoulders and stomach and legs. The scar across his middle is a bright-red gash.

He says, "This would be a helluva lot more fun if you were naked too." And then he dives into the river, so neatly that he barely disturbs the crane. He cuts through the water with broad strokes, like an Olympic swimmer, and I sit on the bank watching him.

He swims so far, he's just a blur. I pull out our notebook and write about the wandering crane and a boy with a red cap who swims in winter. I lose track of time, and when I look up again, Finch is drifting toward me. He floats on his back, arms folded behind his head. "You should come in."

"That's okay. I'd rather not get hypothermia."

"Come on, Ultraviolet Remarkey-able. The water's great."

"What did you call me?"

"Ultraviolet Remarkey-able. Going once, going twice . . ."

"I'm fine right here."

"All right." He swims toward me until he can stand waist-deep. "Where were you this time?"

"I was doing some remodeling." He scoops at the water, as if he's trying to catch something. The crane stands still on the opposite shore, watching us.

"Is your dad back in town?"

Finch seems to catch whatever he's looking for. He studies his cupped hands before letting it go. "Unfortunately."

I can't hear the fire alarm anymore, and I wonder if everyone's gone inside. If so, I'll be counted absent. I should be more worried than I am, especially now that I've gotten detention, but instead I sit there on the bank.

Finch swims toward shore and comes walking toward me. I try not to stare at him, dripping wet and naked, so I watch the crane, the sky, anything but him. He laughs. "I don't guess you've got a towel in that enormous bag you carry around."

"No."

He dries off with his sweater, shakes his hair at me like a dog so that I get sprayed, and then pulls on his clothes. When he's dressed again, he shoves his hat into his back pocket and smooths his hair off his face.

"We should go back to class," I say. His lips are blue, but he's not even shivering.

"I've got a better idea. Want to hear it?" Before he can tell me what it is, Ryan, Roamer, and Joe Wyatt come sliding down the embankment. "Great," Finch says under his breath.

Ryan comes right over to me. "We saw you take off during the fire alarm."

Roamer gives Finch a nasty look. "Is this part of the geography project? Are you wandering the riverbed or just each other?"

Roamer gets up in his face. "Why are you all wet? Decide to finally shower after all this time?"

"No, man, I'm saving that activity for when I see your mom later."

Like that, Roamer jumps on Finch, and the two of them go rolling down the bank into the water. Joe and Ryan just stand there, and I say to Ryan, "Do something."

"I didn't start this."

"Well, do something anyway."

Roamer swings and hits Finch's face with a thud. He swings again and again, his fist smashing into Finch's mouth, into his nose, into his ribs. At first Finch isn't fighting back—he's just blocking the shots. But then he has Roamer's arm twisted behind his back, and he's plunging his head into the water and holding it under.

"Let him go, Finch."

"Grow up, Roamer," I say.

Ryan rubs my arms like he's trying to warm me up. "Are you okay?"

I shrug him off. "Of course I'm okay. You don't need to check up on me."

Finch says, "I didn't kidnap her, if that's what you're worried about."

Roamer says, "Did he ask you?"

Finch looks down at Roamer. He has a good three to four inches on him. "No, but I wish you would."

"Faggot."

"Lay off, Roamer," I snap at him. My heart is battering away because I'm not sure what's going to happen here. "It doesn't matter what he says—you're just looking for a fight." I say to Finch, "Don't make it worse."

He either doesn't hear me or isn't listening. Roamer's legs are thrashing, and Ryan has Finch by the collar of his black sweater, and then by the arm, and is pulling on him. "Wyatt, some help here."

"Let him go." Finch looks at me then, and for a second it's like he doesn't know who I am. "Let him go." I snap it at him like I'm talking to a dog or a child.

Just like that, he lets him go, straightens, picks Roamer up, and drops him onto the bank, where he lies coughing up water. Finch goes stalking up the hill, past Ryan and Joe and me. His face is bloody, and he doesn't wait or look back.

I don't bother going back to school, because the damage is done. Because Mom won't expect me home yet, I sneak over to the parking lot, unlock Leroy, and ride to the east side of town. I cruise up and down the streets until I find the two-story brick colonial. FINCH, it says on the mailbox.

I knock on the door, and a girl with long black hair answers. "Hey," she says to me, like she's not surprised I'm there. "So you must be Violet. I'm Kate."

I'm always fascinated by how the same genes rearrange themselves across brothers and sisters. People thought Eleanor and I were twins, even though her cheeks were narrower and her hair was lighter. Kate looks like Finch, but not. Same coloring, different features, except for the eyes. It's strange seeing his eyes in someone else's face.

"Is he here?"

"I'm sure he's up there somewhere. I'm guessing you know where his room is." She smirks a little, but in a nice way, and I wonder what he's told her about me.

Upstairs, I knock on his door. "Finch?" I knock again. "It's Violet." There's no answer. I try the door, which is locked. I knock again.

I tell myself he must be sleeping or have his headphones on. I knock again and again. I reach into my pocket for the bobby pin I carry with me, just in case, and bend down to examine the lock. The first one I ever picked was to the closet in my mom's office. Eleanor put me up to it because that's where our parents hid the Christmas presents. I discovered lock picking was a skill that comes in handy when you want to disappear during gym class or when you just need some peace and quiet.

I give the knob a shake and then put the bobby pin away. I could probably pick this lock, but I won't. If Finch wanted to let me in, he would.

When I get back downstairs, Kate is standing at the sink smoking a cigarette out the kitchen window, her hand dangling over the sill. "Was he in there?" When I say no, she throws her cigarette down the garbage disposal. "Huh. Well, maybe he's asleep. Or he could have gone running."

"He runs?"

"About fifteen times a day."

It's my turn to say, "Huh."

"You never can tell what that boy's going to do."

FINCH

Day 27 (I am still here)

I stand at the window and watch her climb onto her bike. Afterward, I sit on the shower floor, the water beating down on my head, for a good twenty minutes. I can't even look at myself in the mirror.

I turn on the computer because it's a connection to the world, and maybe that's what I need right now. The brightness of the screen hurts my eyes, and so I dim it way down until the shapes and letters are near shadows. This is better. I sign onto Facebook, which belongs only to Violet and me. I start at the beginning of our message chain and read every word, but the words don't make sense unless I hold my head and repeat them out loud.

I try to read my downloaded version of *The Waves*, and when that isn't any better, I think, *It's the computer. It's not me.* And I find a regular book and thumb through it, but the lines dance across the page like they're trying to get away from me.

I will stay awake.

I will not sleep.

I think of ringing up ol' Embryo. I go so far as to fish his number out from the bottom of my backpack and punch it into my phone. I don't press Call.

I can go downstairs right now and let my mom know how I'm feeling—if she's even home—but she'll tell me to help myself to the Advil in her purse and that I need to relax and stop getting myself worked up, because in this house there's no such thing as being sick unless you can measure it with a thermometer under the tongue.

Things fall into categories of black and white—bad mood, bad temper, loses control, feels sad, feels blue.

You're always so sensitive, Theodore. Ever since you were a little boy. Do you remember the cardinal? The one that kept flying into the glass doors off the living room? Over and over, he knocked himself out, and you said, "Bring him in to live with us so he won't do that anymore." Remember? And then one day we came home and he was lying on the patio, and he'd flown into the door one too many times, and you called his grave a mud nest and said, "None of this would have happened if you'd let him come in."

I don't want to hear about the cardinal again. Because the thing of it is, that cardinal was dead either way, whether he came inside or not. Maybe he knew it, and maybe that's why he decided to crash into the glass a little harder than normal that day. He would have died in here, only slower, because that's what happens when you're a Finch. The marriage dies. The love dies. The people fade away.

I put on my sneakers and bypass Kate in the kitchen. She says, "Your girlfriend was just here looking for you."

"I must have had my headphones on."

"What happened to your lip and your eye? Please tell me she didn't do that."

"I ran into a door."

She stares hard at me. "Everything okay with you?"

"Yeah. Super. I'm just going for a run."

When I get back, the white of my bedroom ceiling is too bright, and so I turn it blue with what's left of the paint.

VIOLET

Six o'clock. Living room of my house. My parents sit across from me, their brows creased and unhappy. It seems Principal Wertz called my mother when I failed to come back for the rest of third period, or show up for my fourth-, fifth-, sixth-, and seventh-period classes.

My dad is still dressed in the suit he wore to work. He does most of the talking. "Where were you?"

"Technically, just across the street from school."

"Where across the street?"

"The river."

"What in the hell were you doing at the river during school, dur-ing *winter*?"

In her even, calm voice, Mom says, "James."

"There was a fire alarm, and we were all outside, and Finch wanted me to see this rare Asian crane . . ."

"Finch?"

"The boy I'm doing the project with. You met him."

"How much is left to do on this project?"

"We have to visit one more place and then we need to put every-thing together."

Mom says, "Violet, we're very disappointed." This is like a knife in my stomach. My parents have never believed in grounding us or taking away our phones or computers, all the things Amanda's par-ents do to her when she gets caught breaking the rules. Instead, they talk to us and tell us how disappointed they are.

Me, I mean. They talk to me.

"This isn't like you." Mom shakes her head.

Dad says, "You can't use losing your sister as an excuse to act out." I wish, just once, they'd send me to my room.

"I wasn't acting out. That wasn't what it was. It's just—I don't cheer anymore. I quit student council. I suck at orchestra. I don't have any friends or a boyfriend, because it's not like the rest of the world stops, you know?" My voice is getting louder, and I can't seem to do anything about it. "Everyone goes on with their lives, and maybe I can't keep up. Maybe I don't want to. The one thing I'm good at I can't do anymore. I didn't even want to work on this project, but it's kind of the only thing I have going on."

And then, because they won't do it, I send myself to my room. I walk away from them just as my dad is saying, "First of all, kiddo, you are good at many things, not just one. . . ."

We eat dinner in almost-silence, and afterward my mother comes up to my bedroom and studies the bulletin board above my desk. She says, "What happened to EleanorandViolet.com?"

"I let it go. There wasn't any point in keeping it."

"I guess not." Her voice is quiet, and when I look up, her eyes are red. "I don't think I'll ever get used to it," she says, and then she sighs, and I've never heard anything like it. It's a sigh full of pain and loss. She clears her throat and taps the paper that reads *New Nameless Web Magazine*. "So talk to me about this."

"I might create another magazine. Or I might not. I think my brain just naturally went there because of EleanorandViolet."

"You liked working on it."

"I did, but if I started another one, I'd want it to be different. Not just the silly stuff, but also real thoughts, real writing, real life."

She taps *Lit, Love, Life.* "And these?"

"I don't know. They might be categories."

She brings a chair over and sits next to me. And then she starts asking questions: Would this be for girls my age, or high school and beyond? Would I want to write all the content or work with contributors? What would be the purpose—why do I want to start another magazine to begin with? *Because people my age need somewhere they can go for advice or help or fun or just to be without anyone worrying about them. Somewhere they can be unlimited and fearless and safe, like in their own rooms.*

I haven't thought most of this out, and so I answer, "I don't know." And maybe the whole thing is stupid. "If I do anything, I have to start over, but all I have is fragments of ideas. Just pieces." I wave at the computer, then at the wall. "Like a germ of an idea for this, and a germ of an idea for that. Nothing whole or concrete."

"'Growth itself contains the germ of happiness.' Pearl S. Buck. Maybe a germ is enough. Maybe it's all you need." She props her chin in her hand and nods at the computer screen. "We can start small. Open up a new document or pull out a blank piece of paper. We'll make it our canvas. Remember what Michelangelo said about the sculpture being in the stone—it was there from the beginning, and his job was to bring it out. Your words are in there too."

For the next two hours we brainstorm and make notes, and at the end of it all, I have a very rough outline of a webzine and a very rough sketch of regular columns falling under the categories of Lit, Love, and Life.

It's nearly ten when she tells me good night. Mom lingers in the doorway and says, "Can you trust this boy, V?"

I turn in my chair. "Finch?"

"Yes."

"I think so. Right now, he's pretty much the only friend I have." I'm not sure if this is a good or a bad thing.

After she goes, I curl up on my bed, computer on my lap. There's no way I'll be able to create all the content. I write down a couple of names, including Brenda Shank-Kravitz, Jordan Gripenwaldt, and Kate Finch with a question mark beside it.

Germ. I do a search, and it's available—www.germmagazine. com. Five minutes later, it's purchased and registered. My stone.

I switch to Facebook and send Finch a message: **I hope you're okay. Came by to see you earlier, but you weren't there. My parents found out about skipping school and aren't happy. I think this may mark the end of our wandering.**

My light is off and my eyes are closed when I realize that for the first time I've forgotten to cross off the day on my calendar. I get up, feet hitting the cool wood floor, and walk over to my closet door. I pick up the black marker that I always leave within reach, uncap it, hold it up. And then my hand freezes in midair. I look at all the days laid out until graduation and freedom and I feel a strange clutching in my chest. They are only a collection of days, less than half a year, and then who knows where I go and what I do?

I cap the marker and grab one corner of the calendar and rip it down. I fold it up and shove it into the back of my closet, tossing the pen in after it. Then I slip out of my room and down the hall.

Eleanor's door is closed. I push it open and go inside. The walls are yellow and covered in pictures of Eleanor and her Indiana friends, Eleanor and her California friends. The California state flag hangs above her bed. Her art supplies are piled in a corner. My parents have been working in here, slowly organizing her things.

I set her glasses down on her dresser. "Thanks for the loan," I say. "But they make my head hurt. And they're ugly." I can almost hear her laughing.

VIOLET
Saturday

The next morning when I come downstairs, Theodore Finch is sitting at the dining-room table with my parents. His red cap is hooked on the back of his chair and he's drinking orange juice, an empty plate in front of him. His lip is split and there's a bruise on his cheek.

"You look better without the glasses," he says.

"What are you doing here?" I stare at him, at my parents.

"I'm eating breakfast. The most important meal of the day. But the real reason I came is that I wanted to explain about yesterday. I told your parents it was my idea and that you didn't want to cut class.

How you were only trying to keep me from getting in trouble by talking me into going back." Finch helps himself to more fruit and another waffle.

My dad says, "We also discussed some ground rules for this project of yours."

"So I can still work on it?"

"Theodore and I have an understanding, don't we?" Dad serves me a waffle and passes my plate down.

"Yes, sir." Finch winks at me.

My dad fixes him with a look. "An understanding not to be taken lightly."

Finch composes himself. "No, sir."

Mom says, "We told him we're putting our trust in him. We appreciate that he's gotten you back in the car again. We want you to have fun, within reason. Just be safe, and go to class."

"Okay." I feel like I'm in a daze. "Thank you."

My father turns to Finch. "We'll need your phone number and contact info for your parents."

"Whatever you need, sir."

"Is your father the Finch of Finch Storage?"

"Yes, sir."

"Ted Finch, former hockey player?"

"That's the one. But we haven't spoken in years. He left when I was ten."

I'm staring at him as my mom says, "I'm so sorry."

"At the end of the day, we're better off without him, but thank you." He gives my mom a sad and wounded smile, and unlike the story he's telling her, the smile is real. "My mother works at Broome

Real Estate and Bookmarks. She isn't home much, but if you have a pen, I'll give you her number."

I'm the one who brings him the pen and the paper, setting it down beside him, trying to catch his eye, but his dark head is bent over the notepad and he's writing in straight block letters: *Linda Finch,* followed by all her numbers, work, home, and cell, and then *Theodore Finch, Jr.,* followed by his own cell. The letters and numbers are neat and careful, like they were drawn by a child expecting to be graded. As I hand the paper to my dad, I want to say, *That's another lie. That's not even his real handwriting. There is nothing about this boy that is neat and careful.*

My mom smiles at my dad, and it's a smile that means "time to lighten up." She says to Finch, "So what are your college plans?" And the conversation turns chatty. When she asks Finch if he's thought about what he wants to do beyond college, as in with his life, I pay attention because I actually don't know the answer.

"It changes every day. I'm sure you've read *For Whom the Bell Tolls*."

Mom answers yes for both of them.

"Well, Robert Jordan knows he's going to die. 'There is only now,' he says, 'and if now is only two days, then two days is your life and everything in it will be in proportion.' None of us knows how long we have, maybe another month, maybe another fifty years—I like living as if I only have that two days." I'm watching my parents as Finch talks. He is speaking matter-of-factly but quietly, and I know this is out of respect for the dead, for Eleanor, who didn't have very long.

My dad takes a drink of coffee and leans back, getting comfortable. "The early Hindus believed in living life to the fullest. Instead of

aspiring to immortality, they aspired to living a healthy, full life. . . ."
He wraps up a good fifteen minutes later, with their earliest concept
of the afterlife, which is that the dead reunite with Mother Nature
to continue on earth in another form. He quotes an ancient Vedic
hymn: " 'May your eye go to the Sun, To the wind your soul . . .' "

" 'Or go to the waters if it suits thee there,' " Finch finishes.

My dad's eyebrows shoot up toward his hairline, and I can see
him trying to figure this kid out.

Finch says, "I kind of have this thing about water."

My father stands, reaches for the waffles, and drops two onto
Finch's plate. Inwardly, I let out a sigh of relief. Mom asks about our
"Wander Indiana" project, and for the rest of breakfast, Finch and
I talk about some of the places we've been so far, and some of the
places we're planning to go. By the time we're done eating, my par-

ents have become "Call me James" and "Call me Sheryl," instead of Mr. and Mrs. Markey. I half expect us to sit there all day with them, but then Finch turns to me, blue eyes dancing. "Ultraviolet, time's a-wastin'. We need to get this show on the road."

Outside, I say, "Why did you do that? Lie to my parents?"

He smooths the hair out of his eyes and pulls on the red cap. "Because it's not a lie if it's how you feel."

"What does that mean? Even your handwriting was lying." For some reason, this makes me maddest. If he's not real with them, maybe he's not real with me. I want to say, *What else is a lie?*

He leans on the open passenger door, the sun behind him so I can't see his face. "Sometimes, Ultraviolet, things feel true to us even if they're not."

FINCH

John Ivers is a polite, soft-spoken grandfather with a white baseball cap and a mustache. He and the missus live on a large farm way out in the Indiana countryside. Thanks to a website called Unusual Indiana, I have his telephone number. I've called ahead, just like the site said to do, and John is in the yard waiting for us. He waves and walks forward, shaking hands and apologizing that Sharon's gone off to the market.

He leads us to the roller coaster he's built in his backyard—actually there are two: the Blue Flash and the Blue Too. Each seats one person, which is the only disappointing thing about it, but otherwise it's really damn cool. John says, "I'm not engineer educated, but I am an adrenaline junkie. Demolition derbies, drag racing, driving fast—when I gave them up, I tried to think of something I could do to replace them, something that would give me that rush. I love the thrill of impending, weightless doom, so I built something to give me those feelings all the time."

As he stands, hands on hips, nodding at the Blue Flash, I think about *impending, weightless doom*. It's a phrase I like and understand. I tuck it away in the corner of my mind to pull out later, maybe for a song.

I say, "You may be the most brilliant man I have ever met." I like the idea of something that can give you those feelings all the time. I want something like that, and then I look at Violet and think: *There she is.*

John Ivers has built the roller coaster into the side of a shed. He says it measures 180 feet in length and climbs to a height of 20 feet. The speeds don't get above 25 mph, and it only lasts ten seconds, but there's an upside-down loop in the middle. To look at it, the Flash is just twisted scrap metal painted baby blue, with a 1970s bucket seat and a frayed cloth lap belt, but something about it makes my palms itch and I can't wait to ride.

I tell Violet she can go first. "No. That's okay. You go." She backs away from the roller coaster like it might reach out and swallow her, and I suddenly wonder if this whole thing was a bad idea.

Before I can open my mouth to say anything, John straps me into the seat and pushes me up the side of the shed till I feel and hear a click, and then up, up, up I go. He says, "You might want to hold on, son," as I reach the top, and so I do as I hover, just for a second, at the very top of the shed, farmland spread out around me, and then off

I shoot, down and into the loop, shouting myself hoarse. Too soon, it's over, and I want to go again, because this is what life should feel like all the time, not just for ten seconds.

I do this five more times because Violet still isn't ready, and whenever I get to the end, she waves her hands and says, "Do it again."

The next time I come to rest, I climb out, legs shaking, and suddenly Violet is taking a seat and John Ivers is strapping her in, and then she's climbing, up to the top, where she hovers. She turns her head to look in my direction, but suddenly she's off and diving and swooping and yelling her head off.

When she comes to a stop, I can't tell if she's going to throw up or climb out and slap me. Instead, she shouts, "Again!" And she's off once more in a blur of blue metal and long hair and long legs and arms.

We trade places then, and I go three times in a row, till the world looks upside down and tilted and I feel the blood pumping hard in my veins. As he unbuckles the lap belt, John Ivers chuckles. "That's a lot of ride."

"You can say that again." I reach for Violet because I'm not too steady on my feet and it's a long way down if I fall. She wraps her arm around me like it's second nature, and I lean into her and she leans into me until we make up one leaning person.

"Want to try the Blue Too?" John wants to know, and suddenly I don't because I want to be alone with this girl. But Violet breaks free and goes right to the roller coaster and lets John strap her in.

The Blue Too isn't nearly so fun, so we ride the Flash twice more. When I step off for the last time, I take Violet's hand and she swings it back and forth, back and forth. Tomorrow I'll be at my dad's for Sunday dinner, but today I'm here.

The things we leave behind are a miniature toy car we got at the dollar store—symbolizing Little Bastard—and two dollhouse figures, a boy and a girl, which we tuck inside an empty pack of American Spirit cigarettes. We cram it all into a magnetized tin the size of an index card.

"So that's it," Violet says, sticking it to the underside of the Blue Flash. "Our last wandering."

"I don't know. As fun as this was, I'm not sure it's what Black had in mind. I'll need to ruminate on it, understand—give it some good, hard thought—but we may need to choose a kind of backup place, just in case. The last thing I want to do is half-ass this, especially now that we have the support of your parents."

On the way home, she rolls down the window, her hair blowing wild. The pages of our wandering notebook rattle in the breeze as she writes, head bent, one leg crossed over the other to make a kind of table. When she's like this for a few miles, I say, "What are you working on?"

"Just making some notes. First I was writing about the Blue Flash, and then about a man who builds a roller coaster in his backyard. But then I had a couple of ideas I wanted to get on paper." Before I can ask about these ideas, her head is bent over the notebook again, and the pen is scratching across the page.

When she looks up again two miles later, she says, "You know what I like about you, Finch? You're interesting. You're different. And I can talk to you. Don't let that go to your head."

The air around us feels charged and electric, like if you were to strike a match, the air, the car, Violet, me—everything might just explode. I keep my eyes on the road. "You know what I like about you, Ultraviolet Remarkey-able? Everything."

"But I thought you didn't like me."

And then I look at her. She raises an eyebrow at me.

I go careening off onto the first exit I see. We roll past the gas station and the fast-food joints and bump across the median into a parking lot. EAST TOWNSHIP PUBLIC LIBRARY, the sign says. I wrench Little Bastard into park and then I get out and walk around to her side.

When I open the door, she says, "What the hell is going on?"

"I can't wait. I thought I could, but I can't. Sorry." I reach across her and unsnap her seat belt, then pull her out so we're standing face to face in this flat, ugly parking lot next to a dark library, a Chick-fil-A right next door. I can hear the drive-through cashier on the speaker asking if they want to add fries and a drink.

"Finch?"

I brush a loose strand of hair off her cheek. Then I hold her face in my hands and kiss her. I kiss her harder than I mean to, so I ease off a little, but then she's kissing me back. Her arms are around my neck, and I'm up against her, and she's against the car, and then I pick her up, and her legs are around me, and I somehow get the back door open, and then I'm laying her down on the blanket that's there, and I close the doors and yank off my sweater, and she pulls off her shirt, and I say, "You are driving me crazy. You have been driving me crazy for weeks."

My mouth is on her neck, and she's making these gasping sounds, and then she says, "Oh my God, where *are* we?" And she's laughing, and I'm laughing, and she's kissing my neck, and my entire body feels like it's going to fucking explode, and her skin is smooth and warm, and I run my hand over the curve of her hip as she bites my ear, and then that hand is sliding into the hollow between her stomach and her jeans. She holds on to me tighter, and when I start undoing my belt, she kind of pulls away, and I want to bang my head against the wall of Little Bastard because, shit. *She's a virgin.* I can tell by the pull-away.

She whispers, "I'm sorry."

"All that time with Ryan?"

"Close, but no."

I run my fingers up and down her stomach. "Seriously."

"Why's it so hard to believe?"

"Because it's Ryan Cross. I thought girls lost it just by looking at him."

She slaps my arm and then lays her hand on top of mine and says, "This is the last thing I thought would happen today."

"Thanks."

"You know what I meant."

I pick up her shirt, hand it to her, pick up my sweater. As I watch her get dressed, I say, "Someday, Ultraviolet," and she actually looks disappointed.

At home in my room, I am overcome by words. Words for songs. Words of places Violet and I will go before time runs out and I'm asleep again. I can't stop writing. I don't want to stop even if I could.

January 31. Method: None. On a scale of one to ten on the how-close-did-I-come scale: zero. Facts: The Euthanasia Coaster doesn't actually exist. But if it did, it would be a three-minute ride that involves a climb nearly a third of a mile long, up to 1,600 feet, followed by a sheer drop and seven loops. That final descent and series of loops takes sixty seconds, but the 10 G centrifugal force that results from the 223-mile-per-hour loops is what kills you.

And then there is this strange fold in time, and I realize I'm not writing anymore. I'm running. I'm still wearing the black sweater and old blue jeans and sneakers and gloves, and suddenly my feet hurt, and somehow I've made it all the way to Centerville, which is the next town over.

I take off my shoes and pull off my hat, and I walk all the way back home because for once I've worn myself out. But I feel good—necessary and tired and alive.

Julijonas Urbonas, the man who thought up the Euthanasia Coaster, claims it's engineered to "humanely—with elegance and euphoria—take the life of a human being." Those 10 Gs create enough centrifugal force on the body so that the blood rushes down instead of up to the brain, which results in something called cerebral hypoxia, and this is what kills you.

I walk through the black Indiana night, under a ceiling of stars, and think about the phrase "elegance and euphoria," and how it describes exactly what I feel with Violet.

For once, I don't want to be anyone but Theodore Finch, the boy she sees. He understands what it is to be elegant and euphoric and a hundred different people, most of them flawed and stupid, part asshole, part screwup, part freak, a boy who wants to be easy for the folks around him so that he doesn't worry them and, most of all, easy for himself. A boy who belongs—here in the world, here in his own skin. He is exactly who I want to be and what I want my epitaph to say: *The Boy Violet Markey Loves.*

FINCH

In gym, Charlie Donahue and I stand on the baseball field, way beyond third base. We've discovered this is the best place to be if you want to have a conversation. Without even looking, he catches a ball that comes zinging our way and flings it back to home. Every athletic coach at Bartlett High has been trying to recruit him since he first walked through the school doors, but he refuses to be a black stereotype. His extracurriculars are chess, yearbook, and euchre club because, as he says, these are things that will make him stand out on college applications.

Right now, he crosses his arms and frowns at me. "Is it true you almost drowned Roamer?"

"Something like that."

"Always finish what you start, man."

"I thought it was a good idea not to get myself incarcerated before I have a chance to get laid again."

"Getting arrested might actually increase your odds of getting laid."

"Not the kind of odds I'm looking for."

"So what's up with you anyway? Look at you."

"I wish I could take the credit, but let's face it, the gym uniform is universally flattering."

"Cheeky wanker." He calls me this even though I'm no longer British. Good-bye, Fiona. Good-bye, flat. Good-bye, Abbey Road. "I mean, you've been Dirtbag Finch for a while now. Before that, you were Badass Finch for a couple weeks. You're slipping."

"Maybe I like Dirtbag Finch." I adjust the knit cap, and it suddenly hits me—which Finch does Violet like? The thought burns a little, and I can feel my mind latch onto it. *Which Finch does she like? What if it's only a version of the real Finch?*

Charlie offers me a cigarette and I shake my head.

"What's going on with you? Is she your girlfriend?"

"Violet?"

"Did you hit that yet, or what?"

"My friend, you are a total and complete pig. And I'm just having a good time."

"Obviously not too good a time."

Roamer comes up to bat, which means we have to pay attention, because not only is he the school's star baseball player (second only to Ryan Cross), he likes to aim right at us. If it wouldn't get him in trouble, he'd probably come over here now and smash my head in with the bat for nearly drowning him.

Sure enough, the ball comes flying at us, and, cigarette between his teeth, Charlie steps backward once, twice, once more, as if he's not in any hurry, as if he knows he's got this. He holds out his glove and the ball falls right into it. Roamer yells about fifteen hundred expletives as Charlie sends it flying right back.

I nod over at Mr. Kappel, our teacher, who also happens to be the baseball coach. "You do know that every time you do that, you make him die just a little."

"Kappy or Roamer?"

"Both."

He flashes me a rare grin. "I do."

In the locker room, Roamer corners me. Charlie is gone. Kappel is in his office. The guys who haven't left yet fade away into the background, like they're trying to go invisible. Roamer leans in so close, I can smell the eggs he had for breakfast. "You're dead, freak."

Much as I would love to kick the shit out of Gabe Romero, I'm not going to. 1) Because he's not worth getting into trouble for. And 2) because I remember the look on Violet's face at the river when she told me to let him go.

So I count. *One, two, three, four, five . . .*
I will hold it in. I won't punch him in the face.
I will be good.

And then he slams me into the locker and, before I can even blink, punches me in the eye, and then again in the nose. It's all I can do to stay on my feet, and I am counting like hell now because I want to kill the son of a bitch.

I wonder, if I count long enough, whether I can go back in time, all the way to the beginning of eighth grade, before I was weird and before anyone noticed me and before I opened my mouth and talked to Roamer and before they called me "freak" and I was awake all the time and everything felt okay and somewhat normal, whatever normal is, and people actually looked at me—not to stare, not to watch for what I'd do next, but looked at me like, *Oh hey, what's up, man, what's up, buddy?* I wonder, if I count backward, whether I can go back and take Violet Markey with me and then move forward with her so we have more time. Because it's time I fear.

And me.

I'm afraid of me.

"Is there a problem here?" Kappel stands a couple of feet away, eyeing us. He's got a baseball bat in his hand, and I can hear him at home telling the wife, "The trouble isn't the freshmen. It's the older ones, once they start working out and hitting those growth spurts. That's when you gotta protect yourself, no matter what."

"No problem," I tell him. "No trouble."

If I know Kappel like I know Kappel, he's never going to take this to Principal Wertz, not when one of his best baseball players is involved. I wait to get blamed for it. I'm all set to hear the details of my detention or expulsion, even if I'm the only one bleeding. But then Kappy says, "We're done here, Finch. You can go."

I wipe the blood off and smile at Roamer as I walk away.

"Not so fast, Romero," I hear Kappy bark, and the sound of Roamer groveling almost makes the pain worth it.

I stop at my locker to get my books, and sitting on top of them is what looks like the Hoosier Hill rock. I pick it up, flip it over, and sure enough: *Your turn*, it says.

"What's that?" Brenda wants to know. She takes it out of my hand and examines it. "I don't get it. 'Your turn'? Your turn for what?"

"It's a private joke. Only the really sexy, really cool people know what it means."

She punches my arm. "Then you must have no clue. What happened to your eye?"

"Your boyfriend. Roamer?"

She makes a face. "I never liked him."

"Really?"

"Shut up. I hope you broke his nose."

"I'm trying to rise above."

"Wuss." She walks with me, chatting away: *Are you totally into Violet Markey, like the forever kind or the she's-interesting-for-right-now kind? What about Suze Haines? Didn't you used to have a thing for her? What about the three Brianas and those macramé girls? What would you do if Emma Watson fell from the sky right now? Would you even want to feel her up or would you tell her to leave you alone? Do you think my hair would look better purple or blue? Do you think I need to lose weight? Be honest. Do you think any guy will ever have sex with me or love me for who I am?*

I answer, "Right," "I don't think so," "Of course," "You never can tell," and all the while I'm thinking about Violet Markey, lock picker.

VIOLET

February 2

Mrs. Kresney folds her hands and smiles her too-broad smile. "How are you, Violet?"

"I'm fine, and you?"

"I'm fine. Let's talk about you. I want to know how you're feeling."

"I'm good actually. Better than I've been in a long time."

"Really?" She's surprised.

"Yes. I've even started writing again. And riding in a car."

"How are you sleeping?"

"Pretty well, I think."

"Any bad dreams?"

"No."

"Not even one?"

"Not in a while now."

For the first time, it's the truth.

In Russian lit, Mrs. Mahone assigns us a five-page paper on Turgenev's *Fathers and Sons*. She looks at me, and I don't mention anything about Extenuating Circumstances or not being ready. I copy down the notes like everyone else. Afterward, Ryan says, "Can I talk to you?"

Mrs. Mahone watches as I walk on by her. I give her a wave. "What's up?" I say to Ryan.

We go out into the hallway and are swept along with the sea

of people. Ryan takes my hand so he doesn't lose me, and I'm like, *Oh God*. But then there's a little break in the crowd and he lets go. "Where are you headed next?"

"Lunch."

We walk together, and Ryan says, "So I just wanted to let you know that I asked Suze out. I thought you should hear it from me before it got all over school."

"That's great." I almost say something about Finch, but then I'm not sure what to say because I don't know what we are or if we're anything. "Thanks for telling me. I hope Suze knows what a good guy you are."

He nods, gives me his signature smile—I can see the dimple—and then says, "I don't know if you heard, but Roamer went after Finch today in gym."

"What do you mean 'went after'?"

"Whatever. Banged him up a little. Roamer's an asshole."

"What happened? Like, to them? Did they get expelled?"

"I don't think so. It was Kappel's class, and he's not going to report Roamer and risk losing him for practice. I gotta go." A few steps away, he turns. "Finch didn't even try to defend himself. He just stood there and took it."

In the cafeteria, I walk past my regular table, past Amanda and Roamer and the audience gathered there. I can hear Roamer talking, but I can't hear what he's saying.

I walk to the other side of the room, toward a half-empty table, but then behind me I hear my name. Brenda Shank-Kravitz is sitting with the three Brianas and a dark-haired girl named Lara at a round table by the window.

"Hey," I say. "Do you mind if I join you?" I feel like I'm the new girl again, trying to make friends and figure out where I fit.

Brenda picks up her backpack and sweater and keys and phone and all the other things that are spilled across the table and dumps them onto the floor. I set my tray down and sit next to her.

Lara is so small, she looks like a freshman, even though I know we're in the same class. She is telling the story of how, just five minutes ago, she accidentally, without meaning to, told her crush she loved him. Instead of crawling under the table, she just laughs and keeps eating.

Then the Brianas are talking about life after high school—one is a musician, one is planning to be a copy editor, and the other is practically engaged to her longtime boyfriend. She says she might run a cookie shop one day or write book reviews, but whatever she does, she's going to enjoy everything she can while she can. The boyfriend joins us, and the two of them sit side by side looking comfortable and happy and like they really might be together forever.

I eat and listen, and at some point Brenda leans over and says in my ear, "Gabe Romero is poison." I raise my water bottle and she raises her soda can. We tap them together and drink.

VIOLET

By now, the wandering is really an excuse to drive somewhere and make out. I tell myself I'm not ready because to me sex is a Big Deal, even if some of my friends have been doing it since ninth grade. But the thing is, my body feels this strange, urgent tug toward Finch like it can't get enough. I add a category to my *Germ* board—*Sex Life*—and write a few pages in our wandering notebook, which is slowly turning into my journal/sounding board/place to brainstorm material for the new webzine.

Before Amanda and I stopped being peripheral semi-friends, I remember sleeping over at her house and talking to her older brothers. They told us that girls who Do are sluts and girls who Don't are teases. Those of us who were there that night took this to heart, because none of the rest of us had older brothers. When we were by ourselves again, Amanda said, "The only way around it is to stay with one guy forever." But does forever have a built-in ending . . . ?

Finch picks me up Saturday morning, and he looks a little battered. We don't even drive that far, just to the Arboretum, where we park the car, and before he reaches for me, I say, "What happened with Roamer?"

"How'd you hear about Roamer?"

"Ryan told me. And it's kind of obvious you were in a fight."

"Does it make me look hotter?"

"Be serious. What happened?"

"Nothing you need to worry about. He was being an asshole.

Big surprise. Now, if we're done talking about him, I've got other things on my mind." He climbs into the back of Little Bastard and pulls me after him.

I feel like I'm living for these moments—the moments when I'm just about to lie down beside him, when I know it's getting ready to happen, his skin on mine, his mouth on mine, and then when he's touching me and the electric current is shooting through me everywhere. It's like all the other hours of the day are spent looking forward to right now.

We kiss until my lips are numb, stopping ourselves at the very edge of Someday, saying not yet, not here, even though it takes willpower I didn't know I had. My mind is spinning with him and with the unexpected Almost of today.

When he gets home, he writes me a message: **I am thinking rather consistently of Someday.**

I write, **Someday soon.**

Finch: **Someday when?**

Me: **????**

Finch: ***#@*!!!**

Me: ☺

Nine a.m. Sunday. My house. When I wake up and go downstairs, my parents are in the kitchen slicing bagels. My mom looks at me over the coffee mug Eleanor and I gave her one year on Mother's Day. *Rock Star Mom*. She says, "You got a package."

"It's Sunday."

"Someone left it on the doorstep."

I follow her into the dining room, thinking that she walks like Eleanor—hair swinging, shoulders back. Eleanor looked more like my dad and I look more like Mom, but she and Mom had the same gestures, same mannerisms, so everyone always said, "Oh my God, she looks just like you." It hits me that my mother may never hear that again.

There's something in brown paper, the kind you wrap fish in, sitting on the dining-room table. It's tied with a red ribbon. The package itself is lumpy. *Ultraviolet*, it reads on one side.

"Do you know who it's from?" My dad is in the doorway, bagel crumbs in his beard.

"James," my mom says, and makes little brushing motions. He rubs at his chin.

I don't have any choice but to open the package in front of them, and I just hope to God it's nothing embarrassing because, from Theodore Finch, you never know.

As I tug off the ribbon and rip at the paper, I'm suddenly six years old at Christmas. Every year, Eleanor knew what she was getting. After we picked the lock to my mom's office closet, my sister would open her gifts and mine too, but not before I left the room. Later, when she wanted to tell me what they were, I wouldn't let her. Those were the days when I didn't mind surprises.

Inside the brown paper is a pair of goggles, the kind you wear swimming.

"Do you have any idea who they're from?" Mom says.

"Finch."

"Goggles," she says. "Sounds serious." She gives me a hopeful little smile.

"Sorry, Mom. He's just a friend."

I don't know why I say this, but I don't want them asking me what he means or what this is, especially when I'm not really sure myself.

"Maybe in time. There's always time," she replies, which is something Eleanor used to say.

I look at my mom to see if she realizes she's quoted her, but if she does realize it, she doesn't show it. She is too busy examining the goggles, asking my dad if he remembers the days he used to send her things when he was trying to convince her to go out with him.

Upstairs, I write, Thanks for the goggles. What are they for? Please tell me you don't want us to use them for Someday.

Finch writes back, **Wait and see. We'll use them soon. We're watching for the first warm day. There's always one that sneaks in during the middle of winter. Once we nail the bastard down, we go. Don't forget the goggles.**

FINCH

The first warm day

The second week of February there's a blizzard that leaves the entire town without power for two days. The best thing about it is that school is canceled, but the worst thing is that the snow is so high and the air so bitter cold, you can barely stay out in it for more than five minutes at a time. I tell myself it's only water in a different form, and I walk all the way to Violet's, where we build the world's largest snowman. We name him Mr. Black and decide he'll be a destination for others to see when they're wandering. Afterward, we sit with her parents around the fire and I pretend I'm part of the family.

Once the roads are clear, Violet and I creep very, very carefully down them to see the Painted Rainbow Bridge, the Periodic Table Display, the Seven Pillars, and the lynching and burial site of the Reno brothers, America's first train robbers. We climb the sheer, high walls of Empire Quarry, where they got the 18,630 tons of stone needed to build the Empire State Building. We visit the Indiana Moon Tree, which is a giant sycamore more than thirty years old that grew from a seed taken to the moon and brought back. This tree is nature's rock star because it's one of only fifty left alive from an original set of five hundred.

We go to Kokomo to hear the hum in the air, and we park Little Bastard in neutral at the base of Gravity Hill and roll to the top. It is like the world's slowest roller coaster, but somehow it works, and minutes later we're at the peak. Afterward, I take her out for a Valentine's Day dinner at my favorite restaurant, Happy Family, which sits at the end of a strip mall about fifteen miles from home. It serves the best Chinese food east of the Mississippi.

The first warm day falls on a Saturday, which is how we end up in Prairieton at the Blue Hole, a three-acre lake that sits on private property. I collect our offerings—the stubs of her SAT number 2 pencils and four broken guitar strings. The air is so warm, we don't even need jackets, just sweaters, and after the winter we've been through so far, it feels almost tropical.

I hold out my hand and lead her up the embankment and down the hill to a wide, round pool of blue water, ringed by trees. It's so private and silent that I pretend we're the only two people on earth, which is how I wish it could be for real.

"Okay," she says, letting out a long breath, as if she's been holding it all this time. The goggles hang around her neck. "What is this place?"

"This," I say, "is the Blue Hole. They say it's bottomless, or that the bottom is quicksand. They say there's a force in the middle of the lake that sucks you down into an underground river that flows right into the Wabash. They say it leads you to another world. That it was a hiding place for pirates burying treasure, and for Chicago bootleggers burying bodies and dumping stolen cars. That in the 1950s a group of teenage boys went swimming here and disappeared. In 1969, two sheriff's deputies launched an expedition to explore the Hole, but they didn't find any cars or treasure or bodies. They also didn't find the bottom. What they did find was a whirlpool that nearly sucked them down."

I've ditched the red cap, gloves, and black sweater, and am wearing a navy pullover and jeans. I've cut my hair shorter, and when she first saw me, Violet said, "All-American Finch. Okay." Now I kick off my shoes and yank off the shirt. It's almost hot in the sun, and I want to go swimming. "Bottomless blue holes exist all over the world, and each one has these kinds of myths associated with it. They were formed as caverns, thousands of years ago during the last ice age. They're like black holes on earth, places where nothing can escape and time and space come to an end. How bloody awesome is it that we actually have one of our own?"

She glances back toward the house and the car and the road, then smiles up at me. "Pretty awesome." She kicks off her shoes and pulls off her shirt and pants so that, in seconds, she is standing there in only her bra and underwear, which are a kind of dull rose color but somehow the sexiest things I've ever seen.

I go totally and utterly speechless and she starts to laugh. "Well, come on. I know you're not shy, so drop your pants and let's do this. I assume you want to see if the rumors are true." My mind draws a blank, and she juts one hip out, Amanda Monk–style, resting a hand on it. "About it being bottomless?"

"Oh yeah. Right. Of course." I slide off my jeans so I'm in my boxers, and I take her hand. We walk to the rock ledge that surrounds part of the Hole and climb up onto it. "What are you most afraid of?" I say before we jump. I can already feel my skin starting to burn from the sun.

"Dying. Losing my parents. Staying here for the rest of my life. Never figuring out what I'm supposed to do. Being ordinary. Losing everyone I love." I wonder if I'm included in that group. She is bouncing on the balls of her feet, as if she's cold. I try not to stare at her chest as she does because, whatever else he is, All-American Finch is not a perv. "What about you?" she asks. She fits the goggles into place. "What are you most afraid of?"

I think, *I'm most afraid of Just be careful. I'm most afraid of the Long Drop. I'm most afraid of Asleep and impending, weightless doom. I'm most afraid of me.*

"I'm not." I take her hand, and together we leap through the air. And in that moment there's nothing I fear except losing hold of her hand. The water is surprisingly warm and, below the surface, strangely clear and, well, blue. I look at her, hoping her eyes are open, and they are. With my free hand, I point below, and she nods, her hair fanning out like seaweed. Together, we swim, still linked, like a person with three arms.

We head down, where the bottom would be if there was one. The deeper we go, the darker the blue becomes. The water feels darker too, as if the weight of it has settled. It's only when I feel her tug at my hand that I let myself be pulled back up to the surface, where we break out of the water and fill our lungs. "Jesus," she says. "You can hold your breath."

"I practice," I say, suddenly wishing I hadn't said it at all, because it's one of those things—like *I am make-believe*—that sounds better in my own head.

She just smiles and splashes me, and I splash her back. We do this for a while, and I chase her around the surface, ducking under, grabbing her legs. She slips through my grasp and breaks into a breaststroke, clean and strong. I remind myself that she's a California girl and probably grew up swimming in the ocean. I suddenly feel jealous of all the years she had before meeting me, and then I swim after her. We tread water, looking at each other, and suddenly there's not enough water in the world to clean away my dirty thoughts.

She says, "I'm glad we came."

We float on our backs, holding hands again, faces to the sun. Because my eyes are closed, I whisper, "Marco."

"Polo," she answers, and her voice sounds lazy and far away.

After a while, I say, "Do you want to go look for the bottom again?"

"No. I like it here, just like this." Then she asks, "When did the divorce happen?"

"Around this time last year."

"Did you know it was coming?"

"I did and I didn't."

"Do you like your stepmother?"

"She's fine. She has a seven-year-old son who may or may not be my dad's, because I'm pretty sure he was cheating with her for the past few years. He left us once, when I was ten or eleven, said he couldn't deal with us anymore. I think he was with her then. He came back, but when he left for good, he made it clear it was our fault. Our fault he came back, our fault he had to leave. He just couldn't have a family."

"And then he married a woman with a kid. What's he like?"

The son I will never be. "He's just a kid." I don't want to talk about Josh Raymond. "I'm going in search of the bottom. Are you okay here? Do you mind?"

"I'm good. You go. I'll be here." She floats away.

I take a breath and dive, grateful for the dark of the water and the warmth against my skin. I swim to get away from Josh Raymond, and my cheating father, and Violet's involved parents who are also her friends, and my sad, deserted mother, and my bones. I close my eyes and pretend it's Violet who surrounds me instead, and then I open my eyes and push myself down, one arm out like Superman.

I feel the strain of my lungs wanting air, but I keep going. It feels a lot like the strain of trying to stay awake when I can feel the darkness sliding under my skin, trying to borrow my body without asking so that my hands become its hands, my legs its legs.

I dive deeper, lungs tight and burning. I feel a distant twinge of panic, but I make my mind go quiet before I send my body deeper. I want to see how far I can go. *She's waiting for me.* The thought fills me, but I can still feel the darkness working its way up, through my fingers, trying to grab hold.

Less than 2 percent of people in the U.S. kill themselves by drowning, maybe because the human body was built to float. The number one country in the world for drowning, accidental or otherwise, is Russia, which has twice as many deaths as the next highest, Japan. The Cayman Islands, surrounded by the Caribbean Sea, has the fewest drownings of all.

I like it deeper, where the water feels heaviest. Water is better than running because it blocks everything out. Water is my special power, my way to cheat the Asleep and stop it from coming on.

I want to go even deeper than this, because the deeper the better. I want to keep going. But something makes me stop. The thought of Violet. The burning sensation in my lungs. I stare longingly at the black of where the bottom should be but isn't, and then I stare up again at the light, very faint but still there, waiting with Violet, over my head.

It takes strength to push myself up, because I need air by now, badly. The panic comes back, stronger this time, and then I aim myself for the surface. *Come on,* I think. *Please come on.* My body wants up, but it's tired. *I'm sorry. I'm sorry, Violet. I won't leave you again. I don't know what I was thinking. I'm coming.*

When I finally hit the air, she is sitting on the bank crying. "Asshole," she says.

I feel my smile go and I swim toward her, head up, afraid to put it under again, even for a second, afraid she'll freak out.

"Asshole," she says, louder this time, standing, still in her underwear. She wraps her arms around herself, trying to get warm, trying to cover up, trying to pull away from me. "What the hell? Do you know how scared I was? I searched everywhere. I went as deep as I could before I ran out of air and had to come back up, like, three times."

I want her to say my name because then I'll know it's okay and I haven't gone too far and I haven't just lost her forever. But she doesn't, and I can feel a cold, dark feeling growing in the pit of my stomach—every bit as cold and dark as the water. I find the outer edge of the Blue Hole where there's suddenly a bottom, and I rise up out of it until I'm next to her, dripping on the bank.

She pushes me hard and then again, so I go jolting backward, but I don't lose my footing. I stand there as she slaps at me, and then she starts to cry, and she is shaking.

I want to kiss her but I've never seen her like this, and I'm not sure what she'll do if I try to touch her. I tell myself, *For once it's not about you, Finch.* So I stand an arm's length away and say, "Let it out, all that stuff you're carrying around. You're pissed off at me, at your parents, at life, at Eleanor. Come on. Let me have it. Don't disappear in there." I mean inside herself, where I'll never get to her.

"Screw you, Finch."

"Better. Keep going. Don't stop now. Don't be a waiting person. You lived. You survived a really horrible accident. But you're just . . . there. You're just *existing* like everyone else. Get up. Do this. Do that. Lather. Rinse. Repeat. Over and over so that you don't have to think about it."

She shoves me again and again. "Stop acting like you know how I feel." She's pounding at me with her fists, but I just stand, feet planted, and take it.

"I know there's more in there, probably years of shit you've been smiling away and keeping down."

She pounds and pounds and then suddenly covers her face. "You don't know how it is. It's like I've got this angry little person inside me, and I can feel him trying to get out. He's running out of room because he's growing bigger and bigger, and so he starts rising up, into my lungs, chest, throat, and I just push him right back down. I don't want him to come out. I can't let him out."

"Why not?"

"Because I hate him, because he's not me, but he's in there and he won't leave me alone, and all I can think is that I want to go up to someone, anyone, and just knock them into space because I'm angry at all of them."

"So don't tell me. Break something. Smash something. Throw something. Or scream. Just get it out of you." I yell again. I yell and yell. Then I pick up a rock and smash it into the wall that surrounds the hole.

I hand her a rock and she stands, palm up, like she's not sure what to do. I take the rock from her and hurl it against the wall, then hand her another. Now she's hurling them at the wall and shouting and stomping, and she looks like a crazy person. We jump up and down the banks and storm around smashing things, and then she turns on me, all of a sudden, and says, "What are we, anyway? What exactly is going on here?"

It's at that moment that I can't help myself, even though she is furious, even though she maybe hates me right now. I pull her in and kiss her the way I've always wanted to kiss her, a lot more R-rated than PG-13. I can feel her tense at first, not wanting to kiss me back, and the thought of it breaks my heart. Before I can pull away, I feel her bend and then melt into me as I melt into her under the warm Indiana sun. And she's still here, and she isn't going anywhere, and it will be okay. *I am carried off. We yield to this slow flood. . . . In and out, we are swept; . . . we cannot step outside its sinuous, its hesitating, its abrupt, its perfectly encircling walls.*

And then I push her away.

"What the hell, Finch?" She is wet and angry and staring at me with large gray-green eyes.

"You deserve better. I can't promise you I'll stay around, not because I don't want to. It's hard to explain. I'm a fuckup. I'm broken, and no one can fix it. I've tried. I'm still trying. I can't love anyone because it's not fair to anyone who loves me back. I'll never hurt you, not like I want to hurt Roamer. But I can't promise I won't pick you apart, piece by piece, until you're in a thousand pieces, just like me. You should know what you're getting into before getting involved."

"In case you haven't noticed, we're already involved, Finch. And in case you haven't noticed, I'm broken too." Then she says, "Where did you get the scar? The real story this time."

"The real story's boring. My dad gets in these black moods. Like, the blackest black. Like, no moon, no stars, storm's coming black. I used to be a lot smaller than I am now. I used to not know how to get out of the way." These are just some of the things I never wanted to say to her. "I wish I could promise you perfect days and sunshine, but I'm never going to be Ryan Cross."

"If there's one thing I know, it's that no one can promise anything. And I don't want Ryan Cross. Let me worry about what I want." And then she kisses me. It's the kind of kiss that makes me lose track of everything, and so it may be hours or minutes by the time we break apart.

She says, "By the way? Ryan Cross is a kleptomaniac. He steals stuff for fun. And not even things he wants, but everything. His room looks like one of those rooms on *Hoarders*. Just in case you thought he was perfect."

"Ultraviolet Remarkey-able, I think I love you."

So that she doesn't feel she has to say it back, I kiss her again, and wonder if I dare do anything else, go any further, because I don't want to ruin this moment. And then, because I'm now the one thinking too much, and because she is different from all other girls and because I really, really don't want to screw this up, I concentrate on kissing her on the banks of the Blue Hole, in the sunshine, and I let that be enough.

VIOLET

The Day Of

Around three o'clock the air turns cool again, and we drive to his house to shower and get warm. His house is empty because everyone comes and goes as they please. He grabs waters from the fridge, and a bag of pretzels, and I follow him upstairs, still damp and shivering.

His bedroom is blue now—walls, ceiling, floor—and all the furniture has been moved to one corner so that the room is divided in two. There's less clutter, no more wall of notes and words. All that blue makes me feel like I'm inside a swimming pool, like I'm back at the Blue Hole.

I shower first, standing under the hot water, trying to get warm. When I come out of the bathroom, wrapped in a towel, Finch has music playing on the old turntable.

Unlike his swim in the Blue Hole, his shower lasts no more than a minute. Before I'm dressed, he reappears, towel around his waist, and says, "You never asked me what I was doing up on that ledge." He stands, open and ready to tell me anything, but for some reason I'm not sure I want to know.

"What were you doing up on that ledge?" It comes out a whisper.

"The same thing you were. I wanted to see what it was like. I wanted to imagine jumping off it. I wanted to leave all the shit behind. But when I did start to imagine it, I didn't like what it looked like. And then I saw you."

He takes my hand and spins me out and then in so I'm tucked

against him, and we sway, and rock a little, but mostly stand still, pressed together, my heart pounding because if I tilt my head back, just like this, he will kiss me like he's doing now. I can feel his lips curving up at the corners, smiling. I open my eyes at the moment he opens his, and his blue-blue eyes are shining so fierce and bright that they're nearly black. The damp hair is falling across his forehead, and he rests his head against mine. And then I realize his towel is lying on the floor and he's naked.

I lay my fingers against his neck, long enough to feel his pulse, which feels just like my own—racing and feverish.

"We don't have to."

"I know."

And then I close my eyes as my own towel drops and the song comes to an end. I still hear it after we are in the bed and under the sheets and other songs are playing.

FINCH

The Day Of

She is oxygen, carbon, hydrogen, nitrogen, calcium, and phosphorus. The same elements that are inside the rest of us, but I can't help thinking she's more than that and she's got other elements going on that no one's ever heard of, ones that make her stand apart from everybody else. I feel this brief panic as I think, *What would happen if one of those elements malfunctioned or just stopped working altogether?* I make myself push this aside and concentrate on the feel of her skin until I no longer see molecules but Violet.

As the song plays on the turntable, I hear one of my own that's taking shape:

You make me love you . . .

The line plays over and over in my head as we move from standing to lying down.

You make me love you
You make me love you
You make me love you . . .

I want to get up and write it down and tack it to the wall. But I don't.

Afterward, as we lie tangled up, kind of winded and Huh and Wow, she says, "I should get home." We lie there a little longer and then she says it again. "I should get home."

In the car, we hold hands and don't talk about what happened. Instead of driving to her house, I take a detour. When I get to the Purina Tower, she wants to know what we're doing.

I grab the blanket and pillow from the back and say, "I'm going to tell you a story."

"Up there?"

"Yes."

We climb up the steel ladder, all the way to the top. The air must be cold because I can see my breath, but I feel warm all the way through. We walk past the Christmas tree and I spread out the blanket. We lie down and wrap ourselves in and then I kiss her.

She is smiling as she pushes me away. "So tell me this story."

We lie back, her head on my shoulder, and, as if I ordered them, the stars are clear and bright. There are millions of them.

I say, "There was this famous British astronomer named Sir Patrick Moore. He hosted a BBC television program called *Sky at Night*, which ran for something like fifty-five years. Anyway, on April 1, 1976, Sir Patrick Moore announced on his show that something extraordinary was getting ready to happen in the skies. At exactly 9:47 a.m., Pluto would pass directly behind Jupiter, in relation to the earth. This was a rare alignment that meant the combined gravitational force of those two planets would exert a stronger tidal pull, which would temporarily counteract gravity here on earth and make people weigh less. He called this the Jovian-Plutonian gravitational effect."

Violet is heavy against my arm, and for a minute I wonder if she's asleep.

"Patrick Moore told viewers that they could experience the phenomenon by jumping in the air at the exact moment the alignment occurred. If they did, they would feel weightless, like they were floating."

She shifts a little.

"At 9:47 a.m., he told everyone, 'Jump now!' Then he waited. One minute passed, and the BBC switchboard lit up with hundreds of people calling in to say they'd felt it. One woman phoned from Holland to say she and her husband had swum around the room together. A man called from Italy to say he and his friends had been seated at a table, and all of them—including the table—rose into the air. Another man called from the States to say he and his children had flown like kites in their backyard."

Violet is propped up now, looking at me. "Did those things actually happen?"

"Of course not. It was an April Fool's joke."

She smacks my arm and lies back down. "You had me believing."

"But I bring it up to let you know that this is the way I feel right now. Like Pluto and Jupiter are aligned with the earth and I'm floating."

In a minute, she says, "You're so weird, Finch. But that's the nicest thing anyone's ever said to me."

VIOLET

The morning after

I wake up before him, and the blanket is cocooned over us like a tent. I lie there for a while, enjoying the feel of his arm around me and the sound of his breathing. He's so still and quiet, I barely recognize him. I watch the way his eyelids twitch as he dreams, and I wonder if he's dreaming of me.

Like he can feel me watching, he opens his eyes.

"You're real," he says.

"That's me."

"Not a Jovian-Plutonian gravitational effect."

"No."

"In that case"—he grins wickedly—"I hear that Pluto and Jupiter and the earth are about to align. I wonder if you want to join me in a floating experiment." He pulls me in closer and the blanket shifts. I blink into the brightness and the cold.

As it hits me.

It's morning.

As in the sun is coming up.

As in the sun went down at some point, and I never went home or called my parents to let them know where I was. As in we are still on top of the Purina Tower, where we have spent the night.

"It's morning," I say, and I feel like I'm going to be sick.

Finch sits up, his face gone blank. "Shit."

"OhmyGodohmyGodohmyGod."

"Shitshitshit."

It feels like years before we are down the twenty-five thousand steps and back on the ground. I phone my parents as Finch tears out of the parking lot. "Mom? It's me." At the other end of the line she bursts into tears, and then my dad is on, saying, "Are you okay? Are you safe?"

"Yes, yes. I'm sorry. I'm coming. I'm almost there."

Finch breaks speed records to get me home, but he doesn't say a word to me, maybe because he's concentrating so hard on the driving. I don't say anything either until we turn the corner onto my street. It hits me all over again, this thing I've done. "Oh my God," I say into my hands. Finch jerks to a stop and we are out of the car and rushing up the walk. The door to the house is standing open, and I can hear voices inside, rising and falling.

"You should go," I tell him. "Let me talk to them."

But at that moment my dad appears, and he looks like he's aged twenty years overnight. His eyes run over my face, making sure I'm okay. He pulls me in and hugs me tight, almost strangling the breath out of me. Then he is saying over my head, "Go inside, Violet. Tell Finch good-bye." It sounds final, the way he says it, like *Tell Finch good-bye because you will never see him again.*

Behind me, I hear Finch: "We lost track of time. It's not Violet's fault, it's mine. Please don't blame her."

My mom is there now, and I say to my dad, "It's not his fault."

But my dad isn't listening. He's still looking over my head at Finch. "I'd get out of here if I were you, son." When Finch doesn't move, my father pushes forward a little, and I have to block him.

"James!" My mom tugs at my dad's arm so he can't go through

me and after Finch, and then we are pushing my dad into the house, and now my mom is the one practically strangling me as she hugs me too tightly and cries into my hair. I can't see anything because once again I'm being smothered, and eventually I hear Finch drive away.

Inside, after my parents and I have all (somewhat) calmed down, I sit facing them. My dad does most of the talking as my mom stares at the floor, her hands resting limply on her knees.

"The boy is troubled, Violet. The boy is unpredictable. He's dealt with anger issues since he was little. This is not the kind of person you need to be spending time with."

"How did you—" But then I remember the numbers Finch gave him, written so neatly, so carefully. "Did you call his mother?"

My mom says, "What were we supposed to do?"

My dad shakes his head. "He lied to us about his father. The parents divorced last year. Finch sees him once a week."

I am trying to remember what Finch said about lies not being lies if they feel true. My mother says, "She called his father."

"Who called—"

"Mrs. Finch. She said he would know what to do, that maybe he would know where Finch was."

My brain is trying to keep up with everything, to put out fires, to think of ways to tell my parents that Finch is not this lying, deceitful boy they seem to think he is. That *that* in itself is a lie. But then my dad says, "Why didn't you tell us he was the one in the bell tower?"

"How did— Did his dad tell you that too?" Maybe I don't have a right to, but my face is going hot and my palms are burning the way they do when I get angry.

"When you weren't home by one a.m. and you didn't answer your phone, we called Amanda to see if you were at her house, or if she'd seen you. She said you were probably with Finch, the boy whose life you saved."

Mom's face is wet, her eyes red. "Violet, we're not trying to be the bad guys here. We're just trying to do what's best."

Best for who, I want to say.

"You don't trust me."

"You know better than that." She looks hurt and also angry. "We think we've been pretty damn cool, all things considered. But you need to take a minute to understand where we're coming from. We're not being overprotective and we're not trying to suffocate you. We're trying to make sure you're okay."

"And that nothing happens to me like it did to Eleanor. Why don't you just keep me locked up in the house forever so you never have to worry again?"

Mom shakes her head at me. My father repeats, "No more seeing him. No more of this driving around. I'll speak to your teacher on Monday if I need to. You can write a report or do something else to make up for the work. Are we understood?"

"Extenuating circumstances." Here I am again.

"Excuse me?"

"Yes. We're understood."

From my bedroom window I watch the street outside, as if Finch might reappear. If he does, I will climb out of my window and tell

him to drive, just drive, as fast and far as he can. I sit there a long time
and he doesn't come. My parents' voices rumble from the first floor,
and I know that they will never trust me again.

FINCH

What follows

I see his SUV before I see him. I almost drive on past my house and just keep going who knows where, but something makes me stop the car and walk on in.

"I'm here," I yell. "Come and get me."

My dad barrels out of the living room like a battering ram, Mom and Rosemarie fluttering behind him. My mom is apologizing to me or to him, it's hard to tell. "What was I supposed to do? . . . The phone rings at two a.m., there must be some emergency. . . . Kate wasn't home. . . . I didn't have a choice. . . ."

My father doesn't say a word to me, just sends me flying across the kitchen and into the door. I stand up, shake it off, and the next time he raises his arm, I laugh. This throws him so much that the arm stops in midair, and I can see him thinking, *He's crazier than I thought he was.*

I say, "Here's the thing. You can spend the next five hours or five days beating me to dust, but I don't feel it. Not anymore." I let him try to get in one last whack, but as his hand moves toward me, I grab it by the wrist. "Just so you know, you will never do that again."

I don't expect it to work, but there must be something in my voice, because he suddenly drops his arm. I say to Mom, "Sorry we worried everyone. Violet's home and she's safe, and I'm going to my room."

I wait for my father to come after me. Instead of locking the door and pushing the dresser in front of it, I leave it open. I wait for my mother to check on me. But no one comes because, in the end, this is my house, which means you don't go out of your way to engage.

I write Violet an apology. **I hope you're okay. I hope they're not too hard on you. I wish that hadn't happened, but I don't regret anything that came before.**

She writes back: **I'm okay. Are you okay? Did you see your dad? I don't regret it either, even though I wish we could go back and get me home on time. My parents don't want me seeing you anymore.**

I write: **We'll just have to convince them to change their minds. By the way? For what it's worth, you showed me something, Ultraviolet— there is such a thing as a perfect day.**

The next morning I'm at Violet's, ringing the bell. Mrs. Markey an-swers, but instead of letting me in, she stands in the doorway, the door pulled close around her. She smiles apologetically. "I'm sorry, Theodore." She shakes her head, and that one gesture says it all. *I'm sorry that you will never be allowed near our daughter again because you are different and strange and a person who cannot be trusted.*

I can hear Mr. Markey from inside. "Is that him?"

She doesn't answer. Instead, her eyes run over my face, as if she's been told to check for bruises or maybe something deeper and even more broken. It's a kind gesture, but something about it makes me feel like I'm not really there. "Are you all right?"

"Sure. I'm fine. Nothing to see here. I'd be even better, though, if I could talk to you and explain and say I'm sorry and see Violet. Just for a couple minutes, nothing more. Maybe if I could just come in . . ." All I need is the chance to sit down with them and talk and tell them it's not as bad as they think, that it'll never happen again, and they weren't wrong to trust me.

Over his wife's shoulder, Mr. Markey frowns at me. "You need to go."

Just like that, they shut the door, and I am on the step, locked out and alone.

At home, I type in **EleanorandViolet.com** and get a message: **Server not found.** I type it again and again, but each time it's the same thing. *She's gone, gone, gone.*

On Facebook, I write: **Are you there?**

Violet: **I'm here.**

Me: **I came to see you.**

Violet: **I know. They're so mad at me.**

Me: **I told you I break things.**

Violet: **This wasn't you—this was us. But it's my fault. I wasn't thinking.**

Me: **I'm lying here wishing I could count us backward to yesterday morning. I want the planets to align again.**

Violet: **Just give them time.**

I write: That's the only thing I don't have. And then I erase it.

FINCH

How to survive quicksand

That night, I move into my walk-in closet, which is warm and cozy, like a cave. I push my hanging clothes to one corner and lay the comforter from my bed on the floor. I set the jug of Mudlavia healing water at the foot and prop Violet's picture against the wall—a shot of her at the Blue Flash—along with the license plate I took from the scene of the accident. Then I turn off the light. I balance my laptop on my knees and stick a cigarette in my mouth unlit because the air's too close in here as it is.

This is Finch Survival Boot Camp. I've been here before and know the drill like the back of my too-large hand. I will stay in here as long as I need to, as long as it takes.

The MythBusters say there is no way to drown in quicksand, but tell that to the young mother who went to Antigua for her father's wedding (to wife number two) and was sucked into the beach as she watched the sunset. Or the teenage boys who were swallowed whole by a man-made quicksand pit on the property of an Illinois businessman.

Apparently, to survive quicksand, you should stay perfectly still. It's only when you panic that you pull yourself under and sink. So maybe if I stay still and follow the Eight Steps to Surviving Quicksand, I'll get through this.

1. *Avoid quicksand.* Okay. Too late. Moving on.
2. *Bring a large stick when going into quicksand territory.* The theory here is that you can use the stick to test the ground in front of you, and even pull yourself out of

it if you sink. The problem with this theory is that you don't always know when you're entering quicksand territory, not until it's too late. But I like the idea of preparedness. I figure I've just left this step and have gone on to:

3. *Drop everything if you find yourself in quicksand.* If you're weighed down by something heavy, you're apt to get pulled to the bottom faster. You need to shed your shoes and anything you're carrying. It's always best to do this when you know ahead of time that you're going to encounter quicksand (see number 2), so, essentially, if you're going anywhere that might even possibly have quicksand, go naked. My removal to the closet is part of the dropping everything.

4. *Relax.* This goes back to the stay-perfectly-still-so-you-don't-sink adage. Additional fact: if you relax, your body's buoyancy will cause you to float. In other words, it's time to be calm and let the Jovian-Plutonian gravitational effect take over.

5. *Breathe deeply.* This goes hand in hand with number 4. The trick, apparently, is to keep as much air in your lungs as possible—the more you breathe, the more you float.

6. *Get on your back.* If you start sinking, you simply fall backward and spread yourself out as far as you can as you try to pull your legs free. Once you're unrooted, you can inch yourself to solid ground and safety.

7. *Take your time.* Wild movements only hurt your cause, so move slowly and carefully until you're free again.

8. *Take frequent breaks.* Climbing out of quicksand can be a long process, so be sure to take breaks when you feel your breath running out or your body beginning to tire. Keep your head high so that you buy yourself more time.

VIOLET
The week after

I go back to school, expecting everyone to know. I walk through the halls and stand at my locker and sit in class and wait for my teachers and classmates to give me a knowing look or say, "Someone's not a virgin anymore." It's actually kind of disappointing when they don't.

The only one who figures it out is Brenda. We sit in the cafeteria picking at the burritos some Indiana kitchen worker has attempted to make, and she asks what I did over the weekend. My mouth is full of burrito, and I am trying to decide whether to swallow it or spit it out, which means I don't answer right away. She says, "Oh my God, you slept with him."

Lara and the three Brianas stop eating. Fifteen or twenty heads turn in our direction because Brenda has a really loud voice when she wants to. "You know he'll never say a word to anyone. I mean, he's a gentleman. Just in case you were wondering." She pops the tab on her soda and drinks half of it down.

Okay, I've been wondering a little. After all, it's my first time but not his. He's Finch and I trust him, but you just never know—guys do talk—and even though the Day Of wasn't slutty, I feel a little slutty, but also kind of grown up.

On our way out of the cafeteria, mostly to change the subject, I tell Brenda about *Germ* and ask if she'd like to be a part of it.

Her eyes go narrow, like she's trying to see if I'm joking or not.

"I'm serious. There's a lot left to figure out, but I know I want *Germ* to be original."

Bren throws back her head and laughs, kind of diabolically. "Okay," she says, catching her breath. "I'm in."

When I see Finch in U.S. Geography, he looks tired, like he hasn't slept at all. I sit beside him, across the room from Amanda and Roamer and Ryan, and afterward he pulls me under the stairwell and kisses me like he's afraid I might disappear. There's something forbidden about the whole thing that makes the electric currents burn stronger, and I want school to be over forever so we don't have to come here at all. I tell myself that we can just take off in Little Bastard and head west or east, north or south, till we've left Indiana far behind. We'll wander the country and then the world, just Theodore Finch and me.

But for now, for the rest of the week, we see each other only at school, kissing under stairwells or in dark corners. In the afternoons we go our separate ways. At night we talk online.

Finch: **Any change?**

Me: **If you mean my parents, no.**

Finch: **What are the odds of them forgiving and forgetting?**

The truth is, the odds aren't very good. But I don't want to say this because he's worried enough, and ever since that night, there's something pulled in about him, as if he's standing behind a curtain.

Me: **They just need time.**

Finch: **I hate to be all Romeo and Juliet about this, but I want to see you alone. As in when we're not surrounded by the entire population of Bartlett High.**

Me: **If you came over here and I sneaked out or sneaked you in, they really would lock me in the house forever.**

We go back and forth for the next hour thinking up wild scenarios for seeing each other, including a faked alien abduction, triggering the citywide tornado alarm, and digging an underground tunnel that would stretch from his side of town to mine.

It's one a.m. when I tell him I have to get some sleep, but I end up lying in bed, eyes open. My brain is awake and racing, the way it used to be before last spring. I turn on my light and sketch out ideas for *Germ*—Ask a Parent, book playlists, monthly soundtracks, lists of places where girls like me can get involved. One of the things I want to create is a Wander section where readers can send in pictures or videos of their favorite grand, small, bizarre, poetic, nothing-ordinary sites.

I email Brenda and send Finch a note, in case he's still awake. And then, even though it's jumping the gun a little, I write to Jordan Gripenwaldt, Shelby Padgett, Ashley Dunston, the three Brianas, and reporter Leticia Lopez, inviting them to contribute. Also

Brenda's friend Lara, and other girls I know who are good writers or artists or have something original to say: *Dear Chameli, Brittany, Rebekah, Emily, Sa'iyda, Priscilla, Annalise . . .* Eleanor and I *were* EleanorandViolet.com, but as far as I'm concerned, the more voices here, the better.

I think about asking Amanda. I write her a letter and leave it in my drafts folder. When I get up the next morning, I delete it.

On Saturday, I eat breakfast with my parents and then I tell them I'm going to ride my bike over to Amanda's house. They don't question me about why I want to hang out with this person I barely like or what we're planning to do or when I'll be back. For some reason, they trust Amanda Monk.

I ride past her house and continue across town to Finch's, and the whole thing is so easy, even though I have this weird stitch in my chest because I just lied to my parents. When I get there, Finch makes me crawl up the fire escape and climb in the window so I don't run into his mom or sisters.

"Do you think they saw?" I brush the dust off my jeans.

"I doubt it. They're not even home." He laughs when I pinch his arm, and then his hands are on my face and he's kissing me, which makes the stitch disappear.

Because his bed is stacked with clothes and books, he drags a comforter out of his closet and we lie on the floor, the blanket wrapped around us. Under the covers, we get naked and heated, and afterward we talk like children, the blanket up over our heads. We lie there whispering, as if someone might hear us, and for the first time

I tell him about *Germ*. "I think this could actually be something, and it's because of you," I say. "When I met you, I was finished with all this. I didn't think it mattered."

"One, you worry about everything being filler, but the words you write will still be here when you're gone. And two, you were finished with a lot of things, but you would have come around whether you met me or not."

For some reason, I don't like the way this sounds, as if a universe could exist in which I wouldn't know Finch. But then we're under the blanket again discussing all the places in the world we want to wander, which somehow turns into all the places in the world we want to Do It.

"We'll take this show on the road," says Finch, tracing lazy circles on my shoulder, down my arm, over to my hip. "We'll wander every state, and after we check them off, we'll go across the ocean and start wandering there. It will be a Wander-a-thon."

"Wander-mania."

"Wander-rama."

Without consulting the computer, we list the places we might go, taking turns. And then for some reason I have that feeling again, as if he's stepped behind a curtain. And then the stitch returns and I can't help thinking of all I'm doing to be here—sneaking around behind my parents' backs, for one, lying to them, for another.

At some point I say, "I should probably go."

He kisses me. "Or you could stay a little longer."

So I do.

VIOLET

Spring break

Noon. NYU campus, New York, New York.

My mom says, "Your father and I are glad to have this time with you, honey. It's good for all of us to get away." She means away from home, but I think, more than that, she means away from Finch.

I'm carrying our wandering notebook so that I can make notes on the buildings and the history and anything interesting that I might want to share with him. My parents are discussing how I can apply for spring admission next year and transfer from whatever school I choose for fall.

I'm more worried about why Finch hasn't answered my last three texts. I wonder if this is the way it will be next year if I come to New York, or wherever I go—me trying to concentrate on college, on life, when all I'm doing is thinking about him. I wonder if he'll come with me, or if our built-in ending is high school.

My mom says, "It'll be here before we know it, and I'm not ready. I don't think I'll ever be ready."

"Don't start crying, Mom. You promised. We've still got lots of time to go, and we don't know where I'm going to end up."

My dad says, "Just an excuse to come see her and spend time in the city." But his eyes go damp too.

Even though they don't say it, I can feel all the expectation and weight surrounding us. It comes from the fact that they didn't get to do this with their older daughter. They never got to take her to college and wish her a good freshman year, be safe, come home and see us, don't forget we're always a phone call away. It's just one more moment they were cheated of, and one more I have to make up for because I'm all that's left.

Before the three of us lose it right there, in the middle of campus, I say, "Dad, what can you tell us about the history of NYU?"

I have my own room at the hotel. It is narrow, with two windows, a dresser, and a giant TV cabinet that looks as if it might fall on you and crush you while you sleep.

The windows are closed tight, but I can still hear the noises of the city, which are so different from the ones I hear in Bartlett—sirens, yelling, music, garbage trucks rattling up and down.

"So, do you have a special boy back home?" my mom's agent asked over dinner.

"No one in particular," I answered her, and my parents exchanged a look of relief and conviction that yes, they did the right thing by chasing Finch away.

The only light in the room is from my laptop. I skim through our notebook, thick with words, and then through our Facebook messages—so many now—and then I write a new one, quoting Virginia Woolf: **"Let us wander whirling to the gilt chairs. . . . Are we not acceptable, moon? Are we not lovely sitting together here . . . ?"**

FINCH

Day 64 of the Awake

On the last Sunday of spring break it snows again, and for an hour or so, everything is white. We spend the morning with Mom. I help Decca in the yard, building a half-snow, half-mud man, and then we walk six blocks to the hill behind my grade school and go sledding. We race each other, and Decca wins every time because it makes her happy.

On the way home she says, "You better not have let me win."

"Never." I throw an arm around her shoulders and she doesn't pull away.

"I don't want to go to Dad's," she says.

"Me neither. But you know deep down it means a lot to him, even though he doesn't show it." This is something my mother has said to me more than once. I don't know that I believe it, but there's a chance Decca might. As tough as she is, she wants to believe in something.

In the afternoon, we head over to my father's house, where we sit inside, scattered around the living room, hockey playing on yet another giant flat screen that has been implanted into the wall.

Dad is alternately shouting at the television and listening to Kate talk about Colorado. Josh Raymond sits at my father's elbow staring at the game and chewing each mouthful forty-five times. I know because I'm so bored, I start counting.

At some point, I get up and go to the bathroom, mainly just to clear my head and text Violet, who comes home today. I sit waiting for her to text me back, flipping the faucets on and off. I wash my hands, wash my face, rummage through the cabinets. I am starting in on the shower rack when my phone buzzes. **Home! Should I sneak over?**

I write: **Not yet. Am currently in hell, but will leave as soon as possible.**

We go back and forth for a little while, and then I set off down the hallway, toward the noise and the people. I pass Josh Raymond's room, and the door is ajar and he's inside. I knock and he squeaks, "Come in."

I go into what must be the largest room for a seven-year-old on the planet. The thing is so cavernous, I wonder if he needs a map, and it's filled with every toy you can imagine, most requiring batteries.

I say, "This is quite a room you have, Josh Raymond." I am trying not to let it bother me because jealousy is a mean, unpleasant feeling that only eats you from the inside, and I do not need to stand here, an almost-eighteen-year-old with a really sexy girlfriend, even if she's not allowed to see me anymore, and worry about the fact that my stepbrother seems to own thousands of Legos.

"It's okay." He is sorting through a chest that contains—believe it or not—more toys, when I see them: two old-fashioned wooden stick horses, one black, one gray, that sit forgotten in a corner. These are my stick horses, the same ones I used to ride for hours when I was younger than Josh Raymond, pretending I was Clint Eastwood from one of the old movies my dad used to watch on our small, non-flat-screen TV. The one, incidentally, we still have and use.

"Those are pretty cool horses," I say. Their names are Midnight and Scout.

He swivels his head around, blinks twice, and says, "They're okay."

"What are their names?"

"They don't have names."

I suddenly want to take the stick horses and march into the living room and whack my father over the head with them. Then I want to take them home with me. I'll pay attention to them every day. I'll ride them all over town.

"Where'd you get them?" I ask.

"My dad got them for me."

I want to say, *Not your dad. My dad. Let's just get this straight right now. You already have a dad somewhere else, and even though mine isn't all that great, he's the only one I've got.*

But then I look at this kid, at the thin face and the thin neck and the scrawny shoulders, and he's seven and small for his age, and I remember what that was like. And I also remember what it was like growing up with my father.

I say, "You know, I had a couple of horses once, not as cool as these here, but they were still pretty tough. I named them Midnight and Scout."

"Midnight and Scout?" He eyes the horses. "Those are good names."

"If you want, you can have them."

"Really?" He is looking up at me with owl eyes.

"Sure."

Josh Raymond finds the toy he's looking for—some sort of robocar—and as we walk out the door, he takes my hand.

Back in the living room, my father smiles his camera-ready *SportsCenter* smile and nods at me like we're buddies. "You should bring your girlfriend over here." He says this like nothing ever happened and he and I are the best of friends.

"That's okay. She's busy on Sundays."

I can imagine the conversation between my father and Mr. Markey.

Your delinquent son has my daughter. At this moment, she is probably lying in a ditch thanks to him.

What did you think would happen? Damn right he's a delinquent, and a criminal, and an emotional wreck, and a major-disappointment-weirdo-fuckup. Be grateful for your daughter, sir, because trust me, you would not want my son. No one does.

I can see Dad searching for something to say. "Well, any day is fine, isn't it, Rosemarie? You just bring her by whenever you can." He's in one of his very best moods, and Rosemarie nods and beams. He slaps his hand against the chair arm. "Bring her over here, and we'll put some steaks on the grill and something with beans and twigs on it for you."

I am attempting not to explode all over the room. I am trying to keep myself very small and very contained. I am counting as fast as I can.

Thankfully, the game comes back on and he's distracted. I sit another few minutes and then I thank Rosemarie for the meal, ask Kate if she can take Decca back to Mom's, and tell everyone else I'll see them at home.

I walk across town to my house, climb inside Little Bastard, and drive. No map, no purpose. I drive for what feels like hours, passing fields of white. I head north and then west and then south and then east, the car pushing ninety. By sunset, I'm on my way back to Bartlett, cutting through the heart of Indianapolis, smoking my fourth American Spirit cigarette in a row. I drive too fast, but it doesn't feel fast enough. I suddenly hate Little Bastard for slowing me down when I need to go, go, go.

The nicotine scrapes at my throat, which is already raw, and I feel like throwing up, so I pull over onto the shoulder and walk around. I bend over, hands on my knees. I wait. When I don't get sick, I look at the road stretched out ahead and start to run. I run like hell, leaving

Little Bastard behind. I run so hard and fast, I feel like my lungs will explode, and then I go harder and faster. I'm daring my lungs and my legs to give out on me. I can't remember if I locked the car, and God I hate my mind when it does that because now I can only think about the car door and that lock, and so I run harder. I don't remember where my jacket is or if I even had one.

It will be all right.

I will be all right.

It won't fall apart.

It will be all right.

It will be okay.

I'm okay. Okay. Okay.

Suddenly I'm surrounded by farms again. At some point, I pass a series of commercial greenhouses and nurseries. They won't be open on Sunday, but I ru... mom-and-pop organization. A two-story white ranoks like a real ... on the back of the property.

The driveway is crowded with trucks and cars, and I can hear the laughter from inside. I wonder what would happen if I just walked in and sat down and made myself at home. I go up to the front door and knock. I am breathing hard, and I should have waited to knock so I could catch my breath, but *No*, I think, *I'm in too much of a hurry*. I knock again, louder this time.

A woman with white hair and the soft, round face of a dumpling answers, still laughing from the conversation she left. She squints at me through the screen, and then opens it because we're in the country and this is Indiana and there is nothing to fear from our neighbors. It's one of the things I like about living here, and I want to hug her for the warm but confused smile she wears as she tries to figure out if she's seen me before.

"Hello there," I say.

"Hello," she says. I can imagine what I must look like, red face, no coat, sweating and panting and gasping for air.

I compose myself as fast as I can. "I'm sorry to disturb you, but I'm on my way home and I just happened to pass your nursery. I know you're closed and you have company, but I wonder if I could pick out a few flowers for my girlfriend. It's kind of an emergency."

Her face wrinkles with concern. "An emergency? Oh dear."

"Maybe that's a strong word, and I'm sorry to alarm you. But winter is here, and I don't know where I'll be by spring. And she's named for a flower, and her father hates me, and I want her to know that I'm thinking of her and that this isn't a season of death but of living."

A man walks up behind her, napkin still tucked into his shirt. "There you are," he says to the woman. "I wondered where you'd gone off to." He nods at me.

She says, "This young man is having an emergency."

I explain myself all over again to him. She looks at him and he looks at me, and then he calls to someone inside, telling them to stir the cider, and out he comes, napkin blowing a little in the cold wind, and I walk beside him, hands in my pockets, as we go to the nursery door and he pulls a janitor's keychain off his belt.

I am talking a mile a minute, thanking him and telling him I'll pay him double, and even offering to send a picture of Violet with the flowers—maybe violets—once I give them to her.

He lays a hand on my shoulder and says, "You don't worry about that, son. I want you to take what you need."

Inside, I breathe in the sweet, living scent of the flowers. I want to stay in here, where it's warm and bright, surrounded by things that are living and not dead. I want to move in with this good-hearted couple and have them call me "son," and Violet can live here too because there's room enough for both of us.

He helps me choose the brightest blooms—not just violets, but daisies and roses and lilies and others I can't remember the names of. Then he and his wife, whose name is Margaret Ann, wrap them in a refrigerated shipping bucket, which will keep the flowers hydrated. I try to pay them, but they wave my money away, and I promise to bring the bucket back as soon as I can.

By the time we're done, their guests have gathered outside to see the boy who must have flowers to give to the girl he loves.

The man, whose name is Henry, drives me back to my car. For some reason, I expect it to take hours, but it only takes a few minutes to reach it. As we circle back around to the other side of the road, where Little Bastard sits looking patient and abandoned, he says, "Six miles. Son, you ran all that way?"

"Yes, sir. I guess I did. I'm sorry to pull you away from dinner."

"That's no worry, young man. No worry at all. Is something wrong with your car?"

"No, sir. It just didn't go fast enough."

He nods as if this makes all the sense in the world, which it probably doesn't, and says, "You tell that girl of yours hello from us. But you drive back home, you hear?"

It's after eleven when I reach her house, and I sit in Little Bastard for a while, the windows rolled down, the engine off, smoking my last cigarette because now that I'm here I don't want to disturb her. The windows of the house are lit up, and I know she is in there with her parents who love her but hate me, and I don't want to intrude.

But then she texts me, as if she knows where I am, and says, **I'm glad to be back. When will I see you?**

I text her: **Come outside.**

She is there in a minute, wearing monkey pajamas and Freud slippers, and a long purple robe, her hair pulled into a ponytail. I come up the walk carrying the refrigerated shipping bucket, and she says, "Finch, what on earth? Why do you smell like smoke?" She looks behind her, afraid they might see.

The night air is freezing, and a few flakes start to fall again. But I feel warm. She says, "You're shivering."

"Am I?" I don't notice because I can't feel anything.

"How long have you been out here?"

"I don't know." And suddenly I can't remember.

"It snowed today. It's snowing again." Her eyes are red. She looks like she's been crying, and this might be because she really hates winter or, more likely, because we're coming up on the anniversary of the accident.

I hold out the bucket and say, "Which is why I wanted you to have these."

"What is it?"

"Open and see."

She sets down the bucket and undoes the latch. For a few seconds, all she does is breathe in the scent of the flowers, and then she turns to me and, without a word, kisses me. When she pulls away, she says, "No more winter at all. Finch, you brought me spring."

For a long time, I sit in the car outside my house, afraid to break the spell. In here, the air is close and Violet is close. I'm wrapped up in the day. I love: the way her eyes spark when we're talking or when she's telling me something she wants me to know, the way she mouths the words to herself when she's reading and concentrating, the way she looks at me as if there's only me, as if she can see past the flesh and bone and bullshit right into the me that's there, the one I don't even see myself.

FINCH

Days 65 and 66

At school, I catch myself staring out the window and I think: *How long was I doing that?* I look around to see if anybody noticed, half expecting them to be staring at me, but no one is looking. This happens in every period, even gym.

In English, I open my book because the teacher is reading, and everyone else is reading along. Even though I hear the words, I forget them as soon as they're said. I hear fragments of things but nothing whole.

Relax.

Breathe deeply.

Count.

After class, I head for the bell tower, not caring who sees me. The door to the stairs opens easily, and I wonder if Violet was here. Once I'm up and out in the fresh air, I open the book again. I read the same passage over and over, thinking maybe if I just get away by myself, I'll be able to focus better, but the second I'm done with one line and move on to the next, I've forgotten the one that came before.

At lunch, I sit with Charlie, surrounded by people but alone. They are talking to me and around me, but I can't hear them. I pretend to be interested in one of my books, but the words dance on the page, and so I tell my face to smile so that no one will see, and I smile and nod and I do a pretty good job of it, until Charlie says, "Man, what is wrong with you? You are seriously bringing me down."

In U.S. Geography, Mr. Black stands at the board and reminds us once again that just because we're seniors and this is our last semester, we do not need to slack off. As he talks, I write, but the same thing happens as when I was trying to read—the words are there one minute, and the next they're gone. Violet sits beside me, and I catch her glancing at my paper, so I cover it up with my hand.

It's hard to describe, but I imagine the way I am at this moment is a lot like getting sucked into a vortex. Everything dark and churning, but slow churning instead of fast, and this great weight pulling you down, like it's attached to your feet even if you can't see it. I think, *This is what it must feel like to be trapped in quicksand.*

Part of the writing is taking stock of everything in my life, like I'm running down a checklist: Amazing girlfriend—check. Decent friends—check. Roof over my head—check. Food in my mouth—check.

I will never be short and probably not bald, if my dad and grandfathers are any indication. On my good days, I can outthink most people. I'm decent on the guitar and I have a better-than-average voice. I can write songs. Ones that will change the world.

Everything seems to be in working order, but I go over the list again and again in case I'm forgetting something, making myself think beyond the big things in case there's something hiding out behind the smaller details. On the big side, my family could be better, but I'm not the only kid who feels that way. At least they haven't thrown me out on the street. School's okay. I could study more, but

I don't really need to. The future is uncertain, but that can be a good thing.

On the smaller side, I like my eyes but hate my nose, but I don't think my nose is what's making me feel this way. My teeth are good. In general, I like my mouth, especially when it's attached to Violet's. My feet are too big, but at least they're not too small. Otherwise I would be falling over all the time. I like my guitar, and my bed and my books, especially the cut-up ones.

I think through everything, but in the end the weight is heavier, as if it's moving up the rest of my body and sucking me down.

The bell rings and I jump, which causes everyone to laugh except Violet, who is watching me carefully. I'm scheduled to see Embryo now, and I'm afraid he'll notice something's up. I walk Violet to class and hold her hand and kiss her and give her the best smile I can find so that she won't watch me that way. And then, because her class is on the opposite side of school from the counseling office and I'm not exactly running to get there, I show up five minutes late to my appointment.

Embryo wants to know what's wrong and why I look like this, and does it have something to do with turning eighteen soon.

It's not that, I tell him. After all, who wouldn't want to be eighteen? Just ask my mom, who would give anything not to be forty-one.

"Then what is it? What's going on with you, Finch?"

I need to give him something, so I tell him it's my dad, which isn't exactly a lie, more of a half-truth because it's only one part of a much bigger picture. "He doesn't want to be my dad," I say, and Embryo listens so seriously and closely, his thick arms crossed over his thick chest, that I feel bad. So I tell him some more truth. "He wasn't happy with the family he had, so he decided to trade us in for a new one he liked better. And he does like this one better. His new wife is pleasant and always smiling, and his new son who may or may not actually be related to him is small and easy and doesn't take up much space. Hell, I like them better myself."

I think I've said too much, but instead of telling me to man up and walk it off, Embryo says, "I thought your father died in a hunting accident."

For a second, I can't remember what he's talking about. Then, too late, I start nodding. "That's right. He did. I meant before he died."

He is frowning at me, but instead of calling me a liar, he says, "I'm sorry you've had to deal with this in your life."

I want to bawl, but I tell myself: *Disguise the pain. Don't call attention. Don't be noticed.* So with every last ounce of energy—energy that will cost me a week, maybe more—I say, "He does the best he can. I mean he did. When he was alive. The best sucks, but at the end of the day, it's got more to do with him than me. And I mean, let's face it, who couldn't love me?"

As I sit across from him, telling my face to smile, my mind recites the suicide note of Vladimir Mayakovski, poet of the Russian Revolution, who shot himself at the age of thirty-six:

My beloved boat
is broken on the rocks of daily life.
I've paid my debts
and no longer need to count

> *pains I've suffered at the hands of others.*
> *The misfortunes*
> *and the insults.*
> *Good luck to those who remain.*

And suddenly Embryo is hunched over his desk staring at me with what could only be called alarm. Which means I must have said this out loud without meaning to.

His voice takes on the slow, deliberate tone of a man talking someone off a ledge. "Were you in the bell tower again today?"

"Jesus, do you guys have, like, security cameras up there?"

"Answer me."

"Yes, sir. But I was reading. Or trying to. I needed to clear my mind, and I couldn't do it down below with all the noise."

"Finch, I hope you know I'm your friend, and that means I want to help you. But this is also a legal matter, and I have an obligation."

"I'm fine. Believe me, if I decide to kill myself, you'll be the first to know. I'll save you a front-row seat, or at least wait till you've got more money for the lawsuit."

Note to self: Suicide is not a laughing matter, particularly for authority figures who are in any way responsible for you.

I rein myself in. "Sorry. Bad taste. But I'm fine. Really."

"What do you know about bipolar disorder?"

I almost say, *What do you know about it?* But I make myself breathe and smile. "Is that the Jekyll-Hyde thing?" My voice sounds flat and even. Maybe a little bored, even though my mind and body are on alert.

"Some people call it manic depression. It's a brain disorder that causes extreme shifts in mood and energy. It runs in families, but it can be treated."

I continue to breathe, even if I'm not smiling anymore, but here is what is happening: my brain and my heart are pounding out different rhythms; my hands are turning cold and the back of my neck is turning hot; my throat has gone completely dry. The thing I know about bipolar disorder is that it's a label. One you give crazy people. I know this because I've taken junior-year psychology and I've seen movies and I've watched my father in action for almost eighteen years, even though you could never slap a label on him because he would kill you. Labels like "bipolar" say *This is why you are the way you are. This is who you are.* They explain people away as illnesses.

Embryo is talking about symptoms and hypomania and psychotic episodes when the bell rings. I stand more abruptly than I mean to, which sends my chair clattering into the wall and onto the floor. If I'm suspended above the room, looking down, I can see how this would be mistaken for a violent act, especially as large as I am. Before I can tell him it was an accident, he is on his feet.

I hold up my hands in a gesture of surrender, and then hold out my hand—an olive branch. It takes him a good minute or two, but he shakes it. Instead of letting go, he jerks my arm forward so we are almost nose to nose—or, given our height difference, nose to chin—and says, "You are not alone." Before I can tell him, *Actually I am, which is part of the problem; we are all alone, trapped in these bodies and our own minds, and whatever company we have in this life is only fleeting and superficial,* he tightens his grip until I worry my arm will snap off. "And we are not done discussing this."

The next morning, after gym, Roamer walks by and says, "Freak," under his breath. There are still a lot of guys milling around, but I don't care. To be more accurate, I don't think. It just happens.

In a flash, I have him up against the locker, my hands around his throat, and I'm choking him until he turns purple. Charlie is behind me, trying to pull me off, and then Kappel is there with his bat. I keep going, because now I'm fascinated by the way Roamer's veins are throbbing, and the way his head looks like a lightbulb, all lit up and too bright.

It takes four of them to get me off him because my fist is like iron. I'm thinking: *You put me here. You did this. It's your fault, your fault, your fault.*

Roamer drops to the floor, and as I'm being dragged away, I lock eyes with him and say, "You will never call me that again."

VIOLET
March 10

My phone buzzes after third period, and it's Finch. He tells me he's waiting outside, near the river. He wants to drive down south to Evansville to see the Nest Houses, which are these huts woven out of saplings that were created by an Indiana artist. They're literally like birds' nests for humans, with windows and doors. Finch wants to see if there's anything left of them. While we're down there, we can cross the Kentucky border and take pictures of ourselves, one foot in Kentucky, one in Indiana.

I say, "Doesn't the Ohio River run the entire border? So we'd have to stand on a bridge—"

But he keeps right on like he doesn't hear me. "As a matter of fact, we should do this with Illinois, Michigan, and Ohio."

"Why aren't you on your way to class?" I'm wearing one of his flowers in my hair.

"I got expelled. Just come out here."

"Expelled?"

"Let's go. I'm wasting gas and daylight."

"It's four hours to Evansville, Finch. By the time we get there, it'll be dark."

"Not if we leave now. Come on, come on, get on out here. We can sleep there." He is talking too fast, as if everything depends on us looking at nest houses. When I ask him what happened, he just says he'll tell me later, but he needs to go now, as soon as possible.

"It's a Tuesday in winter. We're not sleeping in a nest house. We can go Saturday. If you wait for me after school, we can go somewhere a little closer than the Indiana-Kentucky border."

"You know what? Why don't we just forget it? Why don't I go by myself? I think I'd rather go alone anyway." Through the phone, his voice sounds hollow, and then he hangs up on me.

I'm still staring at the phone when Ryan walks past with Suze Haines, hand in hand. "Everything okay?" he says.

"Everything's fine," I answer, wondering what on earth just happened.

FINCH

The Nest Houses aren't there. It's dark by the time I stop in downtown New Harmony, with its brightly painted buildings, and ask everyone I can find about where the houses have gone. Most people haven't heard of them, but one old man tells me, "Sorry you came all this way. I'm afraid they been ate up by weather and the elements."

Just like all of us. The Nest Houses have reached their life expectancy. I think of the mud nest we made for the cardinal, all those years ago, and wonder if it's still there. I imagine his little bones in his little grave, and it is the saddest thought in the world.

***

At home, everyone is asleep. I go upstairs, and for a long time I look at myself in the bathroom mirror, and I actually disappear before my eyes.

I am disappearing. Maybe I'm already gone.

Instead of feeling panicked, I am fascinated, as if I'm a monkey in a lab. What makes the monkey turn invisible? And if you can't see him, can you still touch him if you wave your hand around in the place where he used to be? I lay my hand on my chest, over my heart, and I can feel the flesh and bone and the hard, erratic beating of the organ that is keeping me alive.

I walk into my closet and shut the door. Inside, I try not to take up too much space or make any noise, because if I do, I may wake up the darkness, and I want the darkness to sleep. I'm careful when I breathe so as not to breathe too loudly. If I breathe too loudly, there's no telling what the darkness will do to me or to Violet or to anyone I love.

The next morning I check messages on our home voicemail, the landline my mom and sisters and I share. There is one from Embryo for my mother, left yesterday afternoon. "Mrs. Finch, this is Robert Embry from Bartlett High. As you know, I've been counseling your son. I need to talk to you about Theodore. I'm afraid it's extremely important. Please call me back." He leaves the number.

I play the message two more times and then delete it.

Instead of going to school, I go back upstairs and into my closet, because if I leave, I will die. And then I remember that I've been expelled, so it's not as if I can go to school anyway.

The best thing about the closet: no wide-open space. I sit very quietly and very still and am careful how I breathe.

A string of thoughts runs through my head like a song I can't get rid of, over and over in the same order: *I am broken. I am a fraud. I am impossible to love.* It's only a matter of time until Violet figures it out. *You warned her. What does she want from you? You told her how it was.*

Bipolar disorder, my mind says, labeling itself. *Bipolar, bipolar, bipolar.*

And then it starts all over again: *I am broken. I am a fraud. I am impossible to love. . . .*

I am quiet at dinner, but after *Tell me what you learned today, Decca,
Tell me what you learned today, Theodore,* my mother and Decca are
quiet too. No one notices that I am busy thinking. We eat in silence,
and afterward, I find the sleeping pills in my mom's medicine cabinet. I take the whole bottle back to my room and drop half the contents down my throat and then, in the bathroom, bend over the sink,
washing them down. *Let's see what Cesare Pavese felt. Let's see if there's
any valiant acclamation to this.* I stretch out on the floor of my closet,
the bottle in my hand. I try to imagine my body shutting down, little
by little, going totally numb. I almost feel the heaviness coming over
me, even though I know it's too fast.

I can barely lift my head, and my feet seem miles away. *Stay here,*
the pills say. *Don't move. Let us do our work.*

It's this haze of blackness that settles over me, like a fog, only darker. My body is pressed down by the black and the fog, into the floor. There's no acclamation here. This is what it feels like to be asleep.

I force myself up and drag myself into the bathroom, where I stick my finger down my throat and throw up. Nothing much comes out, even though I just ate. I try again and again, and then I pull on my sneakers and run. My limbs are heavy, and I am running through quicksand, but I am breathing and determined.

I run my regular nighttime route, down National Road all the way to the hospital, but instead of passing it, I run across the parking lot. I push my limbs through the doors of the emergency room and say to the first person I see, "I swallowed pills and can't get them out of me. Get them out of me."

She lays a hand on my arm and says something to a man behind me. Her voice is cool and calm, as if she is used to people running in wanting their stomachs pumped, and then a man and another woman are leading me to a room.

I go black then, but I wake up sometime later and I feel empty but awake, and a woman comes in and, as if she reads my mind, says, "You're awake, good. We're going to need you to fill out some paperwork. We checked you for ID, but you didn't have any on you." She hands me a clipboard, and my hand is shaking as I take it from her.

The form is blank except for my name and age. *Josh Raymond, age 17.* I start to shake harder, and then I realize I'm laughing. Good one, Finch. You're not dead yet.

Fact: Most suicides occur between the hours of noon and six p.m.

Guys with tattoos are more likely to kill themselves with guns.

People with brown eyes are more likely to choose hanging or poison.

Coffee drinkers are less likely to commit suicide than non–coffee drinkers.

I wait till the nurse is gone and then put on my clothes and stroll out of the room and down the stairs and out the door. No need to stick around here anymore. The next thing they'll do is send someone in to look at me and ask me questions. Somehow they'll find my parents, but if they don't, they'll bring out a stack of forms and calls will be made, and before you know it, I won't be allowed to leave. They almost get me, but I'm too quick for them.

I'm too weak to run, so I walk all the way home.

FINCH

Life Is Life meets on the grounds of the arboretum in a nearby Ohio town, which shall remain nameless. This isn't a nature class, but a support group for teens who are thinking about, or have attempted, or have survived, suicide. I found it on the internet.

I get into Little Bastard and drive to Ohio. I am tired. I am avoiding seeing Violet. It's exhausting trying to even myself out and be careful around her, so careful, like I'm picking my way through a minefield, enemy soldiers on every side. *Must not let her see.* I've told her I've come down with some sort of bug and don't want to get her sick.

The Life Is Life meeting takes place in a large room with wood paneling and radiators that jut out from the walls. We sit around two long tables pushed together, as if we're going to be doing homework or taking tests. Two pitchers of water sit at either end, with brightly colored Dixie cups stacked up beside them. There are four plates of cookies.

The counselor is a guy named Demetrius, who is this very pale black guy with green eyes. For those of us who haven't been here before, he tells us he's getting his doctorate at the local college, and Life Is Life is in its twelfth year, even though he's only been running it for the past eleven months. I want to ask what happened to the last counselor, but don't in case it's not a pretty story.

The kids file in, and they look just like the ones we have in Bartlett. I don't recognize any of them, which is why I drove twenty-five miles to get here. Before I take my seat, one of the girls sidles up to me and says, "You are really tall."

"I'm older than I look."

She smiles in what she probably thinks is a seductive way, and I add, "Gigantism runs in my family. After high school, I'm required to join the circus because by the time I'm twenty the doctors predict I'll be over seven feet."

I want her to go away because I'm not here to make friends, and then she does. I sit and wait and wish I hadn't come. Everyone is helping themselves to the cookies, which I don't touch because I know each of those brands may or may not contain something disgusting called bone char, which is from the bones of animals, and then I can't even look at the cookies or at the people eating them. I stare out the window, but the trees of the arboretum are thin and brown and dead, and so I keep my eyes on Demetrius, who sits in the middle where we can all see him.

He recites facts I already know about suicide and teenagers, and then we go around the room and say our names and how old we are and the thing we've been diagnosed with and if we've had any firsthand experience trying to kill ourselves. Then we say the phrase "_____ is life," as in whatever strikes us in that moment as something to celebrate, like "Basketball is life," "School is life," "Friends are life," "Making out with my girlfriend is life." Anything that reminds us how good it is to be alive.

A number of these kids have the slightly dull, vacant look of people on drugs, and I wonder what they're taking to keep them here and breathing. One girl says, "*Vampire Diaries* is life," and a couple of the other girls giggle. Another says, "My dog is life even when she's eating my shoes."

When it's my turn, I introduce myself as Josh Raymond, seventeen, no previous experience beyond my recent halfhearted experiment with sleeping pills. "The Jovian-Plutonian gravitational effect is life," I add, even though no one knows what this means.

At that moment the door opens and someone runs in, letting the cold air in with her. She is hatted and scarved and mittened up tightly, unwrapping herself like a mummy as she finds her seat. We all turn and Demetrius smiles a comforting smile. "Come in, no worries, we're just getting started."

The mummy sits down, losing the scarf, mittens, and hat. She turns away from me, blond ponytail swinging, as she hooks her purse strap over her chair. She settles back, smoothing the loose strands of hair off her cheeks, which are pink from the cold, and leaves her coat on. "I'm sorry," Amanda Monk mouths at Demetrius, at the table. When her eyes get around to me, her face goes completely and immediately blank.

Demetrius nods at her. "Rachel, why don't you go ahead?"

Amanda, as Rachel, avoids looking at me. In a wooden voice, she recites, "I'm Rachel, I'm seventeen, I'm bulimic, and I tried to kill myself twice, both times with pills. I hide myself away with smiles and gossip. I am not happy at all. My mother is making me come here. Secrecy is life." She says this last line to me and then looks away.

The others take their turns, and by the time we get all the way around, it's clear I am the only one here who hasn't tried to really and truly kill himself. It makes me feel superior, even though it shouldn't, and I can't help thinking, *When I actually try, I'm not going to miss.* Even Demetrius has a story. These people are here and trying to get help and they're alive, after all.

But the whole thing is heartbreaking. Between thoughts of bone char, and stories of wrist cutting and hangings, and bitchy Amanda Monk with her little pointed chin jutted out, so exposed and scared, I want to put my head on the table and let the Long Drop just come. I want to get away from these kids who never did anything to anyone except be born with different brains and different wiring, and from the people who aren't here to eat these bone char cookies and share their tales, and the ones who didn't make it and never had a chance. I want to get away from the stigma they all clearly feel just because they have an illness of the mind as opposed to, say, an illness of the lungs or blood. I want to get away from all the labels. *"I'm OCD," "I'm depressed," "I'm a cutter,"* they say, like these are the things that define them. One poor bastard is ADHD, OCD, BPD, bipolar, and on top of it all has some sort of anxiety disorder. I don't even know what BPD stands for. I'm the only one who is just Theodore Finch.

A girl with a fat black braid and glasses says, "My sister died of leukemia, and you should have seen the flowers and the sympathy." She holds up her wrists, and even across the table I can see the scars. "But when I nearly died, no flowers were sent, no casseroles were baked. I was selfish and crazy for wasting my life when my sister had hers taken away."

This makes me think of Eleanor Markey, and then Demetrius talks about medicines that are out there and helpful, and everyone volunteers the names of the drugs that are helping them get through. A boy at the other end of the table says the only thing he hates is feeling like everyone else. "Don't get me wrong—I'd rather be here than dead—but sometimes I feel that everything that, like, makes me up has gone away."

I stop listening after that.

When it's over, Demetrius asks me what I thought, and I tell him it was eye-opening and enlightening and other things along those lines to make him feel good about the work he is doing, and then I chase down Amanda, as Rachel, in the parking lot before she can run away. "I'm not going to say anything to anyone."

"You better not. I'm so serious." Her eyes are wild, her face flushed.

"If I do, you can just tell them I'm a freak. They'll believe you. They'll think I'm just making shit up. Besides, I was expelled, re-member?" She looks away. "So do you still think about it?"

"If I didn't, I wouldn't be here." She looks up. "What about you? Were you really going to jump off the bell tower before Violet talked you down?"

"Yes and no."

"Why do you do that? Don't you get tired of people talking about you?"

"Including you?"

She goes quiet.

"I do it because it reminds me to be here, that I'm still here and I have a say in the matter."

She puts one leg in the car and says, "I guess now you know you're not the only freak." It's the nicest thing she's ever said to me.

VIOLET

March 18

I don't hear from Finch for a day, then two days, then three days. By the time I get home from school on Wednesday, it's snowing. The roads are white, and I've wiped out a half dozen times on Leroy. I find my mom in her office and ask if I can borrow her car.

It takes her a moment to find her voice. "Where are you going?"

"To Shelby's house." Shelby Padgett lives on the other side of town. I'm amazed at how easily the words come out of my mouth. I act like the fact that I'm asking if I can drive her car, when I haven't driven in a year, is no big deal, but my mom is staring at me. She continues to stare as she hands me her keys and follows me to the door and down the sidewalk. And then I can see that she's not just staring, she's crying.

"I'm sorry," she says, wiping at her eyes. "We just weren't sure . . . we didn't know if we'd ever see you drive again. The accident changed a lot of things and it took a lot of things. Not that driving, in the great scheme of life, is so important, but you shouldn't have to think twice about it at your age, except to be careful. . . ."

She's kind of babbling, but she looks happy, which only makes me feel worse about lying to her. I hug her before climbing in behind the wheel. I wave and smile and start the engine and say out loud, "Okay." I pull away slowly, still waving and smiling but wondering what in the hell I think I'm doing.

I'm shaky at first because it's been so long and I wasn't sure I'd ever drive again either. I jerk myself black and blue because I keep hitting the brakes. But then I think of Eleanor beside me, letting me drive home after I got my license. *You can drive me everywhere now, little sister. You'll be my chauffeur. I'll sit in the back, put my feet up, and just enjoy the view.*

I look over at the passenger seat and I can almost see her, smiling at me, not even glancing at the road, as if she doesn't need to look because she trusts me to know what I'm doing without her help. I can see her leaning back against the door, knees under her chin, laughing at something, or singing along with the music. I can almost hear her.

By the time I get to Finch's neighborhood, I'm cruising along smoothly, like someone who's been driving for years. A woman answers the door, and this must be his mother because her eyes are the same bright-sky blue as Finch's. It's strange to think, after all this time, I'm only meeting her now.

I hold out my hand and say, "I'm Violet. It's nice to meet you. I've come to see Finch." It occurs to me that maybe she's never heard of me, so I add, "Violet Markey."

She shakes my hand and says, "Of course. Violet. Yes. He should be home from school by now." *She doesn't know he's been expelled.* She is wearing a suit, but she's in her stocking feet. There's a kind of faded, weary prettiness to her. "Come on in. I'm just getting home myself."

I follow her into the kitchen. Her purse sits on the breakfast table next to a set of car keys, and her shoes are on the floor. I hear a television from the other room, and Mrs. Finch calls, "Decca?"

In a moment I hear a distant "What?"

"Just checking." Mrs. Finch smiles at me and offers me something to drink—water, juice, soda—as she pours herself a glass of wine from a corked bottle in the fridge. I tell her water's fine, and she asks ice or no ice, and I say no ice, even though I like it better cold.

Kate walks in and waves hello. "Hey."

"Hey. I came to see Finch."

They chat with me like everything is normal, like he hasn't been expelled, and Kate pulls something out of the freezer and sets the temperature on the oven. She tells her mother to remember to listen for the buzzer and then tugs on her coat. "He's probably upstairs. You can go on up."

I knock on the door to his room, but don't get any answer. I knock again. "Finch? It's me."

I hear a shuffling, and the door opens. Finch wears pajama bottoms but no shirt, and glasses. His hair spikes up in all directions, and I think, *Nerd Finch.* He gives me a lopsided grin and says, "The only person I want to see. My Jovian-Plutonian gravitational effect." He moves out of the way so I can come in.

The room has been stripped bare, down to the sheets on the bed. It looks like a vacant blue hospital room, waiting to be made up for the next patient. Two medium-sized brown boxes are stacked by the door.

My heart does this weird little flip. "It almost looks like—are you moving?"

"No, I just cleared some things out. Giving a few things to Goodwill."

"Are you feeling okay?" I try not to sound like the blaming girlfriend. *Why won't you spend time with me? Why won't you call me back? Don't you like me anymore?*

"Sorry, Ultraviolet. I'm still feeling kind of under the weather.

Which, when you think about it, is a very odd expression. One that finds its origins in the sea—as in a sailor or passenger feels seasick from the storm, and they send him below to get out of the bad weather."

"But you're better now?"

"It was touch-and-go for a while, but yeah." He grins and pulls on a shirt. "Want to see my fort?"

"Is that a trick question?"

"Every man needs a fort, Ultraviolet. A place to let his imagination run wild. A 'No Trespassing/No Girls Allowed' type of space."

"If no girls are allowed, why are you letting me see it?"

"Because you're not just any girl."

He opens the door to his closet, and it actually looks pretty cool. He's made a kind of cave for himself, complete with guitar and computer and notebooks of staff paper, along with pens and stacks of Post-its. My picture is tacked to the blue wall along with a license plate.

"Other people might call it an office, but I like fort better."

He offers me a seat on the blue comforter and we sit side by side, shoulder to shoulder, backs against the wall. He nods at the opposite wall, and that's when I see the pieces of paper there, kind of like his Wall of Ideas, but not as many or as cluttered.

"So I've discovered I think better in here. It gets loud out there sometimes between Decca's music and my mom yelling at my dad over the phone. You're lucky you live in a house of no yelling." He writes down *House of no yelling* and sticks it onto the wall. Then he hands me a pen and a pad of Post-its. "Want to try?"

"Just anything?"

"Anything. Positive ones go on the wall, negative on the floor over there." He points to this heap of ripped-up paper. "It's important to get those down, but they don't need to hang around after you do. Words can be bullies. Remember Paula Cleary?" I shake my head. "She was fifteen when she moved to the States from Ireland and started dating some idiot guy the other girls loved. They called her 'slut' and 'whore' and worse and wouldn't let her alone until she hanged herself in a stairwell."

I write *Bully* and hand it to Finch, who rips it into a hundred pieces and throws it on the heap. I write *Mean girls* and then shred it to bits. I write *Accidents, Winter, Ice,* and *Bridge,* and tear at the paper until it's only dust.

Finch scribbles something and slaps it to the wall. *Welcome.* He scribbles something else. *Freak.* He shows it to me before destroying it. He writes *Belong,* which goes on the wall, and *Label,* which doesn't. *Warmth, Saturday, Wander, You, Best friend* go up, while *Cold, Sunday, Stand still, Everyone else* go into the heap.

Necessary, Loved, Understood, Forgiven are on the wall now, and then I write *You, Finch, Theodore, Theo, Theodore Finch,* and post them up.

We do this for a long time, and then he shows me how he makes a song out of the words. First he rearranges them into a kind of order that almost makes sense. He grabs the guitar and strums out a tune and, just like that, starts singing. He manages to get every word in, and afterward I clap and he bows with the top half of his body since he's still sitting on the floor, and I say, "You have to write it down. Don't lose it."

"I don't ever write songs down."

"What's all that staff paper there?"

"Ideas for songs. Random notes. Things that'll become songs. Things I might write about someday, or started once but didn't finish because there wasn't enough in them. If a song's meant to stay around, you carry it with you in your bones."

He writes *I, want, to, have, sex, with, Ultraviolet, Remarkey-able*.

I write *Maybe*, which he immediately rips up.

And then I write *Okay*.

He rips this up too.

Yes!

He slaps this onto the wall and then kisses me, his arm circling my waist. Before I know it, I'm on my back and he's looking down at me, and I am pulling off his shirt. Then his skin is on mine, and I'm on top of him, and for a while I forget we're on the floor of a closet because all I can think of is him, us, him and me, Finch and Violet, Violet and Finch, and everything is okay again.

Afterward, I stare up at the ceiling, and when I look over at him, there is this strange look on his face. "Finch?" His eyes are fixed on something above us. I poke him in the ribs. "Finch!"

Finally his eyes turn to mine and he says, "Hey," like he just remembered that I'm there. He sits up and rubs his face with his hands, and then he reaches for the Post-its. He writes *Relax*. Then *Breathe deeply*. Then *Violet is life*.

He fixes them to the wall and reaches for the guitar again. I rest my head against his as he plays, changing the chords a little, but I can't shake this feeling that something happened, like he went away for a minute and only part of him came back.

"Don't tell anyone about my fort, okay, Ultraviolet?"

"Like not telling your family you got expelled?"

He writes *Guilty* and holds it up before ripping it into pieces.

"Okay." Then I write *Trust, Promise, Secret, Safe,* and place them on the wall.

"Ahhhhh, and now I have to start over." He closes his eyes, then plays the song again, adding in the words. It sounds sad the second time, as if he shifted to a minor key.

"I like your secret fort, Theodore Finch." This time I rest my head on his shoulder, looking at the words we've written and the song we've created, and then at the license plate again. I feel this strange need to move closer to him, as if he might get away from me. I lay one hand on his leg.

In a minute he says, "I get into these moods sometimes, and I can't shake them." He's still strumming the guitar, still smiling, but his voice has gone serious. "Kind of black, sinking moods. I imagine it's what being in the eye of a tornado would be like, all calm and blinding at the same time. I hate them."

I lace my fingers through his so that he has to stop playing. "I get moody too. It's normal. It's what we're supposed to do. I mean, we're teenagers." Just to prove it, I write *Bad mood* before tearing it up.

"When I was a kid, younger than Decca, there was this cardinal in our backyard that kept flying into the sliding glass doors of our house, over and over again until he knocked himself out. Each time, I thought he was dead, but then he'd get up again and fly off. This little female cardinal sat and watched him from one of the trees, and I always thought it was his wife. Anyway, I begged my parents to stop him from banging into the glass. I thought he should come inside and live with us. Kate called the Audubon Society, and the man there said if it was his guess, the cardinal was probably just trying to get back to his tree, the one that had been standing there before someone came along and knocked it down and built a house on top of it."

He tells me about the day the cardinal died, about finding the body on the back deck, about burying him in the mud nest. "There was nothing to make him last a long time," Finch told his parents afterward. He said he always blamed them because he knew they could have been the thing that made the cardinal last if they'd only let it in like he'd asked them to.

"That was the first black mood. I don't remember much that happened after that, not for a little while at least."

The worried feeling is back. "Have you ever talked to anyone? Do your parents or Kate—or maybe one of the counselors . . . ?"

"Parents, no. Kate, not really. I've been talking to a counselor at school."

I look around the closet, at the comforter we're sitting on, at the pillows, the water jug, the energy bars, and that's when it hits me. "Finch, are you living in here?"

"I've been in here before. Eventually, it works. I'll wake up one morning and feel like coming out." He smiles at me, and the smile seems hollow. "I kept your secret; you keep mine."

When I get home, I open the door to my closet and walk inside. It's larger than Finch's but packed full of clothes, shoes, purses, jackets. I try to imagine what it would be like to live in here and feel I couldn't come out. I lie down flat and stare up at the ceiling. The floor is hard and cold. In my head, I write: *There was a boy who lived in a closet. . . .* But that's as far as I get.

I'm not claustrophobic, but when I open the door and walk back into my room, I feel like I can breathe again.

At dinner, my mom says, "Did you have a fun time with Shelby?" She raises her eyebrows at my dad. "Violet drove to Shelby's house after school. As in *drove.*"

My dad clinks his glass against mine. "Proud of you, V. Maybe it's time we talk about getting you a car of your own."

They're so excited over this that I feel even guiltier about lying. I wonder what they'd do if I told them where I really was—having sex with the boy they don't want me to see in the closet where he's living.

FINCH

"The cadence of suffering has begun."—Cesare Pavese
  I
  am
  in
  pieces.

VIOLET

March 20

After U.S. Geography, Amanda tells Roamer to go on ahead and she'll catch up. I haven't spoken a word to him since Finch got expelled. "I need to tell you something," she says to me.

"What?" I haven't said much to her either.

"You can't tell anyone."

"Amanda, I'm going to be late for class."

"Promise first."

"Fine, I promise."

She's talking so low I almost can't hear her. "I saw Finch at this group I go to. I've been going a while, even though I don't really need to, but my mom is, like, making me." She sighs.

"What's the group?"

"It's called Life Is Life. It's this—it's a support group for teenagers who've either thought about suicide or tried it."

"And you saw Finch there? When?"

"Sunday. He said he was there because he swallowed a bunch of pills and had to go to the hospital. I thought you should know."

I stay through last period, only because I have a test. Afterward, I grab Leroy and ride directly to Finch's house. He doesn't know I'm coming, and when I get there, no one answers the door. I find some pebbles in the driveway and throw them at his window, and with every *ping ping* against the glass, my heart jumps. Then I sit down on the front step, hoping his mom or his sisters will appear and let me in. I'm still sitting there twenty minutes later, the house as closed up and silent as when I arrived, and finally I head home.

In my room, I don't even bother taking off my coat and scarf. I open my laptop and send Finch a Facebook message. He answers right away, like he's been waiting. **So tomorrow's my birthday. . . .**

I want to ask where he was and was he there the whole time and did he know that I was outside his house. I want to ask about the hospital, but I'm worried if I ask anything he'll go quiet and disappear, so instead I write: **How should we celebrate?**

Finch: **It's a surprise.**

Me: **But it's your birthday, not mine.**

Finch: **Doesn't matter. Come over at six. Be hungry.**

VIOLET

I knock on the door to his room but don't get any answer. I knock again. "Finch?" I knock again and again, and finally I hear a shuffling, a crash as something is dropped, a *goddammit,* and the door opens. Finch is wearing a suit. His hair is cut short, buzzed very close, and between that and the stubble on his jaw, he looks different, older, and, yes, hot.

He gives me a lopsided grin and says, "Ultraviolet. The only person I want to see." He moves out of the way so I can come in.

The room is still hospital bare, and I have a sinking feeling because he's been to the hospital but didn't tell me, and there's something about all that blue that makes me feel suffocated.

I say, "I need to talk to you."

Finch kisses me hello, and his eyes are brighter than the other night, or maybe it's that he isn't wearing glasses. Every time he changes, it takes getting used to. He kisses me again and leans sexily against the door, as if he knows how good he looks.

"First things first. I need to know how you feel about space travel and Chinese food."

"In that order?"

"Not necessarily."

"I think one is interesting and the other is really great to eat."

"Good enough. Shoes off."

I take my shoes off, which drops me an inch or two.

"Clothes off, midget."

I swat at him.

"Later then, but I won't forget. Okay. Please close your eyes."

I close my eyes. In my mind, I'm going over the best way to bring up Life Is Life. But he's so much like himself again, even if he looks different, that I tell myself that when I open my eyes, the walls of his room will be painted red and the furniture will be back where it was and the bed will be made because that's where he sleeps.

I hear the door to the closet open and he leads me forward a few steps. "Keep them closed." Out of instinct, I reach my hands out in front of me, and Finch lowers them to my sides. The Slow Club is playing, a band I like, all plucky and bittersweet and kind of offbeat. *Like Finch*, I think. *Like us.*

He helps me sit, and I'm on what feels like a stack of pillows. I hear him and feel him moving around me as the door closes, and then his knees are pressed to mine. I'm ten years old again, back in my fort-building days.

"Open."

I open.

And I'm in space, everything glowing like the Emerald City. The walls and ceiling are painted with planets and stars. Our Post-its still hang on one wall. The blue comforter is at our feet, so the whole floor glows. Plates and silverware and napkins are stacked next to containers of food. A bottle of vodka sits on ice.

"How did you . . ."

Finch points to the black-light bulb in the ceiling. "If you'll notice," he says, holding a hand up to the skies, "Jupiter and Pluto are perfectly aligned in relation to earth. It's the Jovian-Plutonian gravitational chamber. Where everything floats indefinitely."

The only thing that comes out of my mouth is "Oh my God." I've been so worried about him, this boy I love, more worried than I knew until right this moment, staring up at the solar system. This is the single loveliest thing anyone's ever done for me. It's movie lovely. It feels somehow epic and fragile, and I want the night to last forever, and knowing it can't already has me sad.

The food is from Happy Family. I don't ask how he got it, if he actually drove out there himself or maybe got Kate to pick it up for him, but I tell myself that he was the one who went all that way because he doesn't have to stay in this closet if he doesn't want to.

He opens the vodka and we pass the bottle back and forth. It tastes dry and bitter, like autumn leaves. I like the way it burns my nose and throat on the way down.

"Where did you get this?" I hold up the bottle.

"I have my ways."

"It's perfect. Not just this—all of it. But it's your birthday, not mine. I should be doing something like this for you."

He kisses me.

I kiss him.

The air is full of things we aren't saying, and I wonder if he feels it too. He's being so easy and Finch-like that I tell myself to let it go, don't think so much. Maybe Amanda's wrong. Maybe she only told me about that group to get me upset. Maybe she made the whole thing up.

He fills our plates, and as we eat, we talk about everything except for how he's feeling. I tell him what he's missed in U.S. Geography and talk about the places left to wander. I give him his birthday present, a first edition of *The Waves* I found in a little bookstore in New York. I inscribed it: *You make me feel gold, flowing too. I love you. Ultra-violet Remarkey-able.*

He says, "This is the book I was looking for at Bookmarks, at the Bookmobile Park. Anytime I went into a bookstore."

He kisses me.

I kiss him.

I can feel the worries fading away. I'm relaxed and happy—happier than I've been in a while. I am in the moment. I am here.

After we finish the food, Finch takes off his jacket and we lie side by side on the floor. While he examines his book, and reads sections aloud to me, I stare up at the sky. Eventually, he lays the book on his chest and says, "You remember Sir Patrick Moore."

"The British astronomer with the TV show." I raise my arms toward the ceiling. "The man we have to thank for the Jovian-Plutonian gravitational effect."

"Technically, we have ourselves to thank, but yeah, that's him. So on one of his shows, he explains the concept of a giant black hole in the center of our galaxy. Understand this is a very big deal. He's the first person to explain the existence of a black hole in a way that the average person can understand. I mean, he explains it in a way that even Roamer could get."

He grins at me. I grin at him. He says, "Shit, where was I?"

"Sir Patrick Moore."

"Right. Sir Patrick Moore orders that a map of the Milky Way be drawn on the TV studio floor. With the cameras rolling, he walks toward the center describing Einstein's general theory of relativity and goes into some facts—black holes are the remnants of former stars; they're so dense that not even light can escape; they lurk inside every galaxy; they're the most destructive force in the cosmos; as a black hole passes through space, it engulfs everything that comes too close to it, stars, comets, planets. I mean everything. When planets, light, stars, whatever, pass that point of no return, it's what's called the event horizon—the point after which escape is impossible."

"It sounds kind of like a blue hole."

"Yeah, I guess it does. So as he's explaining all this, Sir Patrick Moore pulls the greatest feat ever—he walks right into the heart of the black hole and disappears."

"Special effects."

"No. It's, like, the damnedest thing. The cameraman and others who were there say he just vanished." He reaches for my hand.

"How then?"

"Magic."

He grins at me.

I grin at him.

He says, "Being sucked into a black hole would pretty much be the coolest way to die. It's not like anyone has firsthand experience, and scientists can't decide if you would spend weeks floating past the event horizon before being torn apart or soar into a kind of maelstrom of particles and be burned alive. I like to think of what it would be like if we were swallowed, just like that. Suddenly none of this would matter. No more worrying about where we're going or what's to become of us or if we'll ever disappoint another person again. All of it—just . . . gone."

"So there's nothing."

"Maybe. Or maybe it's a whole other world, one we can't even imagine."

I feel the way his hand, warm and firm, fits around mine. He may keep changing, but that never does.

I say, "You're the best friend I've ever had, Theodore Finch." And he is, even more so than Eleanor.

Suddenly I'm crying. I feel like an idiot because I hate to cry, but I can't help it. All the worry comes out and just spills all over the floor of his closet.

Finch rolls over and kind of scoops me into him. "Hey now. What gives?"

"Amanda told me."

"Told you what?"

"About the hospital and the pills. About Life Is Life."

He doesn't let go of me but his body goes stiff. "She told you?"

"I'm worried about you, and I want you to be okay, but I don't know what to do for you."

"You don't need to do anything." Then he does let go. He pulls away and sits up, staring at the wall.

"But I have to do something, because you might need help. I don't know anyone who goes into the closet and stays there. You need to talk to your counselor, or maybe Kate. You can talk to my parents if you want."

"Yeah—that's not happening." In the ultraviolet light, his teeth and eyes are glowing.

"I'm trying to help you."

"I don't need help. And I'm not Eleanor. Just because you couldn't save her, don't try to save me."

I'm starting to get mad. "That's not fair."

"I just meant I'm doing okay."

"Are you?" I hold my hands up at the closet.

He looks at me with this hard, awful smile. "Do you know I'd give anything to be you for a day? I'd just live and live and never worry and be grateful for what I have."

"Because I have nothing to worry about?" He just looks at me. "Because what could Violet possibly have to worry about? After all, Eleanor's the one who died. Violet's still here. She was spared. She's lucky because she has her whole life ahead of her. Lucky, lucky Violet."

"Listen, I'm the freak. I'm the weirdo. I'm the troublemaker. I start fights. I let people down. Don't make Finch mad, whatever you do. Oh, there he goes again, in one of his moods. Moody Finch. Angry Finch. Unpredictable Finch. Crazy Finch. But I'm not a compilation of symptoms. Not a casualty of shitty parents and an even shittier chemical makeup. Not a problem. Not a diagnosis. Not an illness. Not something to be rescued. I'm a person." He smiles the awful smile again. "I bet by now you're pretty sorry you picked that particular ledge that particular day."

"Don't do that. Don't be like this."

Like that, the smile is gone. "I can't help it. It's what I am. I warned you this would happen." His voice turns cold instead of angry, which is worse because it's like he's stopped feeling. "You know, right now this closet is feeling pretty tight, like maybe there's not as much room in here as I thought."

I stand. "It just so happens I can help you with that."

And I slam out the door knowing full well he can't follow me, even though I tell myself: *If he really loves you, he'll find a way.*

At home, my parents are in the family room watching TV. "You're home early," Mom says. She gets up from the couch to make room for me.

"There's something you need to know." She sits back down in the exact same spot and my father clicks the television off. I immediately feel bad because before I walked in they were having a peaceful, happy evening, and now they are worried because they can tell by my voice that whatever it is isn't going to be good.

"On the first day of school after Christmas break, I climbed up on the bell tower ledge. That's where I met Finch. He was up there too, but he was the one who talked me down, because once I realized where I was, I was scared and I couldn't move. I might have fallen off if he wasn't there. But I didn't fall off, and that's thanks to him. Well, now he's up on that ledge. Not literally," I say to my dad before he can jump for the phone. "And we need to help him."

Mom says, "So you've been seeing him?"

"Yes. And I'm sorry, and I know you're mad and disappointed, but I love him, and he saved me. You can tell me later how unhappy you are with me and how I've let you down, but right now I need to do what I can to make sure he'll be okay."

I tell them everything, and afterward my mom is on the telephone, calling Finch's mom. She leaves a message, and when she hangs up, she says, "Your dad and I will figure out what to do. There's a psychiatrist at the college, a friend of your father's. He's talking to him now. Yes, we're disappointed in you, but I'm glad you told us. You did the right thing by telling us."

I lie awake in my bedroom for at least an hour, too upset to sleep.
When I do drift off, I toss and turn and my dreams are a twisted,
unhappy jumble. At some point I wake up. I roll over and drift off
again, and in my dreams I hear it—the faint, faraway sound of rocks
hitting the window.

I don't get out of bed, because it's cold and I'm half asleep and
anyway the sound isn't real. *Not now, Finch,* I say in the dream. *Go
away.*

And then I wake up fully and think, *What if he was really here?
What if he actually got out of the closet and drove to see me?* But when I
look out the window, the street is empty.

I spend the day with my parents, obsessively checking Facebook for a new message when I'm not pretending to focus on homework and *Germ*. The contributor replies come in from all the girls—*yes, yes, yes*. They sit in my inbox unanswered.

My mother is on the phone periodically, trying to reach Mrs. Finch. When she hasn't heard from her by noon, Mom and Dad head to Finch's house. No one answers the door and they're forced to leave a note. The psychiatrist has (somewhat) better luck. He is able to talk to Decca. She leaves the doctor on the line while she checks Finch's bedroom and closet, but she says he isn't there. I wonder if he's hiding somewhere. I send him a text, telling him I'm sorry. By midnight, he still hasn't texted back.

On Monday, Ryan finds me in the hall and walks me to Russian literature. "Have you heard from all your colleges yet?" he wants to know.

"Only a couple."

"What about Finch? Do you think you'll wind up at the same place?" He's trying to be nice, but there's something else there—maybe the hope that I'll tell him no, Finch and I broke up.

"I'm not sure what he's going to do. I don't think he knows."

He nods and shifts his books to the other hand so that his free hand is now next to mine. Every now and then I feel the brush of his skin. For each step we take, about five people call out to him or nod a what's-up. Their eyes move past him to me, and I wonder what they see.

Eli Cross is having a party. You should come with me.

I wonder if he remembers that it was his brother's party Eleanor and I were leaving when we had the accident. Then I wonder for a minute what it would be like to be with him again, if a person could ever go back to someone like good, steady Ryan after being with Theodore Finch. No one will ever call Ryan Cross a freak or say mean things about him behind his back. He wears the right clothes and says the right things and is going to the right college after all of this is said and done.

When I get to U.S. Geography, Finch isn't there, of course, because he's been expelled, and I can't concentrate on anything Mr. Black is saying. Charlie and Brenda haven't heard from Finch in a couple of days, but they don't seem worried because this is how he is, this is what he does, this is the way he's always been.

Mr. Black starts calling on us, one by one, down the rows, asking for progress reports on our projects. When he gets to me, I say, "Finch isn't here."

"I know very well . . . he's not here and that he won't . . . be coming back to school. . . . How are you . . . coming along on . . . your work, Miss Markey?"

I think of all the things I could mention: Theodore Finch is living in his closet. I think there's something seriously wrong with him. We haven't been able to wander lately, and we still have four or five places left on our map.

I say, "We're learning a lot about this state of ours. I'd never seen much of Indiana before I started, but now I know it really well."

Mr. Black seems happy with this, and then he's on to the next person. Under my desk, I text Finch: **Please let me know you're okay.**

When I don't hear from him by Tuesday, I ride over to his house. This time a little girl answers the door. She has short, dark hair sliced into a bob and the same blue eyes as Finch and Kate. "You must be Decca," I say, sounding like one of those grown-ups I hate.

"Who are you?"

"Violet. I'm a friend of your brother's. Is he here?" She opens the door wider and steps out of the way.

Upstairs, I pass the wall of Finches and knock but don't wait for an answer. I push the door open and rush in, and right away I can feel it: No one is here. It's not just that the room is bare—it's that there's a strange, dead stillness to the air, as if the room is an empty shell left behind by an animal.

"Finch?" My heart is starting to pound. I knock on the closet door, and then I'm standing in the closet, and he's not there. The comforter is gone, along with his guitar and amp, the notebooks of staff paper, the stacks of blank Post-its, the jug of water, his laptop, the book I gave him, the license plate, and my picture. The words we wrote are on the walls, and the planets and stars he created are there, but they're dead and still and no longer glowing.

I can't do anything but turn around and around, looking for something, anything he might have left to let me know where he's gone. I pull out my phone and call him, but it goes right to voice-mail. "Finch, it's me. I'm in your closet, but you're not here. Please call me back. I'm worried. I'm sorry. I love you. But not sorry I love you because I could never be sorry for that."

In his room I start opening drawers. In his bathroom I open cabinets. He's left some things behind, but I don't know if this means he's coming back or if these are just things he doesn't want anymore.

In the hallway I pass his school pictures, his eyes following me as I run down the stairs so fast I nearly fall. My heart is beating so hard and loud that I can't hear anything except the drumming of it, which fills my ears. In the living room I find Decca staring at the television, and I say, "Is your mom home?"

"Not yet."

"Do you know if she got the messages from my mom?"

"She doesn't check the phone much. Kate probably got them."

"Is Kate here?"

"Not yet. Did you find Theo?"

"No. He's not there."

"He does that sometimes."

"Goes away?"

"He'll be back. He always comes back." *That's just his thing. It's what he does.*

I want to say to her and Charlie and Brenda, to Kate, to his mom: *Doesn't anyone care* why *he comes and goes? Have you ever stopped to think that something might be wrong with this?*

I go into the kitchen, where I check the fridge and center island in case he left a note, because these seem like note-leaving places, and then I open the door to the garage, which is empty. Little Bastard is gone too.

I find Decca again and tell her to let me know if she hears from her brother, and I give her my number. On the street outside I look up and down for his car, but it's not there either.

I pull out my phone. The voicemail picks up again. "Finch, where are you?"

FINCH

Day 80
(a muthaf#@*ing world record)

In his poem "Epilogue," Robert Lowell asked, "Yet why not say what happened?"

To answer your question, Mr. Lowell, I'm not sure. Maybe no one can say. All I know is what I wonder: Which of my feelings are real? Which of the *mes* is me? There is only one me I've ever really liked, and he was good and awake as long as he could be.

I couldn't stop the cardinal's death, and this made me feel responsible. In a way, I was—we were, my family and I—because it was our house that was built where his tree used to be, the one he was trying to get back to. But maybe no one could have stopped it.

"You have been in every way all that anyone could be. . . . If anybody could have saved me it would have been you."

Before he died, Cesare Pavese, believer in the Great Manifesto, wrote, *"We do not remember days, we remember moments."*

I remember running down a road on my way to a nursery of flowers.

I remember her smile and her laugh when I was my best self and she looked at me like I could do no wrong and was whole. I remember how she looked at me the same way even when I wasn't.

I remember her hand in mine and how that felt, as if something and someone belonged to me.

VIOLET

The rest of March

The first text comes in on Thursday. **The thing is, they were all perfect days.**

As soon as I read it, I call Finch, but he's already turned the phone off and I go to voicemail. Instead of leaving a message, I text him back: **We're all so worried. I'm worried. My boyfriend is a missing person. Please call me.**

Hours later, I hear from him again: **Not missing at all. Found.**

I write immediately: **Where are you?** This time he doesn't answer.

My dad is barely speaking to me, but my mom talks with Mrs. Finch, who says Finch has been in touch to let her know he's okay, not to worry, and he promises to check in every week, which implies that he's going to be gone for a while. No need to call in psychiatrists (but thanks so much for the concern). No need to call the police. After all, he does this sometimes. It appears my boyfriend isn't missing.

Except that he is.

"Did he say where he went?" As I ask it, I suddenly can see that my mom looks worried and tired, and I try to imagine what would be happening right now if it was me and not Finch who'd disappeared. My parents would have every cop within five states out looking.

"If he did, she didn't tell me. I don't know what else we can do. If the parents aren't even worried . . . well. I guess we need to trust that Finch means what he says and that he's all right." But I can hear all the things she isn't saying: *If it were my child, I'd be out there myself, bringing him home.*

At school, I'm the only one who seems to notice he's gone. After all, he's just another troublemaker who's been expelled. Our teachers and classmates have already forgotten about him.

So everyone acts as if nothing has happened and everything's fine. I go to class and play in an orchestra concert. I hold my first *Germ* meeting, and there are twenty-two of us, all girls, except for Briana Boudreau's boyfriend, Adam, and Lizzy Meade's brother, Max. I hear from two more colleges—Stanford, which is a no, and UCLA, which is a yes. I pick up the phone to tell Finch, but his voicemail is full. I don't bother texting him. Whenever I write back, it takes him a long time to respond, and when he does, it's never in answer to anything I've said.

I'm starting to get mad.

Two days later, Finch writes: **I am on the highest branch.**

The next morning: **We are written in paint.**

Later that night: **I believe in signs.**

The next afternoon: **The glow of Ultraviolet.**

The day after that: **A lake. A prayer. It's so lovely to be lovely in Private.**

And then everything goes quiet.

VIOLET
April

April 5 is Easter Sunday. My parents and I drive to the A Street Bridge and climb down to the dried-up riverbed that runs below to lay some flowers on the spot where Eleanor was killed. Embedded in the ground is a license plate, one that suddenly looks familiar, and circling this is a small garden where someone has planted flowers. *Finch*.

I go cold all over, not just from the damp air. It's been one year, and even though my parents don't say much as we're standing there, we've survived.

On the way home, I wonder when Finch was there—when he first found the license plate, when he came back. I wait for my parents to ask about the garden or talk about Eleanor, to call her by name today of all days. When they don't, I say, "It was my idea to see Boy Parade during spring break. Eleanor wasn't crazy about them, but she said, 'If you want to see Boy Parade, then let's really see them. Let's follow them all over the Midwest.' She was good at that, taking things one step further and making them bigger and more exciting than they would have been." *Like someone else I know.*

I start to sing my favorite Boy Parade song, the one that most reminds me of her. My mom looks at my dad, his eyes fixed on the road, and then she joins in.

Back at home, I sit at my desk thinking about my mother's question: *Why do I want to start a magazine?*

I stare at the board on my wall. My notes are spilling over and across the wall itself and reaching toward the closet. I open the wandering notebook and flip through the pages. On the first empty one, I write: *Germ—noun \ˈjərm\ the origin of something; a thing that may serve as the basis of further growth or development.*

I read this over and add: *Germ is for everyone....*

I cross this out.

I try again: *Germ is meant to entertain, inform, and keep you safe....*

I cross this out too.

I think of Finch and Amanda, and then I look at the closet door, where you can still see the thumbtack holes from my calendar. I think of the big black "X"s that marked off the days because all I wanted was for them to be behind me.

I turn to a new page and write: *Germ Magazine. You start here.* And then I rip it out and add it to my wall.

I haven't heard anything from Finch since March. I'm not worried anymore. I'm angry. Angry at him for leaving without a word, angry at myself for being so easy to leave and for not being enough to make him want to stick around. I do the normal post-breakup things— eating ice cream out of the carton, listening to better-off-without-him music, choosing a new profile photo for my Facebook page. My bangs are finally growing out, and I'm starting to look like my old self, even if I don't feel like her. On April 8, I gather the few things I have of his, pack them into a box, and slide them into the back of my closet. No more Ultraviolet Remarkey-able. I'm Violet Markey once again.

Wherever Finch is, he has our map. On April 10, I buy another one so that I can finish this project, which I have to do whether he's here or not. Right now the only things I have are memories of places. Nothing to show for them except a couple of pictures and our notebook. I don't know how to put all of what we've seen and done together into one comprehensive something that will make sense to anyone but me. It—whatever we did and were—doesn't even make sense to me.

On April 11, I borrow Mom's car, and she doesn't ask where I'm going, but as she hands me the keys, she says, "Call or text when you get there and when you're on your way home."

I head to Crawfordsville, where I make a halfhearted attempt to visit the Rotary Jail Museum, but I feel like a tourist. I call my mother to check in, and afterward I drive. It's a warm Saturday. The sun is bright. It almost feels like spring, and then I remember that, technically, it is. As I drive, I keep my eye out for a Saturn SUV, and every time I spot one, my heart does this wild leap into my throat, even though I tell myself: *I'm done. I'm over him. I'm moving on.*

I remember what he said about how he loved driving, the forward motion of it, like you might go anywhere. I picture the look on his face if he could see me behind the wheel right now. "Ultraviolet," he'd say, "I always knew you had it in you."

When Ryan and Suze break up, he asks me out. I say yes, but only as friends. On April 17, we eat dinner at the Gaslight, which is one of the fancier restaurants in Bartlett.

I pick at my meal and do my best to focus on Ryan. We talk about college plans and turning eighteen (his birthday's this month, mine's in May), and while it's not the most exciting conversation

I've ever had, it is a nice, normal date, with a nice, normal guy, and there's something to be said for that right now. I think about how I've labeled Ryan just like everyone labeled Finch. I suddenly like his solidness and sense of permanence, as if what you see is what you get, and he will always be and do exactly what you expect him to be and do. Except for the stealing, of course.

When he walks me to my door, I let him kiss me, and when he calls me the next morning, I answer.

On Saturday afternoon, Amanda shows up at my house and asks if I want to hang out. We end up playing tennis in the street, like we did when I first moved here, and afterward we walk up to the Dairy Queen and order Blizzards. That night, we go to the Quarry, just Amanda and me, and then I text Brenda and Shelby and Lara and the three Brianas, and they meet us there. An hour later, Jordan

Gripenwaldt and some of the other *Germ* girls have joined us. We dance till it's time to go home.

Friday, April 24, Brenda and I go to the movies, and when she invites me to sleep over, I do. She wants to talk about Finch, but I tell her I'm trying to put him behind me. She hasn't heard from him either, so she lets me be, but not before she says, "Just so you know, it's not you. Whatever reason he had for leaving, it must have been a good one."

We stay up till four a.m. working on *Germ*, me on my laptop, Brenda flat on her back on the floor, legs up the wall. She says, "We can help guide our readers into adulthood like Sherpas on Mount Everest. We give them the truth about sex, the truth about college life, the truth about love." She sighs. "Or at least the truth about what to do when boys are complete and total prats."

"Do we even know what to do when that happens?"

"Not at all."

I have fifteen emails from girls at school wanting to be contributors, because *Violet Markey, bell tower hero and creator of Eleanorand Violet.com (Gemma Sterling's favorite blog site), has started another magazine.* I read them aloud, and Brenda says, "So this is what it's like to be popular."

By now, she's pretty much my closest friend.

VIOLET
April 26

On Sunday, around ten thirty in the morning, Kate Finch shows up at our door. She looks as if she hasn't slept in weeks. When I invite her in, she shakes her head. "Do you have any idea where Theo might be?"

"I don't hear from him anymore."

She starts nodding. "Okay." She nods and nods. "Okay. Okay. It's just that he's been checking in every Saturday with Mom or me, either by email or voicemail when he knows he won't get us live. I mean, every Saturday. We didn't hear from him yesterday, and then this morning we get this weird email."

I try not to feel jealous of the fact that he's been checking in with them but not me. After all, they're his family. I'm only me, the most important person in his life, for a while at least. But okay. I get it. He's moved on. I've moved on too.

She hands me a piece of paper. It's the email, sent at 9:43 a.m. I'm remembering the time we went to Indianapolis to eat at that pizza place, the one with the organ that came up out of the floor. Kate must have been eleven, I was ten, Decca was a baby. Mom was there. Dad too. When the organ started playing—so loud the tables shook—the light show started. Remember? It was like the aurora borealis. But what stays with me most is all of you. We were happy. We were good. Each and every one of us. The happy times went away for a while, but they're coming back. Mom, forty-one's not old. Decca, sometimes there's beauty in the tough words—it's all in how you read them. Kate, be careful with your own heart, and remember that you're better than some guy. You're one of the best there is. You all are.

"I thought you might know why he wrote this, or maybe you might have heard from him."

"I don't, and I haven't. I'm sorry." I hand her the email and promise to let her know if by some miracle he gets in touch with me, and then she goes away, and I shut the door. I lean against it because for some reason I feel the need to catch my breath.

My mom appears, the skin between her eyebrows pinched. "Are you okay?"

I almost say sure, yes, great, but I feel myself folding in two, and I just hug her and rest my head on her shoulder and let her momness surround me for a few minutes. Then I go upstairs and turn on the computer and sign onto Facebook.

There's a new message, as of 9:47 a.m., four minutes after he sent the email to his family.

The words are written in The Waves: "If that blue could stay for ever; if that hole could remain for ever; if this moment could stay for ever. . . . I feel myself shining in the dark. . . . I am arrayed. I am prepared. This is the momentary pause; the dark moment. The fiddlers have lifted their bows. . . . This is my calling. This is my world. All is decided and ready. . . . I am rooted, but I flow. . . . 'Come,' I say, 'come.'"

I write the only thing I can think of: **"Stay,"** I say, **"stay."**

I check every five minutes, but he doesn't reply. I call him again, but the voicemail is still full. I hang up and call Brenda. She answers on the first ring. "Hey, I was getting ready to call you. I got this weird email from Finch this morning."

Brenda's was sent at 9:41 and said simply, **Some guy will definitely** love you for who you are. **Don't settle.**

The one to Charlie was sent at 9:45 and read, **Peace, you todger.** Something is wrong.

I tell myself it's only the heartbreak at being left, the fact that he disappeared without saying good-bye.

I pick up the phone to call Kate and realize I don't have her number, so I tell my mom I'll be back, and I drive to Finch's house.

Kate, Decca, and Mrs. Finch are there. When she sees me, Mrs. Finch starts to cry, and then before I can stop her, she's hugging me too hard and saying, "Violet, we're so glad you're here. Maybe you can figure this out. I told Kate maybe Violet will know where he is."

Through Mrs. Finch's hair, I look at Kate: *Please help me.*

She says, "Mom," and touches her once, on the shoulder. Mrs. Finch moves away from me, dabbing at her eyes and apologizing for being so emotional.

I ask Kate if I can speak with her alone. She leads me through sliding glass doors, outside to the patio, where she lights a cigarette. I wonder if this is the same patio where Finch found the cardinal.

She frowns at me. "What's going on?"

"He just wrote me. Today. Minutes after the email he sent you. He also sent emails to Brenda Shank-Kravitz and Charlie Donahue." I don't want to share his message with her, but I know I have to. I pull out my phone, and we stand in the shade of a tree as I show her the lines he wrote.

"I didn't even know he was on Facebook," she says, and then goes quiet as she reads. When she's finished, she looks at me, lost.

"Okay, what does all that mean?"

"It's a book we discovered. By Virginia Woolf. We've been quoting the lines to each other off and on."

"Do you have a copy of the book? Maybe there's a clue in the part that comes before or after this."

"I brought it with me." I pull it out of my bag. I've already marked the words, and now I show her where he got them. He's taken them out of sequence, picking and choosing certain lines over a series of pages and putting them together in his own way. Just like his Post-it songs.

Kate has forgotten about her cigarette, and the ash dangles, as long as a fingernail. "I can't figure out what the hell these people are doing"—she gestures at the book—"much less see how it might relate to where he is." She suddenly remembers her cigarette and takes a long drag. As she exhales, she says, "He's supposed to go to NYU, you know."

"Who?"

"Theo." She drops the cigarette onto the patio and crushes it with her shoe. "He got early acceptance."

NYU. Of course. What are the odds we were both supposed to be there, but now neither one of us is going?

"I didn't—he never told me about college."

"He didn't tell me or Mom either. The only reason we found out is that someone from NYU tried to contact him during the fall and I got to the message first." She forces a smile. "For all I know, he's in New York right now."

"Do you know if your mom ever got the messages? The ones from my mom and the psychiatrist?"

"Decca mentioned the doctor, but Mom almost never checks the home phone. I would have picked up the messages if there were any."

"But there weren't."

"No."

Because he erased them.

We go back inside, and Mrs. Finch is lying on the couch, eyes closed, while Decca sits nearby arranging pieces of paper across the floor. I can't help but watch her, because it's so much like Finch and his Post-its. Kate notices and says, "Don't ask me what she's doing. Another one of her art projects."

"Do you mind if I take a look at his room while I'm here?"

"Go for it. We've left everything the way it was—you know, for when he comes back."

If he comes back.

Upstairs, I shut the door to his bedroom and stand there a moment. The room still smells like him—a mix of soap and cigarettes and the heady, woodsy quality that is distinctly Theodore Finch. I open the windows to let some air in because it's too dead and stale, and then I close them again, afraid the scent of soap and cigarettes and Finch will escape. I wonder if his sisters or mom have even set foot in this room since he's been gone. It looks so untouched, the drawers still open from when I was here last.

I search through the dresser and desk again, and then the bathroom, but there's nothing that can tell me anything. My phone buzzes, and I jump. It's Ryan, and I ignore it. I walk into the closet, where the black light has been replaced by a regular old bulb. I go through the shelves and the remaining clothes, the ones he didn't take with him. I pull his black T-shirt off a hanger and breathe him in, and then I slip it into my purse. I close the door behind me, sit down, and say out loud, "Okay, Finch. Help me out here. You must have left something behind."

I let myself feel the smallness and closeness of the closet pressing in on me, and I think about Sir Patrick Moore's black hole trick, when he just vanished into thin air. It occurs to me that this is exactly what Finch's closet is—a black hole. He went inside and disappeared.

Then I examine the ceiling. I study the night sky he created, but it looks like a night sky and nothing more. I look at our wall of Post-its, reading every single one until I see there's nothing new or added. The short wall, the one opposite the door, holds an empty shoe rack, which he used to hang his guitar from. I sit up and scoot back and check the wall I was leaning against. There are Post-its here too, and for some reason I didn't notice them the last time.

Just two lines across, each word on a separate piece of paper. The first reads: *long, last, nothing, time, there, make, was, to, a, him.*

The second: *waters, thee, go, to, it, suits, if, the, there.*

I reach for the word "nothing." I sit cross-legged and hunched over, thinking about the words. I know I've heard them before, though not in this order.

I take the words from line one off the wall and start moving them around:

Nothing was to him a long time there make last.

Last a long time make there nothing was to him.

There was nothing to make him last a long time.

On to the second line now. I pluck "go" from the wall and place it first. "To" moves next, and so on until it reads: *Go to the waters if it suits thee there.*

By the time I'm back downstairs, it's just Decca and Mrs. Finch. She tells me Kate has gone out to look for Theo and there's no telling when she'll be back. I have no choice but to talk to Finch's mom. I ask if she'd mind coming upstairs. She climbs the steps like a much older person, and I wait for her at the top.

She hesitates on the landing. "What is it, Violet? I don't think I can handle surprises."

"It's a clue to where he is."

She follows me into his room and stands for a moment, looking around as if she's seeing it for the first time. "When did he paint everything blue?"

Instead of answering, I point at the closet. "In here."

We stand in his closet, and she covers her mouth at how bare it is, how much is gone. I crouch in front of the wall and show her the Post-its.

She says, "That first line. That's what he said after the cardinal died."

"I think he's gone back to one of the places we wandered, one of the places with water." **The words are written in The Waves,** he wrote on Facebook. At 9:47 a.m. The same time as the Jovian-Plutonian hoax. The water could be the Bloomington Empire Quarry or the Seven Pillars or the river that runs in front of the high school or about a hundred other places. Mrs. Finch stares blankly at the wall, and it's hard to know if she's even listening. "I can give you directions and tell you exactly where to look for him. There are a couple of places he could have gone, but I have a pretty good idea where he might be."

Then she turns to me and lays her hand on my arm and squeezes it so hard, I can almost feel the bruise forming. "I hate to ask you, but can you go? I'm just so—worried, and—I don't think I could—I mean, in case something were to—or if he were." She is crying again, the hard and ugly kind, and I'm ready to promise her anything as long as she stops. "I just really need you to bring him home."

VIOLET
April 26 (part two)

I don't go for her or for his dad or for Kate or for Decca. I go for me. Maybe because I know, somehow, what I'll find. And maybe because I know whatever I find will be my fault. After all, it's because of me he had to leave his closet. I was the one who pushed him out by talking to my parents and betraying his trust. He never would have left if it hadn't been for me. Besides, I tell myself, Finch would want me to be the one to come.

I call my parents to tell them I'll be home in a while, that I've got something to do, and then I hang up on my dad, even as he's asking me a question, and drive. I drive faster than I normally do, and I remember the way without looking at the map. I am scarily, eerily calm, as if someone else is doing the driving. I keep the music off. This is how focused I am on getting there.

"If that blue could stay for ever; if that hole could remain for ever."

There was nothing to make him last.

The first thing I see is Little Bastard, parked on the side of the road, right wheels, front and back, on the embankment. I pull up behind it and turn off the engine. I sit there.

I can drive away right now. If I drive away, Theodore Finch is still somewhere in the world, living and wandering, even if it's without me. My fingers are on the ignition key.

Drive away.

I get out of the car, and the sun is too warm for April in Indiana. The sky is blue, after nothing but gray for the past few months except for that first warm day. I leave my jacket behind.

I walk past the NO TRESPASSING signs and the house that sits off the road and up a driveway. I climb up the embankment and go down the hill to the wide, round pool of blue water, ringed by trees. I don't know how I didn't notice it the first time—the water is as blue as his eyes.

The place is deserted and peaceful. So deserted and peaceful that I almost turn around and go back to the car.

But then I see them.

His clothes, on the bank, folded neatly and stacked, collared shirt on top of jeans on top of leather jacket on top of black boots. It's like a greatest hits of his closet. Only there. On the bank.

For a long time, I don't move. Because if I stand here like this, Finch is still somewhere.

Then: I kneel beside the stack of clothes and lay my hand on them, as if by doing so I can learn where he is and how long ago he came. The clothes are warm from the sun. I find his phone tucked into one of the boots, but it's completely dead. In the other boot, his nerd glasses and car keys. Inside the leather jacket, I find our map, folded as neatly as the clothes. Without thinking, I put it in my bag.

"Marco," I whisper.

Then: I stand.

"Marco," I say louder.

I pull off my shoes and coat and set my keys and phone beside the neat stack of Finch's clothing. I climb onto the rock ledge and dive into the water, and it knocks the breath out of me because it's cold, not warm. I tread circles, head up, until I can breathe. And then I take a breath and go under, where the water is strangely clear.

I go as deep as I can, heading straight for the bottom. The water feels darker the deeper I go, and too soon I have to push up to the surface and fill my lungs. I dive again and again, going as deep as I dare before running out of breath. I swim from one end of the hole to the other, back and forth. I come up and then go down again. Each time, I can stay a little longer, but not as long as Finch, who can hold his breath for minutes.

Could hold.

Because at some point, I know: he's gone. He's not somewhere. He's nowhere.

Even after I know, I dive and swim and dive and swim, up and down and back and forth, until finally, when I can't do it anymore, I crawl up onto the bank, exhausted, lungs heaving, hands shaking.

As I dial 9-1-1, I think: *He's not nowhere. He's not dead. He just found that other world.*

The sheriff for Vigo County arrives with the fire department and an ambulance. I sit on the bank wrapped in a blanket someone has given me, and I think about Finch and Sir Patrick Moore and black holes and blue holes and bottomless bodies of water and exploding stars and event horizons, and a place so dark that light can't get out once it's in.

Now these strangers are here and milling around, and they must be the ones who own this property and this house. They have children, and the woman is covering their eyes and shooing them away, telling them to get on back in there and don't come out, whatever you do, not till she says so. Her husband says, "Goddamn kids," and he doesn't mean his, he means kids in general, kids like Finch and me.

Men are diving over and over, three or four of them—they all look the same. I want to tell them not to bother, they're not going to find anything, he's not there. If anyone can make it to another world, it's Theodore Finch.

Even when they bring the body up, swollen and bloated and blue, I think: *That's not him. That's someone else. This swollen, bloated, blue thing with the dead, dead skin is not anyone I know or recognize.* I tell them so. They ask me if I feel strong enough to identify him, and I say, "That's not him. That is a swollen, bloated, dead, dead blue thing, and I can't identify it because I've never seen it before." I turn my head away.

The sheriff crouches down beside me. "We're going to need to call his parents."

He is asking for the number, but I say, "I'll do it. She was the one who asked me to come. She wanted me to find him. I'll call."

But that's not him, don't you see? People like Theodore Finch don't die. He's just wandering.

I call the line his family never uses. His mother answers on the first ring, as if she's been sitting right there waiting. For some reason, this makes me mad and I want to slam the phone off and throw it into the water.

"Hello?" she says. "Hello?" There's something shrill and hopeful and terrified in her voice. "Oh God. *Hello?!*"

"Mrs. Finch? It's Violet. I found him. He was where I thought he would be. I'm so sorry." My voice sounds as if it's underwater or coming from the next county. I am pinching the inside of my arm, making little red marks, because I suddenly can't feel anything.

His mother lets out a sound I've never heard before, low and guttural and terrible. Once again, I want to throw the phone into the water so it will stop, but instead I keep saying "I'm sorry" over and over and over, like a recording, until the sheriff pries the phone from my hand.

As he talks, I lie back against the ground, the blanket wrapped around me, and say to the sky, "May your eye go to the Sun, To the wind your soul. . . . You are all the colors in one, at full brightness."

VIOLET

May 3

I stand in front of the mirror and study my face. I am dressed in black. Black skirt, black sandals, and Finch's black T-shirt, which I've belted. My face looks like my face, only different. It is not the face of a carefree teenage girl who has been accepted at four colleges and has good parents and good friends and her whole life ahead of her. It is the face of a sad, lonely girl something bad has happened to. I wonder if my face will ever look the same again, or if I'll always see it in my reflection—Finch, Eleanor, loss, heartache, guilt, death.

But will other people be able to tell? I take a picture with my phone, fake smiling as I pose, and when I look at it, there's Violet Markey. I could post it on Facebook right now, and no one would know that I took it After instead of Before.

My parents want to go with me to the funeral, but I say no. They are hovering too much and watching me. Every time I turn around, I see their worried eyes, and the looks they give each other, and there's something else—anger. They are no longer mad at me, because they're furious with Mrs. Finch, and probably Finch too, although they haven't said so. My dad, as usual, is more outspoken than my mom, and I overhear him talking about *That woman*, and how he'd like to give her a piece of his *goddamn mind*, before Mom shushes him and says, *Violet might hear you.*

His family stands in the front row. And it is raining. This is the first time I've seen his dad, who is tall and broad-shouldered and movie-star handsome. The mousy woman who must be Finch's stepmom stands next to him, her arm around a very small boy. Next to him is Decca, and then Kate, and then Mrs. Finch. Everyone is crying, even the dad.

Golden Acres is the largest cemetery in town. We stand at the top of a hill next to the casket, my second funeral in just over a year's time, even though Finch wanted to be cremated. The preacher is quoting verses from the Bible, and the family is weeping, and everyone is weeping, even Amanda Monk and some of the cheerleaders. Ryan and Roamer are there, and about two hundred other kids from school. I also recognize Principal Wertz and Mr. Black and Mrs. Kresney and Mr. Embry from the counseling office. I stand off to the side with my parents—who insisted on coming—and Brenda and Charlie. Brenda's mom is there, her hand resting on her daughter's shoulder.

Charlie is standing with his hands folded in front of him, staring at the casket. Brenda is staring at Roamer and the rest of the crying herd, her eyes dry and angry. I know what she's feeling. Here are these people who called him "freak" and never paid attention to him, except to make fun of him or spread rumors about him, and now they are carrying on like professional mourners, the ones you can hire in Taiwan or the Middle East to sing, cry, and crawl on the ground. His family is just as bad. After the preacher is finished, everyone moves toward them to shake their hands and offer condolences. The family accepts them as if they've earned them. No one says anything to me.

And so I stand quietly in Finch's black T-shirt, thinking. In all his words, the preacher doesn't mention suicide. The family is calling his death an accident because they didn't find a proper note, and so the preacher talks about the tragedy of someone dying so young, of a life ended too soon, of possibilities never realized. I stand, thinking how it wasn't an accident at all and how "suicide victim" is an interesting term. The victim part of it implies they had no choice. And maybe Finch didn't feel like he had a choice, or maybe he wasn't trying to kill himself at all but just going in search of the bottom. But I'll never really know, will I?

Then I think: *You can't do this to me. You were the one who lectured me about living. You were the one who said I had to get out and see what* was right in front of me and make the most of it and not wish my time away and find my mountain because my mountain was waiting, and all that adds up to life. But then you leave. You can't just do that. Especially when you know what I went through losing Eleanor.

I try to remember the last words I said to him, but I can't. Only that they were angry and normal and unremarkable. What would I have said to him if I'd known I would never see him again?

As everyone begins to break apart and walk away, Ryan finds me to say, "I'll call you later?" It's a question, so I answer it with a nod. He nods back and then he's gone.

Charlie mutters, "What a bunch of phonies," and I'm not sure if he's talking about our classmates or the Finch family or the entire congregation.

Bren's voice is brittle. "Somewhere, Finch is watching this, all

I pat her like you would pat a child, and then Mr. Finch is there, and he is hugging me with his big arms, his chin on my head. I can't breathe, and then I feel someone pulling me away, and my father says, "I think we'll take her home." His voice is curt and cold. I let myself be led to the car.

At home, I pick at my dinner and listen to my parents talk about the Finches in controlled, even voices that have been carefully chosen so as not to upset me.

Dad: I wish I could have given those people a piece of my mind today.

Mom: She had no right to ask Violet to do that.

She glances at me and says too brightly, "Do you need more

'What do you expect?' I hope he's flipping them off."

Mr. Finch was the one to officially ID the body. The paper reported that, by the time Finch was found, he'd probably been dead several hours.

I say, "Do you really think he's somewhere?" Brenda blinks at me. "Like anywhere? I mean, I like to think wherever he is, maybe he can't see us because he's alive and in some other world, better than this. The kind of world he would have designed if he could have. I'd like to live in a world designed by Theodore Finch." I think: *For a while, I did.*

Before Brenda can answer, Finch's mother is suddenly beside me, red eyes peering into my face. She sweeps me into a hug and holds on like she never plans to let go. "Oh, Violet," she cries. "Oh, dear girl. Are you okay?"

vegetables, honey?"

Me: No, thank you.

Before they can start in on Finch, and the selfishness of suicide, and the fact that he took his life when Eleanor had hers taken from her, *when she didn't get a say in the matter*—such a wasteful, hateful, stupid thing to do—I ask to be excused, even though I've barely touched my food. I don't have to help with the dishes, so I go upstairs and sit in my closet. My calendar is shoved into a corner. I unfold it now, smoothing it out, and look at all the blank days, too many to count, that I didn't mark off because these were days I had with Finch.

I think:

I hate you.

If only I'd known.

If only I'd been enough.

I let you down.

I wish I could have done something.

I should have done something.

Was it my fault?

Why wasn't I enough?

Come back.

I love you.

I'm sorry.

VIOLET

At school, the entire student body seems to be in mourning. There is a lot of black being worn, and you can hear sniffling in every classroom. Someone has built a shrine to Finch in one of the large glass cases in the main hallway, near the principal's office. His school picture has been blown up, and they have left the case open so that we can all post tributes around it—*Dear Finch,* they all begin. *You are loved and missed. We love you. We miss you.*

I want to tear them all down and shred them up and put them in the pile with the rest of the bad, false words, because that's exactly where they belong.

Our teachers remind us there are just five more weeks of school, and I should be happy, but instead I feel nothing. I feel a lot of nothing these days. I've cried a few times, but mostly I'm empty, as if whatever makes me feel and hurt and laugh and love has been surgically removed, leaving me hollowed out like a shell.

I tell Ryan we can only ever be friends, and it's just as well because he doesn't want to touch me. No one does. It's like they're afraid I might be contagious. This is part of the suicide-by-association phenomenon.

I sit with Brenda, Lara, and the Brianas at lunch until the Wednesday after Finch's funeral, when Amanda walks over, sets her tray down, and, without looking at the other girls, says to me, "I'm sorry about Finch."

For a minute, I think Brenda is going to hit her, and I kind of want her to, or at least I want to see what would happen if she did. But when Bren just sits there, I nod at Amanda. "Thanks."

"I shouldn't have called him a freak. And I want you to know I broke up with Roamer."

"Too little, too late," Brenda mutters. She stands suddenly, knocking into the table, making everything rattle. She grabs her tray, tells me she'll see me later, and marches off.

On Thursday, I meet with Mr. Embry because Principal Wertz and the school board are requiring all friends and classmates of Theodore Finch to have at least one session with a counselor, even though The Parents, as my mother and father refer to Mr. Finch and Mrs. Finch, are insisting it was an accident, which, I guess, means we're free to mourn him out in the open in a normal, healthy, unstigma-tized way. No need to be ashamed or embarrassed since suicide isn't involved.

I ask for Mr. Embry instead of Mrs. Kresney because he was Finch's counselor. From behind his desk, he frowns at me, and I suddenly wonder if he's going to blame me like I blame myself.

I should never have suggested we take the A Street Bridge. What if we'd gone the other way instead? Eleanor would still be here.

Mr. Embry clears his throat. "I'm sorry about Finch. He was a good, screwed-up kid who should have had more help."

This gets my attention.

Then he adds, "I feel responsible."

I want to send his computer and books crashing to the floor. *You can't feel responsible. I'm responsible. Don't try to take that from me.*

He continues, "But I'm not. I did what I felt I could do. Could I have done more? Possibly. Yes. We can always do more. It's a tough question to answer, and, ultimately, a pointless one to ask. You might be feeling some of the same emotions and having some of these same thoughts."

"I know I could have done more. I should have seen what was going on."

"We can't always see what others don't want us to. Especially when they go to great lengths to hide it." Mr. Embry plucks a thin booklet off his desk and reads: "'You are a survivor, and as that unwelcome designation implies, your survival—your *emotional* survival—will depend on how well you learn to cope with your tragedy. The bad news: Surviving this will be the second worst experience of your life. The good news: The worst is already over.'"

He hands the booklet to me. *SOS: A Handbook for Survivors of Suicide.*

"I want you to read it, but I also want you to come talk to me, talk to your parents, talk to your friends. The last thing we want you to do is bottle all this in. You were closest to him, which means you're going to feel all the anger and loss and denial and grief that you would feel over any death, but this death is different, so don't be hard on yourself."

"His family says it was an accident."

"So maybe it was. People are going to deal with it however they can. My only concern is you. You can't be responsible for everyone—not your sister, not Finch. What happened to your sister—she didn't have a choice. And maybe Finch felt like he didn't either, even though he did." He frowns at a spot just over my shoulder, and I can see him going back over it all in his mind—every conversation or meeting with Finch—the same way I've been doing since it happened.

The thing I can't, won't, mention to him is that I see Finch everywhere—in the hallways at school, on the street, in my neighborhood. Someone's face will remind me of him, or someone's walk or someone's laugh. It's like being surrounded by a thousand different Finches. I wonder if this is normal, but I don't ask.

At home, I lie on my bed and read the entire book, and because it's only thirty-six pages, it doesn't take long. Afterward, the thing that sticks in my mind are these two lines: *Your hope lies in accepting your life as it now lies before you, forever changed. If you can do that, the peace you seek will follow.*

Forever changed.

I am forever changed.

★ ★ ★

At dinner, I show my mom the book Mr. Embry gave me. She reads it as she eats, not saying a word, while my dad and I try to carry on a conversation about college.

"Have you decided which school you're going to, V?"

"Maybe UCLA." I want to tell my dad to choose a school for me, because what does it matter? They're all the same.

"We should probably let them know soon."

"I guess. I'll be sure to get right on that."

My dad looks at my mom for help, but she is still reading, her food forgotten. "Have you given any thought to applying to NYU for spring admission?"

I say, "No, but maybe I should go work on that now. Do you guys mind?" I want to get away from the booklet and from them and any talk of the future.

My dad looks relieved. "Of course not. Go." He is glad I'm going, and I'm glad I'm going. It's easier this way, because otherwise we might all have to face each other and Eleanor and this thing that has happened with Finch. In that moment, I'm thankful I'm not a parent and I wonder if I ever will be. What a terrible feeling to love someone and not be able to help them.

Actually, I know exactly how that feels.

At an all-school assembly the second Thursday after Finch's funeral, they bring in a martial arts expert from Indianapolis to talk to us about safety and how to defend ourselves, as if suicide is something that might attack us on the street, and then they show us this film about teenagers on drugs. Before they turn off the lights, Principal Wertz announces that some of the content is pretty graphic, but that it's important we see the realities of drug use.

As the movie starts up, Charlie leans over and tells me the only reason they're showing it is because there's a rumor going around that Finch was on something, and this is why he died. The only people who know this isn't true are Charlie, Brenda, and me.

When one of the teen actors overdoses, I walk out. Outside the auditorium, I throw up in one of the trash cans.

"Are you okay?" Amanda is sitting on the floor, leaning against the wall.

"I didn't see you there." I move away from the trash can.

"I couldn't get through five minutes of that."

I sit down on the floor, a couple of feet away from her. "What goes through your mind when you're thinking about it?"

"About . . ."

"Killing yourself. I want to know what that feels like, what a person thinks about. I want to know why."

Amanda stares at her hands. "I can only tell you how I felt. Ugly. Disgusting. Stupid. Small. Worthless. Forgotten. It just feels like there's no choice. Like it's the most logical thing to do because what else is there? You think, 'No one will even miss me. They won't know I'm gone. The world will go on, and it won't matter that I'm not here. Maybe it's better if I was never here.'"

"But you don't feel that way all the time. I mean, you're Amanda Monk. You're popular. Your parents are nice to you. Your brothers are nice to you." *Everyone's nice to you,* I think, *because they're too afraid not to be.*

She looks at me. "In those moments, none of it matters. It's like that stuff is happening to someone else because all you feel is dark inside, and that darkness just kind of takes over. You don't even really think about what might happen to the people you leave behind, because all you can think about is yourself." She wraps her arms around her knees. "Did Finch ever see a doctor?"

"I don't know." There's still so much I don't know about him. I guess now I'll never know it. "I don't think his parents wanted to admit anything was wrong."

"He was trying to fix himself because of you."

I know she wants to make me feel better, but this only makes me feel worse.

The next day, in U.S. Geography, Mr. Black stands at the board, where he writes JUNE 4 and underlines it. "The time has come . . . people . . . your projects are due soon . . . so focus, focus . . . focus. Please come to . . . me with any . . . questions, otherwise I will . . . expect you to . . . turn them in on time . . . if not before."

When the bell rings, he says, "I'd like to . . . talk to you, Violet." I sit in my seat, next to the desk Finch once sat in, and wait. After the last person leaves, Mr. Black closes the door and sinks into his chair. "I wanted to check in . . . with you to see . . . if you need any help . . . and also to tell you . . . to feel free to turn in whatever . . . you have so far . . . I obviously . . . understand . . . that there are extenuating . . . circumstances."

Extenuating Circumstances. That is me. That is Violet Markey. Poor forever-changed Violet and her Extenuating Circumstances.

Must treat her carefully, because she is fragile and might break if expected to do the same as everyone else.

"Thanks, but I'm okay." I can do this. I can show them I'm not some china doll, handle with care. I just wish Finch and I had pulled together all our wanderings, and maybe documented each one a little better. We were so busy being in the moment that I don't have much to show for it except a half-filled notebook, a few pictures, and a marked-up map.

That evening, I torture myself by reading our Facebook messages, going back to the very beginning. And then, even though I know he'll never read it, I open our notebook and start to write.

Letter to Someone Who Committed Suicide
by Violet Markey

Where are you? And why did you go? I guess I'll never know this. Was it because I made you mad? Because I tried to help? Because I didn't answer when you threw rocks at my window? What if I had answered? What would you have said to me? Would I have been able to talk you into staying or talk you out of doing what you did? Or would that have happened anyway?

Do you know my life is forever changed now? I used to think that was true because you came into it and showed me Indiana and, in doing that, forced me out of my room and into the world. Even when we weren't wandering, even from the floor of your closet, you showed the world to me. I didn't know that my life forever changing would be because you loved me and then left, and in such a final way.

So I guess there was no Great Manifesto after all, even though you made me believe there was. I guess there was only a school project.

I'll never forgive you for leaving me. I just wish you could forgive me. You saved my life.

And, finally, I simply write: *Why couldn't I save yours?*

I sit back, and above my desk are the storyboard Post-its for *Germ*. I've added a new category: Ask an Expert. My eyes move past these to the piece of paper that describes what the magazine is about. They rest on the last line: *You start here.*

In a minute, I am up and out of my seat and searching my room.

At first, I can't remember what I've done with the map. I feel this white rush of panic, which leaves me shaky, because what if I've lost it? It will be another piece of Finch, gone.

And then I find it in my bag, on my third time checking, as if it appeared out of thin air. I spread it out and look at the remaining points that are circled. There are five more places to see on my own. Finch has written numbers beside each one so that there's a kind of order.

VIOLET
Remaining wanderings 1 and 2

Milltown, population 815, sits close to the Kentucky border. I have to stop and ask someone how to get to the shoe trees. A woman named Myra points me toward a place called Devils Hollow. It doesn't take long to run out of paved road, and soon I'm driving down a narrow dirt trail, looking up, which is what Myra told me to do. Just when I think I'm lost, I come to a four-way intersection that sits surrounded by woods.

I pull the car over and get out. In the distance, I can hear the sound of kids yelling and laughing. Trees stand at all four corners, their branches filled with shoes. Hundreds and hundreds of shoes.

Most are draped across the limbs by the laces like oversized Christmas ornaments. Myra said she wasn't sure how it began, or who left the first pair, but people travel from all over just to decorate the trees. There's a rumor that Larry Bird, the basketball player, left a pair up there somewhere.

The quest is simple: leave a pair behind. I've brought a pair of green Chuck Taylors from my closet, and a pair of yellow Keds from Eleanor's. I stand, head tilted back, trying to decide where to put them. I'll hang them together on the original tree, the one heaviest with shoes, which has been struck by lightning more than once—I can tell because the trunk looks dead and black.

I pull a Sharpie from my pocket and write *Ultraviolet Remarkeyable* and the date on the side of one of the Chuck Taylors. I hang them low on the original tree, which looks too fragile to climb. I have to jump a little to reach the branch, and the shoes bob and twist before settling. I hang Eleanor's Keds beside them.

That's it then. Nothing more to see. It's a long way to drive for trees of old shoes, but I tell myself not to look at it that way. There might be magic here too. I stand watching for it, shading my eyes against the sun, and just before I walk back to the car I see them: way up on the highest branch of the original tree, hanging all alone. A pair of sneakers with fluorescent laces, *TF* in black on both shoes. A package of blue American Spirits pokes up from the inside of one.

He was here.

I look around as if I might see him right now, but it's just me and the kids who are laughing and hollering from someplace nearby. When did he come? Was it after he left? Was it before that?

Something nags at me as I stand there. *The highest branch,* I think. *The highest branch.* I reach for my phone, but it's in the car, and so I run the short distance, throw open the door, and lean across the seat. I sit half in, half out, scrolling through my texts from Finch. Because there aren't many recent ones, it doesn't take long to find it. **I am on the highest branch.** I look at the date. A week after he left.

He was here.

I read through the other texts: **We are written in paint. I believe in signs. The glow of Ultraviolet. It's so lovely to be lovely in Private.**

I find the map, my finger following the route to the next place. It's hours away, northwest of Muncie. I check the time, turn on the engine, and drive. I have a feeling I know where I'm headed, and I hope it's not too late.

The World's Biggest Ball of Paint sits on the property of Mike Carmichael. Unlike the shoe trees, it's a designated tourist attraction. The ball not only has its own website, it's listed in the *Guinness Book of World Records*.

It's a little after four o'clock by the time I get to Alexandria. Mike Carmichael and his wife are expecting me because I called them from the road. I pull up to the structure where the ball apparently lives—in a kind of barnlike shed—and knock on the door, my heart beating fast.

When there's no answer, I try the handle, but it's locked, and so I walk up to the house, heart going faster because what if someone has been there since? What if they've painted over whatever Finch might have written? It'll be gone then, and I'll never know, and it will be like he was never even here.

I bang harder than I mean to on the front door, and at first I think they aren't home, but then a man with white hair and an expectant smile comes walking out, talking and shaking my hand and telling me to call him Mike.

"Where are you from, young lady?"

"Bartlett." I don't mention that I've just come from Milltown.

"That's a nice town, Bartlett. We go there sometimes to the Gaslight Restaurant."

My heart is beating into my ears, and it's so loud, I actually wonder if he can hear it. I follow him to the barn-shed, and he says, "I started this ball of paint nearly forty years ago. The way it came about, I was working in this paint store back in high school, back before you were born, maybe back before your parents were born. I was playing catch in the store with a friend and the baseball knocked over this can of paint. I thought, I wonder what would happen if I painted it one thousand coats? So that's what I did." Mike says he donated that ball to the Knightstown Children's Home Museum, but in 1977 he decided to start another one.

He nods at the barn and unlocks the door and we walk into a big, bright room that smells like paint. There, in the middle, hangs this enormous ball, the size of a small planet. Paint cans cover the floor and wall, and another wall is lined with photographs of the ball in different stages. Mike tells me how he tries to paint it every day, and I cut him off and say, "I'm so sorry, but a friend of mine was here recently, and I wanted to see if you remembered him, and if maybe he might have written something on the ball."

I describe Finch, and Mike rubs his chin and starts nodding. "Yep, yep. I remember him. Nice young man. Didn't stay long. Used this paint over here." He leads me to a can of purple paint, the color written on the lid: *Violet*.

I look at the ball, and it isn't purple. It's as yellow as the sun. I feel my heart sink. I look at the floor and almost expect to see it lying there.

"The ball's been painted over," I say. I'm too late. Too late for Finch. Too late once again.

"Anyone who wants to write something, I get them to paint over it before they leave. That way it's ready for the next person. A clean slate. Do you want to add a layer?"

I almost say no, but I didn't bring anything to leave, and so I let him hand me a roller. When he asks what color I want, I tell him blue like the sky. As he searches the cans, I stand in place, unable to move or breathe. It's like losing Finch all over again.

Then Mike is back and he has found a color that is the color of Finch's eyes, which he can't possibly know or remember. I dip the roller into the tray and cover the yellow with blue. There's something soothing about the mindless, easy motion of it.

When I'm finished, Mike and I stand back and look at my work. "Don't you want to write anything?" he says.

"That's okay. I'll only have to cover it up." And then no one will know I was here either.

I help him put the paint away and clean up a bit, and he tells me facts about the ball, like that it weighs nearly 4,000 pounds and is made up of over 20,000 coats of paint. Then he hands me a red book and a pen. "Before you leave, you have to sign."

I flip through the pages until I find the first blank spot where I can write my name and the date and a comment. My eyes run over the page, and then I see that only a few people were here in April. I flip back a page, and there it is—there he is. *Theodore Finch, April 3. "Today is your day. You're off to Great Places! You're off and away!"*

I run my fingers over the words, the ones he wrote just weeks ago when he was here and alive. I read them again and again, and then, on the first blank line, I sign my name and write: *"Your mountain is waiting. So . . . get on your way!"*

As I head home to Bartlett, I sing what I can remember of Finch's Dr. Seuss song. When I pass through Indianapolis, I think of trying to find the nursery where he collected flowers in winter, but instead I keep driving east. They won't be able to tell me anything about Finch or why he died or what he wrote on the ball of paint. The only thing that makes me feel better is that, whatever Finch wrote, it will always be there, underneath the layers.

I find my mom and dad in the family room, my dad listening to music on his headphones, my mom grading papers. I say, "I need us to talk about Eleanor and not to forget that she existed." My dad removes his headphones. "I don't want to pretend like everything's fine if it isn't, like we're fine if we're not. I miss her. I can't believe I'm here and she isn't. I'm sorry we went out that night. I need you to know that. I'm sorry I told her to take the bridge home. She only went that way because I suggested it."

When they try to interrupt me, I talk louder. "We can't go backward. We can't change anything that happened. I can't bring her back or bring Finch back. I can't change the fact that I sneaked around to see him when I told you it was over. I don't want to tiptoe around her or him or you anymore. The only thing it's doing is making it harder for me to remember the things I want to remember. It's making it harder for me to remember her. Sometimes I try to concentrate on her voice just so I can hear it again—the way she always said, 'Hey there' when she was in a good mood, and 'Vi-o-let' when she was annoyed. For some reason, these are the easiest ones. I concentrate on them, and when I have them, I hold on to them because I don't ever want to forget how she sounded."

My mom has started to cry, very, very quietly. My father's face has gone gray-white.

"Like it or not, she was here and now she's gone, but she doesn't have to be completely gone. That's up to us. And like it or not, I loved Theodore Finch. He was good for me, even though you think he wasn't and you hate his parents and you probably hate him, and even though he went away and I wish he hadn't, and I can never bring him back, and it might have been my fault. So it's good and it's bad and it hurts, but I like thinking about him. If I think about him, he won't be completely gone either. Just because they're dead, they don't have to be. And neither do we."

My dad sits like a marble statue, but my mom gets up and kind of stumbles toward me. She draws me in, and I think: *That's how she used to feel before any of this happened—strong and sturdy, like she could withstand a tornado.* She is still crying, but she is solid and real, and just in case, I pinch her skin, and she pretends not to notice.

She says, "Nothing that happened is your fault."

And then I'm crying, and my dad is crying, one stoic tear at a time, and then his head is in his hands and my mom and I move like one person over to him, and the three of us huddle together, rocking a little back and forth, taking turns saying, "It's okay. We're okay. We're all okay."

VIOLET

Remaining wanderings 3 and 4

The Pendleton Pike Drive-In is one of the last of its kind. What's left of it sits in an overgrown field on the outskirts of downtown Indianapolis. Now it's like a graveyard, but in the 1960s the drive-in was one of the most popular sites around—not just a movie theater, but a kiddie park with a mini roller coaster and other rides and attractions.

The screen is the only thing that remains. I park on the roadside and approach it from the back. It's an overcast day, the sun hidden behind thick, gray clouds, and even though it's warm, I shiver. The place gives me the spooks. As I tramp over weeds and dirt, I try to picture Finch parking Little Bastard where I parked my car and walking to the screen, which blocks the horizon like a skeleton, just as I'm walking now.

I believe in signs, he texted.

And that's what the screen looks like—a giant billboard. The back is covered with graffiti, and I pick my way across broken beer bottles and cigarette butts.

Suddenly I'm having one of those moments that you have after losing someone—when you feel as if you've been kicked in the stomach and all your breath is gone, and you might never get it back. I want to sit down on the dirty, littered ground right now and cry until I can't cry anymore.

But instead I walk around the side of the screen, telling myself I may not find anything. I count my steps past it until I'm a good thirty paces in. I turn and look up, and the wide white face says in red letters, *I was here. TF.*

In that moment, my knees give out and down I sink, into the dirt and the weeds and the trash. What was I doing when he was here? Was I in class? Was I with Amanda or Ryan? Was I at home? Where was I when he was climbing up on the sign and painting it, leaving an offering, finishing our project?

I get to my feet and take a picture of the skeleton screen with my phone, and then I walk up to the sign, closer and closer, until the letters are huge and towering above me. I wonder how far away they reach, if someone miles from here can read them.

There is a can of red spray paint sitting on the ground, the cap neatly on. I pick it up, hoping for a note or anything to let me know he left it for me, but it's just a can.

He must have climbed up by the steel latticework posts that anchor the thing in place. I rest one foot on a rung, tuck the paint can under my arm, and pull myself up. I have to climb one side and then the other in order to finish it. I write: *I was here too. VM.*

When I'm done, I stand back. His words are neater than mine, but they look good together. There we are, I think. This is our project. We started it together, and we end it together. And then I take another picture just in case they ever tear it down.

Munster is almost as far north and west as you can get and still be in Indiana. It's called a bedroom community of Chicago because it's only thirty miles outside the city. The town is bordered by rivers, something Finch would have liked. Our Lady of Mount Carmel

Monastery sits on a large, shaded property. It looks like a regular church in the middle of some pretty woods.

I roam around the grounds until a balding man in a brown robe appears. "May I help you, young lady?"

I tell him I'm there for a school project, but I'm not sure exactly where I'm supposed to go. He nods like he understands this and leads me away from the church and toward what he calls "the shrines." As we walk, we pass sculpted tributes of wood and copper to a priest from Auschwitz, and also St. Therese of Lisieux, who was known as "The Little Flower of Jesus."

The friar tells me how the church and the tributes and the grounds we are walking on were designed and built by former chaplains from the Polish army, who came to the States after World War II and fulfilled their dream of creating a monastery in Indiana. I wish

Finch were here so we could say, *Who dreams of building a monastery in Indiana?*

But then I remember him standing next to me at Hoosier Hill, smiling out at the ugly trees and the ugly farmland and the ugly kids as if he could see Oz. *Believe it or not, it's actually beautiful to some people. . . .*

So I decide to see it through his eyes.

The shrines are actually a series of grottoes built out of sponge rock and crystals so that the exterior walls sparkle in the light. The sponge rock gives the place a kind of oyster-shell, cave quality that makes it seem ancient and folk-arty at the same time. The friar and I walk through an arched doorway, a crown and stars painted across the top of the face, and then he leaves me on my own.

Inside, I find myself in a series of underground hallways, cobbled in the same sponge rock and crystals and lit up by hundreds of candles. The walls are decorated with marble sculptures, stained-glass windows, and quartz and fluorites that capture the light and hold it. The effect is beautiful and eerie, and the place seems to glow.

I come out into the cool air again and go down into another grotto, another series of tunnels, this one with similar stained-glass windows and crystals built into the rock walls, and angel statues, heads bowed, hands folded in prayer.

I pass through a room arranged like a church, rows of seats facing the altar, where a marble Jesus lies on his deathbed above a base of glittering crystals. I pass another marble Jesus, this one tied to a pillar. And then I step into a room that glows from floor to ceiling.

The archangel Gabriel and Jesus are raising the dead. It's hard to describe—hands reach upward and dozens of yellow crosses race across the ceiling like stars or airplanes. The black-light walls are lined with plaques paid for by families of the dead who are asking the angels to bring their loved ones back to life and give them a happy eternity.

In the outstretched palm of Jesus, I see it—a plain, non-glittering rock. It's the one thing that looks out of place, and so I pick it up and exchange it for the offering I've brought—a butterfly ring that once belonged to Eleanor. I stay awhile longer and then go blinking into the daylight. In front of me are two sets of stairs, side by side, and a sign: PLEASE BE REVERENT. DO NOT WALK ON THE HOLY STAIRS! YOU MAY ASCEND ON YOUR KNEES. THANK YOU!

I count twenty-eight steps. No one is around. I could probably walk right up them, but I think of Finch being here before me and know he wouldn't have cheated. So I drop to my knees and go up.

At the top, the friar appears and helps me to my feet. "Did you enjoy the shrines?"

"They're beautiful. Especially the black-light room."

He nods. "The Ultraviolet Apocalypse. People travel hundreds of miles to see it."

The Ultraviolet Apocalypse. I thank him, and on my way to the car, I remember the rock, which I'm still holding. I open my palm and there it is, the one he first gave to me, and later I gave to him, and now he has given me back: *Your turn.*

That night, Brenda and Charlie and I meet at the base of the Purina Tower. I've invited Ryan and Amanda to join us, and after we've climbed to the top, the five of us sit in a circle, holding candles.

Brenda lights them, one by one, and as she lights them, we each say something about Finch.

When it's Bren's turn, she closes her eyes and says, " 'Leap! leap up, and lick the sky! I leap with thee; I burn with thee!' " She opens her eyes again and grins. "Herman Melville." Then she hits something on her phone, and the night is filled with music. It's a greatest hits of Finch—Split Enz, the Clash, Johnny Cash, and on and on.

Brenda jumps up and starts to dance. She waves her arms and kicks out her legs. She jumps higher and then up and down, up and down, both feet at a time like a kid having a tantrum. She doesn't know it, but she's flip-flapping like Finch and I once did in the children's section of Bookmarks.

Bren shouts along to the music, and all of us are laughing, and I have to lie back and hold my sides because the laughter has taken me by surprise. It's the first time I remember laughing like this in a long, long time.

Charlie pulls me to my feet, and now he is jumping and Amanda is jumping, and Ryan is doing this weird step-hop, step-hop, and shake-shake-shake, and then I join in, leaping and flip-flapping and burning across the roof.

When I get home, I'm still wide-awake, and so I spread out the map and study it. One more place left to wander. I want to save this wandering and hang on to it, because once I go there, the project is over, which means there's nothing left to find from Finch, and I still haven't found anything except evidence that he saw these places without me.

The location is Farmersburg, which is just fifteen miles away from Prairieton and the Blue Hole. I try to remember what we planned to see there. The text from him that should correspond—if it lines up the way the others have—is the last one I received: **A lake. A prayer. It's so lovely to be lovely in Private.**

I decide to look up Farmersburg, but I can't find any sites of interest. The population is barely one thousand, and the most remarkable thing about it seems to be that it's known for its large number of TV and radio transmitter towers.

We didn't choose this place together.

When I realize it, the hairs on the back of my neck stand up.

This is a place Finch added without telling me.

VIOLET

The last wandering

I'm up and out of the house early the next morning. The closer I get to Prairieton, the heavier I feel. I have to drive past the Blue Hole to reach Farmersburg, and I almost turn around and go home because it's too much and this is the last place I want to be.

Once I get to Farmersburg, I'm not sure where to go. I drive around and around this not-very-big place looking for whatever it is Finch wanted me to see.

I look for anything lovely. I look for anything having to do with praying, which I assume means a church. I know from the internet there are 133 "places of worship" in this tiny town, but it seems odd that Finch would choose one for the last wander.

Why should it seem odd? You barely knew him.

Farmersburg is one of these small and quiet Indiana cities filled with small and quiet houses and a small and quiet downtown. There are the usual farms and country roads, and numbered streets. I get nowhere, so I do what I always do—I stop on Main Street (every place has one) and hunt for somebody who can help me. Because it's a Sunday, every shop and restaurant is dark and closed. I walk up and down, but it's like a ghost town.

I'm back in the car and driving past every church I find, but none of them are particularly lovely, and I don't see any lakes. Finally, I pull into a gas station, and the boy there—who can't be much older than me—tells me there are some lakes up north a ways off US 150.

"Are there any churches out there?"

"At least one or two. But we got some here too." He smiles a watery smile.

"Thanks."

I follow his directions to US 150, which takes me away from town. I punch on the radio, but all I get is country music and static, and I don't know which is worse. I listen to the static for a while before turning it off. I spot a Dollar General on the side of the road and pull over because maybe they'll be able to tell me where these lakes are.

A woman works behind the counter. I buy a pack of gum and a water, and I tell her I'm looking for a lake and a church, someplace lovely. She screws up her mouth as she jabs at the cash register. "Emmanuel Baptist Church is just up the highway there. They got a lake not far past it. Not a very big one, but I know there's one because my kids used to go up there swimming."

"Is it private?"

"The lake or the church?"

"Either. This place I'm looking for is private."

"The lake's off of Private Road, if that's what you mean."

My skin starts to prickle. In Finch's text, "Private" is capitalized.

"Yes. That's what I mean. How do I get there?"

"Keep heading north up US 150. You'll pass Emmanuel Baptist on your right, and you'll see the lake past that, and then you'll come to Private Road. You just turn off, and there it is."

"Left or right?"

"There's only one way to turn—right. It's a short road. AIT Training and Technology is back in there. You'll see their sign."

I thank her and run to the car. *I'm close. I'll be there soon, and then it will all be over—wandering, Finch, us, everything.* I sit for a few seconds, making myself breathe so I can focus on every moment. I could wait and save it for later—whatever it is.

But I won't because I'm here now and the car is moving, and I'm heading in that direction, and there's Emmanuel Baptist Church, sooner than I expected, and then the lake, and here is the road, and I'm turning down it, and my palms are damp against the steering wheel, and my skin has gone goose-pimply, and I realize I'm holding my breath.

I pass the sign for AIT Training and Technology and see it up ahead at the end of the road, which is already here. I've dead-ended, and I roll past AIT with a sinking feeling because there's nothing lovely about it, and this can't be the place. But if this isn't the place, then where am I supposed to be?

The car crawls back along Private Road the way I came, and that's when I see the bend in the road that I didn't take, a kind of fork. I follow this now, and there's the lake, and then I see the sign: TAYLOR PRAYER CHAPEL.

A wooden cross, tall as a man, sits in front of the sign by a few feet, and behind the cross and the sign is a tiny white chapel with a tiny white steeple. I can see houses beyond, and the lake to one side, the top of it green with algae.

I turn off the engine and sit for a few minutes. I lose track of how long I'm there. Did he come here the day he died? Did he come here the day before? When was he here? How did he find this place?

Then I am out of the car and walking to the chapel, and I can hear my heart and, somewhere in the distance, the sounds of birds in the trees. The air is already heavy with summer.

I turn the knob, and the door opens, just like that, and inside the chapel smells fresh and clean, as if it has been aired out recently. There are only a few pews, because the entire place is smaller than my bedroom, and at the front a wooden altar with a painting of Jesus and two vases of flowers, two potted plants, and an open Bible.

The long, narrow windows let in the sunlight, and I sit in one of the pews and look around, thinking: *What now?*

I walk to the altar, and someone has typed up and laminated a history of the church, which is propped against one of the vases of flowers.

Taylor Prayer Chapel was created as a sanctuary for weary travelers to stop and rest along their way. It was built in memoriam to those who have lost their lives in

auto accidents, and as a place of healing. We remember those who are no longer here, who were taken from us too soon, and who we will always keep with us in our hearts. The chapel is open to the public day and night, and on holidays. We are always here.

And now I know why Finch chose this place—for Eleanor and for me. And for him too, because he was a weary traveler who just needed rest. Something pokes out of the Bible—a white envelope. I turn to the page, and someone has underlined these words: *"Then you will shine among them like stars in the sky."*

I pick up the envelope, and there is my name: "Ultraviolet Remarkey-able."

I think of taking it to the car to read what's inside, but instead

I sit down in one of the pews, grateful for the sturdy, solid wood underneath me.

Am I ready to hear what he thought of me? To hear how I let him down? Am I ready to know exactly how much I hurt him and how I could have, should have, saved him, if only I'd paid more attention and read the signs and not opened my big mouth and listened to him and been enough and maybe loved him more?

My hands are shaking as I open the envelope. I pull out three sheets of thick staff paper, one covered in musical notes, the other two covered in words that look like lyrics.

I begin to read.

> *You make me happy,*
> *Whenever you're around I'm safe inside your smile,*

You make me handsome,
Whenever I feel my nose just seems a bit too round,
You make me special, and God knows I've longed to be that
    kind of guy to have around,
You make me love you,
And that could be the greatest thing my heart was ever fit to
    do. . . .

I am crying—loud and hiccuping, as if I've been holding my breath for a very long time and finally, finally can breathe.

    You make me lovely, and it's so lovely to be lovely
        to the one I love. . . .

I read and reread the words.

You make me happy . . .
You make me special . . .
You make me lovely . . .

I read and reread them until I know the words by heart, and then I fold up the papers and slide them back into the envelope. I sit there until the tears stop, and the light begins to change and fade, and the soft, pink glow of dusk fills the chapel.

It's dark by the time I drive home. In my bedroom, I pull out the staff paper once again and play the notes on my flute. The tune finds its way into my head and stays there, like it's a part of me, so that, days later, I'm still singing it.

I don't need to worry that Finch and I never filmed our wanderings. It's okay that we didn't collect souvenirs or that we never had time to pull it all together in a way that made sense to anyone else but us.

The thing I realize is that it's not what you take, it's what you leave.

VIOLET

June 20

It's a white-hot summer day. The sky is a pure, bright blue. I park the car and walk up the embankment and stand for a long time on the grassy shore of the Blue Hole. I half expect to see him.

I kick off my shoes and cut through the water, diving deep. I'm looking for him through my goggles, even though I know I won't find him. I swim with my eyes open. I come back up to the surface under the great wide sky, take a breath, and down I go again, deeper this time. I like to think he's wandering in another world, seeing things no one can ever imagine.

In 1950, poet Cesare Pavese was at the peak of his literary career, applauded by his peers and his country as the greatest living Italian author. In August of that year, he took a lethal dose of sleeping pills, and even though he kept a daily journal, no one could ever truly explain why he did it. The writer Natalia Ginzburg remembered him after his death: *"It seemed to us that his sadness was that of a boy, the voluptuous heedless melancholy of a boy who has still not come down to earth, and moves in the arid, solitary world of dreams."*

It was an epitaph that could have been written for Finch, except that I've written one for him myself:

Theodore Finch—I was alive. I burned brightly. And then I died, but not really. Because someone like me cannot, will not, die like everyone else. I linger like the legends of the Blue Hole. I will always be here, in the offerings and people I left behind.

I tread water on the surface under the wide, open sky and the sun and all that blue, which reminds me of Theodore Finch, just like everything else reminds me of him, and I think of my own epitaph, still to be written, and all the places I'll wander. No longer rooted, but gold, flowing. I feel a thousand capacities spring up in me.

Every forty seconds, someone in the world dies by suicide. Every forty seconds, someone is left behind to cope with the loss.

Long before I was born, my great-grandfather died of a self-inflicted gunshot wound. His oldest child, my grandfather, was just thirteen. No one knew if it was intentional or accidental—and being from a small town in the South, my grandfather and his mother and sisters never discussed it. But that death has affected our family for generations.

Several years ago, a boy I knew and loved killed himself. I was the one who discovered him. The experience was not something I wanted to talk about, even with the people closest to me. To this day, many of my family and friends still don't know much, if anything, about it. For a long time, it was too painful to even think about, much less talk about, but it is important to talk about what happened.

In *All the Bright Places,* Finch worries a lot about labels. There is, unfortunately, a good deal of stigma surrounding suicide and mental illness. When my great-grandfather died, people gossiped. Although his widow and his three children never spoke about what happened that day, they felt silently judged and, to some extent, ostracized. I lost my friend to suicide a year before I lost my father to cancer. They were both ill at the same time, and they died within fourteen months of each other, but the reaction to their illnesses and deaths could not have been more different. People rarely bring flowers to a suicide.

It was only when writing this book that I learned my own label—Survivor After Suicide, or Survivor of Suicide. Fortunately, there are numerous resources to help me make sense of this tragic thing that happened and how it affects me, just as there are numerous resources to help anyone, teen or adult, who is struggling with emotional upheaval, depression, anxiety, mental instability, or suicidal thoughts.

Often, mental and emotional illnesses go undiagnosed because the person suffering symptoms is too ashamed to speak up, or because their loved ones either fail to or choose not to recognize the signs. According to Mental Health America, an estimated 2.5 million Americans are known to have bipolar disorder, but the actual number is a good two to three times higher than that. As many as 80 percent of people with this illness go undiagnosed or misdiagnosed.

If you think something is wrong, speak up.
You are not alone.
It is not your fault.
Help is out there.

SUICIDE PREVENTION

American Association of Suicidology (AAS)—suicidology.org

American Foundation for Suicide Prevention (AFSP)—afsp.org

IMAlive—imalive.org

National Suicide Prevention Lifeline—suicidepreventionlifeline.org
(1-800-273-TALK)

DIAGNOSING MENTAL ILLNESS IN TEENS

Helpguide—helpguide.org

Mental Health America (MHA)—mentalhealthamerica.net

National Alliance on Mental Illness (NAMI)—nami.org

National Institute of Mental Health (NIMH)—nimh.nih.gov

Teen Mental Health—teenmentalhealth.org

SURVIVORS

Mayo Clinic—mayoclinic.com/health/suicide/MH00048

SOS: A Handbook for Survivors of Suicide by Jeffrey Jackson (published by AAS)—available online, along with other helpful resources, at www. suicidology.org/suicide-survivors/suicide-loss-survivors

BULLYING

Stomp Out Bullying—stompoutbullying.org

StopBullying—stopbullying.gov

ABUSE

Childhelp—childhelpusa.org

National Child Abuse Hotline—1-800-4-A-CHILD (1-800-422-4453)

ACKNOWLEDGMENTS

In June of 2013, two days after finishing up work on my seventh book and sending it off to my New York publisher, I had an idea for another story, in spite of the fact that I was burned out and ready for a much-needed break—I've been writing back-to-back books for the past couple of years.

This idea was different, however. For one thing, it was personal. For another, it was YA. I've spent my career in adult fiction and non-fiction but, creatively, I was ready for something different.

I wanted to write something edgy.

I wanted to write something contemporary.

I wanted to write something tough, hard, sad, but funny.

I wanted to write from a boy's point of view.

In July, I signed with the most wonderful and amazing agent (champion, partner, editor) a girl could have. Thank you to the incomparable Kerry Sparks for believing in that first fifty pages and me. No one will ever know what her belief and enthusiasm meant at that particular time in my life. I wake up every day counting my lucky stars for Kerry and all the fantastic folks at Levine Greenberg Rostan (especial thanks to Monika Verma and Elizabeth Fisher). They make me lovely.

So does Allison Wortche, my brilliant editor, who is as savvy and insightful as she is warm and kind, and who is as invested in Finch and Violet as I am. Their story would not be the same without her skilled hand. She and the entire team at Knopf and Random House Children's Books (President and Publisher Barbara Marcus; Vice President and Publishing Director Nancy Hinkel; Senior Vice President and Associate Publisher Judith Haut; Isabel Warren-Lynch, Alison Impey, and Stephanie Moss in Design; Artie Bennett, as well as aces Renée Cafiero and Katharine Wiencke, in Copyediting; Managing Editor Shasta Clinch; Tim Terhune and Barbara Cho in Production; Pam White and Jocelyn Lange in Sub Rights; Felicia Frazier, John Adamo, Kim Lauber, Lynn Kestin, Stephanie O'Cain, Adrienne Waintraub, Laura Antonacci, Dominique Cimina, Lydia Finn, and the rest of Sales, Marketing, and Publicity) have created the brightest of places for me to live, breathe, and work, and I am thrilled out of my head to be there.

I'm also thrilled to be working with my wondrous film agent, Sylvie Rabineau, and RWSG Literary Agency.

Thank you to my family and friends for unwavering support, even when I am insufferably consumed by my work (which is most of the time). I couldn't do it without you. Special thanks to my favorite cousin, Annalise von Sprecken, my consultant on all things teen-related and the person who gave me "_____ is life."

Thank you to Louis, love of my life and partner in more ways than one, who has had to endure hours of worrying, brainstorming, outlining, suicide-fact reciting, querying ("What if Violet and Finch met on the bell tower ledge?" "What if Finch and Roamer used to be friends?" "What if Amanda was at Life Is Life too?"), not to mention hours of One Direction listening (my own personal *Boy Parade*). He, more than anyone else (with the exception of our three literary cats), has lived this book with me.

Thank you, John Ivers (Blue Flash, *Blue Too*) and Mike Carmi-

Suicidology, the Mayo Clinic, and the National Institute of Mental Health.

Thanks most of all to my beautiful mother and fellow author, Penelope Niven, who made the world lovelier just by being in it. She was my best friend. She was my best everything. We used to say to each other, "You are my best." And she was. And she always will be. She taught me from childhood that my mountain was waiting, and she never stopped encouraging me to keep climbing. Her unexpected death on August 28, 2014, was the single worst event of my life. This book, and all the books to follow, are because of her and for her. To quote Theodore Finch, *You are all the colors in one, at full brightness.*

Lastly, thanks to my great-grandfather Olin Niven. And to the boy I loved who died too soon, but who left me a song.

chael (World's Biggest Ball of Paint), for creating such uniquely awe-some, wander-worthy sites, and for letting me use your real names.

Thank you to my very first editor, Will Schwalbe, who remains a wise mentor and cherished friend. And to Amanda Brower and Jennifer Gerson Uffalussy for leading me to Kerry Sparks.

Thank you, Briana Harley, for being my go-to one-girl band of a YA focus group. Thank you, Lara Yacoubian, for being the World's Best Assistant Ever.

Thanks to the *Germ* girls and guys for all you are and do, particularly Louis, Jordan, Briana Bailey, Shannon, Shelby, and Lara. You are the prettiest girls (and boys) anywhere.

Thank you to the generous people (who wish to remain name-less) who shared their personal stories of mental illness, depression, and suicide. And to the experts at the American Association of

And in two weeks we'll fly again,
perhaps a Chinese dinner then.
You make me happy, you make me smile.

And in two weeks we'll fly again,

perhaps a Chinese dinner then,

You make me happy, you make me smile.

ABOUT THE AUTHOR

All the Bright Places is Jennifer Niven's first book for young adult readers, but she has written four novels for adults—*American Blonde, Becoming Clementine, Velva Jean Learns to Fly,* and *Velva Jean Learns to Drive*—as well as three nonfiction books—*The Ice Master, Ada Blackjack,* and *The Aqua Net Diaries,* a memoir about her high school experiences. Although she grew up in Indiana, she now lives with her fiancé and three literary cats in Los Angeles, which remains her favorite place to wander. For more information, visit JenniferNiven.com and GermMagazine.com, or find her on Facebook.

LOVE VIOLET AND FINCH?
MEET LIBBY AND JACK.

Turn the page to read an excerpt from
Jennifer Niven's new novel....

JENNIFER NIVEN

Author of All the Bright Places

HOLDING

UP THE

UNIVERSE

A New York Times Bestseller

• • •

I'm not a shitty person, but I'm about to do a shitty thing. And you will hate me, and some other people will hate me, but I'm going to do it anyway to protect you and also myself.

This will sound like an excuse, but I have something called prosopagnosia, which means I can't recognize faces, not even the faces of the people I love. Not even my mom. Not even myself.

Imagine walking into a room full of strangers, people who don't mean anything to you because you don't know their names or histories. Then imagine going to school or work or, worse, your own home, where you should know everyone, only the people there look like strangers too.

That's what it's like for me: I walk into a room and I don't know anyone. That's every room, everywhere. I get by on how a person walks. By gestures. By voice. By hair. I learn people by identifiers. I tell myself, *Dusty has ears that stick out and a red-brown Afro,* and then I memorize this fact so it helps me find my little brother, but I can't actually call up an image of him and his big ears and his Afro unless he's in front of me. Remembering people is like this superpower everyone seems to have but me.

Have I been officially diagnosed? No. And not just because I'm guessing this is beyond the pay grade of Dr. Blume, town pediatrician. Not just because for the past few years my parents have had more than their share of shit to deal with. Not just because it's better *not* to be the freak. But because there's a part of me that hopes it isn't true. That maybe it will clear up and go away on its own. For now, this is how I get by:

Nod/smile at everyone.

Be charming.

Be "on."

Be goddamn hilarious.

Be the life of the party, but don't drink. Don't risk losing control (that happens enough when sober).

Pay attention.

Do whatever it takes. Be lord of the douche. Anything to keep from being the prey. Always better to hunt than be hunted.

I'm not telling you all this as an excuse for what I'm about to do. But maybe you can keep it in mind. This is the only way to stop my friends from doing something worse, and it's the only

of me that hopes it isn't true. That maybe it will clear up and go

away on its own. For now, this is how I get by:

PS. You're the only person who knows what's wrong with me.

Do whatever it takes. Be lord douche. Anything to keep **Jack**

from being the prey. Always bette **Sincerely yours,** hunted.

to happen. telling you all this as an excuse for what I'm about to

anyone. *That's not why.* Even though that's the thing that's going

way to stop this stupid game. Just know that I don't want to hurt

* * *

Prosopagnosia (pro-suh-pag-NO-zhuh) *noun:* 1. an inability to recognize the faces of familiar people, typically as a result of damage to the brain. 2. when everyone is a stranger.

18 HOURS EARLIER

LIBBY

If a genie popped out of my bedside lamp, I would wish for these three things: my mom to be alive, nothing bad or sad to ever happen again, and to be a member of the Martin Van Buren High School Damsels, the best drill team in the tristate area.

But what if the Damsels don't want you?

It is 3:38 a.m., and the time of night when my mind starts running around all wild and out of control, like my cat, George, when he was a kitten. All of a sudden, there goes my brain, climbing the curtains. There it is, swinging from the bookshelf. There it is, with its paw in the fish tank and its head underwater.

I lie on my bed, staring up into the dark, and my mind bounces across the room.

What if you get trapped again? What if they have to knock down the cafeteria door or the bathroom wall to get you out? What if your dad gets married and then he dies and you're left with the new wife and stepsiblings? What if you die? What if there is no heaven and you never see your mom again?

I tell myself to sleep.

I close my eyes and lie very still.

Very still.

For minutes.

I make my mind lie there with me and tell it, *Sleep, sleep, sleep.*

What if you get to school and realize that things are different and kids are different, and no matter how much you try, you will never be able to catch up to them?

I open my eyes.

My name is Libby Strout. You've probably heard of me. You've probably watched the video of me being rescued from my own house. At last count, 6,345,981 people have watched it, so there's a good chance you're one of them. Three years ago, I was America's Fattest Teen. I weighed 653 pounds at my heaviest, which means I was approximately 500 pounds overweight. I haven't always been fat. The short version of the story is that my mom died and I got fat, but somehow I'm still here. This is in no way my father's fault.

Two months after I was rescued, we moved to a different neighborhood on the other side of town. These days I can leave the house on my own. I've lost 302 pounds. The size of two entire people. I have around 190 left to go, and I'm fine with that. I like who I am. For one thing, I can run now. And ride in the car. And buy clothes at the mall instead of special-ordering them. And I can twirl. Aside from no longer being afraid of organ failure, that may be the best thing about now versus then.

Tomorrow is my first day of school since fifth grade. My new title will be high school junior, which, let's face it, sounds a lot better than America's Fattest Teen. But it's hard to be anything but TERRIFIED OUT OF MY SKULL.

I wait for the panic attack to come.

JACK

Caroline Lushamp calls before my alarm goes off, but I let her go to voice mail. I know whatever it is, it's not going to be good and it will be my fault.

She calls three times but only leaves one message. I almost delete it without listening, but what if her car broke down and she's in trouble? This is, after all, the girl I've dated off and on for the past four years. (We're *that* couple. That on-again, off-again everyone-assumes-we'll-end-up-together-forever couple.)

Jack, it's me. I know we're taking a break or whatever but she's my cousin. My COUSIN. I mean, MY COUSIN, JACK! If you wanted to get back at me for breaking up with me, then congratulations, jerkwad, you've done it. *If you see me in class today or in the hallways or in the cafeteria or ANYWHERE ELSE ON EARTH, do not talk to me. Actually, just do me a favor and go to hell.*

Three minutes later, the cousin calls, and at first I think she's crying, but then you can hear Caroline in the background, and the cousin starts yelling and Caroline starts yelling. I delete the message.

Two minutes later, Dave Kaminski sends a text to warn me that Reed Young wants to kick my face in for making out with his girlfriend. I text, *I owe you.* And I mean it. If I'm keeping score, Kam's helped me out more times than I've helped him.

All this fuss over a girl who, if we're being honest, looked so much like Caroline Lushamp that—at least at first—I thought it *was* her, which means in some weird way Caroline should be flattered. It's like admitting to the world that I want to get back together with her even though she dumped me the first week of summer so that she could go out with Zach Higgins.

I think of texting this to her, but instead I turn off my phone and close my eyes and see if I can't transport myself right back into July. The only thing I had to worry about then was going to work, scavenging the local scrap yard, building (mind-blowing) projects in my (kick-ass) workshop, and hanging out with my brothers. Life would be so much easier if it was just Jack + scrap yard + kick-ass workshop + mind-blowing projects.

You should never have gone to the party. You should never have had a drink. You know you can't be trusted. Avoid alcohol. Avoid crowds. Avoid people. You only end up pissing them off.

LIBBY

It's 6:33 a.m. and I am out of bed and standing in front of the mirror. There was a time, a little over two years ago, when I couldn't, wouldn't look at myself. All I saw was the bunched-up face of Moses Hunt, yelling at me across the playground: *No one will ever love you because you're fat!* And the faces of all the other fifth graders as they started to laugh. *You're so big you block the moon. Go home, Flabby Stout, go home to your room. . . .*

Today, for the most part, I only see me—adorable navy dress, sneakers, medium-longish brown hair that my sweet but slightly demented grandmother once described as "the exact color of Highland cattle." And the reflection of my giant dirty cotton ball of a cat. George stares at me with wise gold eyes, and I try to imagine what he might say to me. Four years ago, he was diagnosed with heart failure and given six months to live. But I know him well enough to know that only George will decide when it's time for George to go. He blinks at me.

Right now, I think he would tell me to breathe.

So I breathe.

I've gotten really good at breathing.

I look down at my hands and they're steady, even if the fingernails are bitten to the quick, and, weirdly, I feel pretty calm, considering. I realize: the panic attack never came. This is something to celebrate, so I throw on one of my mom's old albums and dance. Dancing is what I love most and dancing is what I plan to do with my life. I haven't taken lessons since I was ten, but *the dance is in me,* and no lack of training can make that go away.

I tell myself, *Maybe this year you can try out for the Damsels.*

My brain goes zooming up the wall, where it hangs, shaking. *What if it never happens? What if you die before anything good or wonderful or amazing ever happens to you?* For the past two and a half years, the only thing I've had to worry about has been my survival. The focus of every single person in my life, including me, has been: *We just need to get you better.* And now I'm better. *So what if I let them down after all the time and energy they've invested in me?*

I dance harder to push the thoughts out until my dad thumps on the door. His head appears. "You know I love a good Pat Benatar song first thing in the morning, but the question is: how do the neighbors feel?"

I turn it down a little but keep on moving. When the song is over, I find a marker and decorate one shoe. *As long as you live, there's always something waiting; and even if it's bad, and you know it's bad, what can you do? You can't stop living. (Truman Capote, In Cold Blood)* Then I reach for the lipstick my grandmother gave me for my birthday, lean into the mirror, and paint my lips red.

JACK

I hear the shower running and voices downstairs. I pull the pillow over my face, but it's too late—I'm awake.

I turn on my phone and text first Caroline, then Kam, then Reed Young. The thing I say to all of them is that I was very drunk (an exaggeration) and it was very dark (it was) and I don't remember anything that happened because I was not only drunk, I was upset. *There's just this shit happening at home that I can't talk about right now, so if you can bear with me and find it in your heart to forgive me, I'll be forever in your debt.* The shit happening at home part is completely true.

For Caroline, I throw in some compliments and ask her to please apologize to her cousin for me. I say I don't want to contact her directly because I've already made a mess of things and I don't want to do anything else to make things worse between Caroline and me. Even though *Caroline* was the one who broke up with *me,* and even though we're currently in an off-again phase, and even though I haven't seen her *since June,* I basically eat crow and then throw it up all over my phone. This is the price I pay for trying to keep everyone happy.

I drag myself down the hall to the bathroom. The thing I need most in this world is a long, hot shower, but what I get instead is a trickle of warm water followed by a blast of Icelandic cold. Sixty seconds later—because that's all I can bear—I get out, dry off, and stand in front of the mirror.

So this is me.

I think this every time I see my reflection. Not in a *Damn, that's me* way, but more like *Huh. Okay. What have we got here?* I lean in, trying to put the pieces of my face together.

The guy in the mirror isn't bad-looking—high cheekbones, strong jaw, a mouth that's hitched up at one corner like he just got done telling a joke. Somewhere in the neighborhood of pretty. The way he tilts his head back and gazes out through half-open eyelids makes it seem like he's used to looking down on everyone, like he's smart and he knows he's smart, and then it hits me that what he really looks like is an asshole. Except for the eyes themselves. They're too serious and there are circles under them, like he hasn't slept. He's wearing the same Superman shirt I've been wearing all summer.

What does this mouth (Mom's) mean with this nose (also Mom's) and these eyes (a combination of Mom's and Dad's)? My eyebrows are darker than my hair but they aren't as dark as Dad's. My skin is a kind of middle brown color, not dark like Mom's, and not light like Dad's.

The other thing that doesn't match up here is the hair. It's this enormous lion's mane Afro that looks like it's allowed to do whatever the fuck it wants. If he's anything like me, the guy in the mirror calculates everything. Even though this hair *cannot be contained*, he's grown it for a reason. So he can find himself.

Something about the way these features add up is how people find each other in the world. Something about the combination makes them go, *There's Jack Masselin.*

"What's your identifier?" I say to my reflection, and I mean the real identifier, not this giant lion fro. I'm having a right serious moment, but then I hear a distinct snicker, and a tall, skinny blur goes breezing by. That would be my brother Marcus.

"My name's Jack and I'm so pretty," he sings all the way down the stairs.

opposite team, setting the all-time park record for Most Disastrous and Humiliating Debut Ever.

3. That time I'd been working with our high school sports therapist because of a shoulder injury, and, in the middle of Walmart, told the man I thought was my baseball coach, *I could use another massage,* only to discover it was actually Mr. Temple, Mom's boss.

4. That time I hit on Jesselle Villegas, and it turned out to be Miss Arbulata, substitute teacher.

5. That time I made out with Caroline Lushamp and it was actually her cousin.

TOP 5 MOST EMBARRASSING MOMENTS OF MY LIFE

by Jack Masselin

1. That time my mom picked me up from kindergarten (after getting her hair cut), and in front of my teacher, the other kids, the other parents, and the principal, I accused her of trying to kidnap me.

2. That time I joined the pickup (uniform-free) soccer game at Reynolds Park and passed every ball to the